# WIND
# FALLS

# WINTER FALLS

book 1 of the twin willows trilogy

## NICOLE MAGGI

**MEDALLION PRESS**

Medallion Press, Inc.
Printed in USA

For all my Italian mamas, especially Grandma Rosie

Published 2014 by Medallion Press, Inc.

The MEDALLION PRESS LOGO
is a registered trademark of Medallion Press, Inc.

Names, characters, places, and incidents are the products of the author's imagination or are used fictionally. Any resemblance to actual events, locales, or persons, living or dead, is entirely coincidental.

Typeset in Adobe Garamond Pro
Printed in the United States of America
ISBN #978-160542683-9

10 9 8 7 6 5 4 3 2 1
First Edition

# Acknowledgments

Writing is a solitary profession, and yet without many people this book would not exist.

First, to Her Excellency, the Queen of All Agents, Irene Goodman, for encouraging me, supporting me, kicking my ass when it needed to be kicked, and for believing in me even when I didn't believe in myself. There aren't enough words in the English language to express how grateful I am.

To my fantastic editors, Lorie Jones and Emily Steele, for caring as much about Alessia's journey as I do. To the wonderful Medallion marketing team, especially Brigitte Shepard and Paul Ohlson, for leading me through the publication process with such patience and enthusiasm. To Jim Tampa and the Medallion design team, especially Michal Wlos for creating my gorgeous cover.

To Linda Gerber, Julie O'Connell, and Ginger Calem for nurturing my writing at the very beginning. To Barb Wexler for always being there for me, for my awesome website, and for being the best long-distance writing buddy a girl could ever have. To Anne Van, Lizzie Andrews, Will Frank, and Jen Klein for being such an integral part of the growth of this book and for celebrating my successes and supporting me during my woes. Deep, deep gratitude to Romina Garber, my other brain, for knowing this story better than I do, for endless hours of brainstorming over spoonfuls of Noisella at LPQ, and for talking me off the ledge more than once.

To the wonderful and vibrant Los Angeles kid-lit community for being such great cheerleaders on this journey. To the Class of 2k14 for your support and general fabulousness.

To my family for loving me no matter what.

Last, and most of all, to Chris and Emilia. You are the reason my soul can take flight, the inspiration behind every word on the page.

# Table of Contents

*"I am a Benandante because I go with the others to fight . . . I go . . . in spirit and the body remains behind . . ."*

—From the trial of Paolo Gasparutto
in the city of Cividale, region of Friuli, Italy
June 27, 1580

# Chapter One

*The Newcomers*

The town of Twin Willows was a tiny dot on a large map, a speck of nothing in the middle of nowhere. I paused on the steps of the town hall and surveyed the short strip of Main Street, the blood in my veins sizzling with frustration like hot oil. A discarded newspaper blew down the potholed street, carried off by the autumn wind to some distant place that someday—*someday*—I promised myself I would get to.

I sighed and pushed open the door. "I hate Mondays."

Inside the overheated hall, the radiators banged in rhythm with the voices of the people gathered there. I spotted my best friend, Jenny, in the back row, her thumbs working furiously over the keypad of her cell phone. I plunked into the chair next to her.

She clicked her phone off. "I hate Mondays. Why does Clemens insist on torturing us?"

"Because he has no life and wants to ruin ours." I unwrapped my scarf and flung it over the chair next to me.

As an ongoing homework assignment for our

1

government class, we were required to attend weekly town hall meetings. As if anything ever happened in Twin Willows. Every week these meetings were the same. Someone was mad at someone else for an out-of-control tree limb that dangled over their property line, and what was Mayor Lawson going to do about it? Well, I could tell them exactly what Mayor Lawson would do about it because she did the same thing every week. She made some wishy-washy decision that would satisfy everyone so that everything could reset to Boring. One of these days, the monotony of it was going to make me scream right in the middle of the meeting.

"What's cooking in Lidia's kitchen tonight?" Jenny asked. Lidia was my mother. Although I called her Mom to her face, in my head and with my friends she was always Lidia.

"Baked ziti." I looked at the clock. It was five past six. Great. The meeting was running late. As if it wasn't bad enough that I had to be here at all. My stomach growled.

Jenny rolled her eyes back and made a drooling sound. "My mom is making vegan, gluten-free meat loaf. When I left the house she was crushing cashews to use in place of breadcrumbs."

"I think I just felt Lidia shudder," I said with a laugh. My mother was an incredible purist when it came to food. I'd heard her mutter many times about burning the "weirdo" cookbooks in Jenny's house.

The door behind us opened, and a harsh wind gusted in, blowing my scarf off the chair. I bent down to pick it up, and as I straightened Jenny grabbed my arm. "Who are *they*?" she hissed.

I turned in the direction of her gaze.

Standing in the doorway was a couple I had never seen before. The man looked like he had walked right off the cover of *Fortune*, with his overstyled black hair and cashmere coat. His wife stood next to him, her deep red locks glinting under the yellow lights. As they moved down the aisle, they revealed two kids standing behind them. The girl was willowy with raven-colored hair like her father's. But when I saw the boy beside her, my breath left me in one whoosh.

He turned his head and met my stare, long enough for me to notice that his eyes were the color of the forest in springtime. I swallowed hard, my mouth dry as paper. His sister nudged him. He looked away and ran his hand through his dark hair, messing it so the ends stuck out in all directions.

"Where did they come from?" Jenny asked as though she had just seen a unicorn.

"I-I don't know." My voice was shaky, like I hadn't used it in a while. I cleared my throat and straightened my shoulders. I wasn't the kind of girl who got weak-kneed at the sight of a cute boy, and there was no way I was ruining my reputation now.

Still, I couldn't help staring at the family. New people

were rare in Twin Willows, and they garnered a lot of looks and murmurs. The father nodded to everyone as he walked to the front of the hall, but there was nothing friendly about his manner. The wife stared straight ahead as she followed, ignoring everything. The two kids slid into seats in the front row next to their parents without ever speaking to them.

A skinny young man in a pin-striped suit way too expensive for the Twin Willows flannel-and-baseball-cap crowd greeted the father and handed him a stack of note cards.

Mayor Lawson stepped up to the podium, and the room quieted. "We have an exciting agenda tonight," she announced.

"Maybe she's right for once," Jenny said under her breath.

Mayor Lawson gestured to the father of the new family. "I'd like to introduce Travis Wolfe, who comes to us from the Guild Incorporated."

"Whoa." I leaned forward, gripping the edge of the empty seat in front of me. I wasn't a CNN junkie or anything, but I didn't live under a rock. The Guild was one of those companies always in the news, with arms reaching all over the world. I'd just read a story on the Internet about some controversial security contract they had won in the Middle East.

Mayor Lawson held a hand up to quiet down the hum that had started in the hall. "Mr. Wolfe has an exciting venture for Twin Willows. Let's all give him our attention." She nodded to Mr. Wolfe.

He stood and removed his luxurious coat, revealing a sharply angled dark suit. A gold watch flashed on his wrist as he straightened his bright silk tie. He climbed the steps to the podium, and the man in the pinstripes positioned himself in the shadows behind Mr. Wolfe, his fingers poised over the keyboard of a BlackBerry.

"Thank you, Mayor Lawson," Mr. Wolfe said, his voice rolling over us like an oil slick. "I'm thrilled to be here, representing the Guild."

"Oh, my God, just guild me now," moaned Jenny.

"Shut up," I whispered. "What on earth is a huge company like them doing in *Twin Willows*?"

"Maybe they've located the world's richest oil pipeline right down Main Street, and they're going to blow up the town," Jenny said with a yawn.

I rolled my eyes. "Be serious."

"Serious? *Moi*?" She grinned. "The only thing I'm serious about is how cute Monsieur Wolfe's son is."

I glanced at the black-haired boy sitting in the front row and felt another punch to the gut. The thought of sitting next to that beautiful boy in class made my insides fall to pieces. "I wonder if he—they—are in our grade. They look our age."

"The Guild is involved in many industries across the globe," Mr. Wolfe said, his voice breaking my attention away from his son.

I wrestled my focus back to the podium.

"We create jobs and empower communities. From the Congo to Venezuela, men, women, and children have benefited from our presence." Mr. Wolfe lowered his notes and swept his gaze over the hall. His cheeks shone with a translucent rosiness, like a light switch had gone on inside him. "We touch lives. And we are here in Twin Willows to touch you."

"Ew." Jenny stuck her tongue out. "That sounds slightly pornographic."

I stifled a giggle.

"Our team of engineers at the Guild has located a unique confluence of water sources that we think would provide the perfect location for a hydroelectric power plant."

Low muttering broke out across the room.

Mr. Wolfe tapped the cards on the edge of the podium. "Before anyone jumps to any conclusions, let me clarify a few things. This isn't the kind of hydroelectric power plant that you've seen before. This is a brand-new technology that the Guild has been developing for years. We are on the cutting edge of the future. We're going to build something the world has never seen!"

I stared at Mr. Wolfe. Damn, but he had drunk a lot of Kool-Aid.

The assistant behind him coughed quietly.

Mr. Wolfe half turned and gave a little nod. He took a deep breath. When he spoke again, his voice was even, automated. "The Guild's plant will not involve building a dam or the displacement of the population. We simply

want to harness the power of the water to bring afford-
able and sustainable energy to the area."

I hugged one leg up to my chest. There was a place
in the woods near my house—a special place—but they
couldn't possibly mean there. As far as I knew, I was the
only person alive who knew about it. I rested my chin
on my knee, focusing on the Wolfe family. As though
he sensed me, the boy turned around. My brain told me
to look away, but my body wouldn't cooperate. His eyes
found mine. Something broke inside me, but I quickly
set it right again and forced myself to look away. After a
few minutes, when I dared to glance back, the Wolfe boy
had faced front.

Mr. Wolfe finished his pitch. "I know you all have a
lot of questions, which I will be happy to answer in the
public forums I will be scheduling in the near future.
The Guild has a policy of being open and honest with
the communities it serves." He smiled for the first time
that night, and it gave me a headache, like I had eaten a
Popsicle too fast.

"Yeah, right," Jenny muttered.

"What?"

"My mother has been signing petitions against the
Guild for years. She's going to have a conniption fit
when she finds out they're invading our town. It's gonna
be like Berkeley 1969 revisited."

I watched Mr. Wolfe step down from the podium
and sit next to his wife. She didn't even acknowledge

him. In fact, the whole family seemed to shift away from him. "I do kinda get a weird feeling from him."

"Yeah. It's too bad the son is so hot." Jenny gave a big dramatic sigh. "I'm gonna let *you* have him. It looks like there's baggage there, and you know I don't do heavy lifting."

I swatted at her, but she ducked away, laughing.

At the end of the meeting, Jenny and I dawdled, letting the hall empty out until the Wolfe family was halfway up the aisle with Mayor Lawson. When she spotted us, she waved us down. "These are students from the local high school."

"It's wonderful to see young people take an interest in their town," Mr. Wolfe said. He threw us a thousand-watt smile. Now that I saw him up close, I noticed his smile didn't reach any other part of his face.

Jenny pushed me into the aisle. "Our government teacher makes us come," she said.

Mayor Lawson shot her a stony look.

Mr. Wolfe buttoned his suit jacket and smoothed the lapels. "Ah, well. Still."

"What year did you say your children are in school?" Mayor Lawson asked Mrs. Wolfe.

Mr. Wolfe answered before his wife could speak. "Bree and Jonah are juniors. They're twins."

His assistant stepped in, knocking Mayor Lawson off-balance. By the time she righted herself, the two men had stepped off to the side, their heads bent over the assistant's BlackBerry. The mayor sidled over to them, obviously eager to be part of their club.

"We're juniors too," Jenny said to the remaining Wolfes. "Jenny Sands. And this is Alessia Jacobs."

Bree crossed her arms over her chest and looked away.

"We're going to Joe's, the coffee shop across the street," Jenny continued.

I looked at her; we had no such plans.

"There's probably other kids from school over there if you guys want to come."

"We still have unpacking to do." Mrs. Wolfe spoke for the first time all night. Her voice was brittle, like a piece of splintered wood.

"Go ahead, kids," Mr. Wolfe said, not looking up from the BlackBerry.

The twins looked from one parent to the other and seemed to decide collectively to follow their father's instruction. I fell in step with the Wolfe twins as we followed Jenny outside. I couldn't help sneaking looks at Jonah, and when he caught me looking, my skin turned hot.

Jenny stopped on the sidewalk in front of the town hall. "Is that your car?" she asked, pointing to a sleek silver sedan parked at the curb. It looked like something out of a James Bond movie.

"Yeah, so?" Bree said.

"It's in a no-parking zone," Jenny said and marched across the street to Joe's Coffee Shop.

I followed her. Bond or no Bond, that car wouldn't

help them once the snows came. There was a reason that most people in Twin Willows drove trucks.

The bell over the door to Joe's jangled when we entered. One of the large corner booths was crammed with a bunch of our friends from school, and we wound through the packed tables.

"Where were you tonight?" Jenny asked our friend Carly, who was squeezed in between two sophomore boys trying to have simultaneous conversations with her.

"I had my piano lesson, and my mother wouldn't let me out of it." Carly's parents were determined to make her a concert pianist, even though Carly was the first to admit her musical talent was mediocre at best. "Can you fill me in?"

"Well—" I glanced at Bree who stood beside me, her lip curled as she surveyed the other kids in the booth. "Um, this is Bree Wolfe. Her family just moved to town." I looked past her, scanning the restaurant. "Where'd your brother go?"

"Why?" Bree slid her gaze up and down the full length of my body, making me flush. "Got a crush?"

My jaw dropped.

Before I could answer, Jenny stepped in front of me. "Look, *Wolfe*," she said, bringing her face almost nose to nose with Bree, "we're just trying to be nice. But if you want to make enemies with the entire school before your first day, be my guest." She spun around, whipping Bree in the face with her long blonde hair, and climbed over one of the sophomores to squish in next to Carly.

Bree seemed about to claw Jenny's eyes out, thought the better of it, and stalked out of the coffee shop.

Jenny snorted and bent her head toward Carly, the two of them whispering.

I pressed my lips together. Jenny was the best friend a girl could have, but sometimes she had problems with compassion. It had to be hard coming to a new school; I didn't want Bree to think she wasn't welcome. I slipped away from the table and headed to the door.

Darkness had swept over Main Street, and the dim streetlamps lit the pavement with pools of yellow light. I spotted Bree half a block down from Joe's and hurried to catch up, my shoulders hunched against the evening chill. "Hey!"

She tossed her hands in the air and gave an exaggerated sigh. "What's your problem?"

"I don't have one," I said. "I just came out here to make sure you were okay. Sensitivity isn't always Jenny's strong suit."

"I'm fine. Like you care." Bree shook her head slightly and smirked. "You small-town girls are all the same. The minute the new-kid novelty wears off, I'll be invisible."

"Maybe we're different. You'll never know until you give us a chance."

She dug inside her coat and pulled out a pack of cigarettes.

I made a face; I hated smokers.

Bree lit her cigarette, her gaze still on me. "I don't need to give you a chance. We'll be gone soon enough." She took a pull on her cigarette and blew a cloud of smoke right in my face.

I coughed and stumbled back a step. Standing against the door of the closed hardware store, hidden by the shadows, was Jonah. "Oh!" I pressed a hand to my chest. "I didn't see—have you been there this whole time?"

He pushed away from the wall. A slant of lamplight fell across his face. "Yeah. Sorry. I didn't mean to scare you." His voice was soft as just-fallen snow. He was close enough now that I could see flecks of gold in his deep green eyes. He stared at me for a moment before he turned to Bree. "I think we should go home."

"Yeah, we're done here," she said, flicking her half-finished cigarette on the ground. She stepped off the curb and walked down the middle of the street without looking back.

"Listen, I know how Bree comes off," Jonah said. "But she's not really like that. She's pissed because this is the fourth time we've moved this year."

"Wow." I shifted a little closer to him. "Doesn't that piss you off too?"

He shrugged one shoulder and tucked his hands in his pockets. "Yeah, but I just show it in a different way." His smile, unlike his father's, reached into every part of his face, lighting up his eyes and cheeks from within.

Without meaning to, I felt myself smiling back. "Like how?"

He leaned in close to me. "Oh, you know. The usual. Sneaking out in the middle of the night to break into the library, borrowing the car without asking to go to the museum."

I laughed. "Stealing money out of your mom's purse to give to the local orphanage . . ."

"Exactly." I could see myself in the reflection of his eyes. "You get it."

"Jonah, come *on*." Bree's disembodied voice rang out from the shadows across the street.

"Coming," Jonah answered. He gave my arm just the whisper of a touch. "Nice to meet you, Alessia." The way he said my name tingled my skin.

I watched him disappear down the dusky street until I could no longer hear his footsteps. I thought about going back to Joe's, but I wasn't ready to face Jenny's interrogation about Jonah. I rubbed my hand over my chest. An odd feeling lingered there, like something inside me was trying to break free.

Somewhere in the distance, a wolf howled. The night shuddered all around me.

As I walked home, I kept seeing Jonah's smile in my head, hearing him say my name over and over. *Stop it*, I told myself. *He's just a boy*. And pretty soon he would move away, and I would still be stuck in this dead-end town where two new kids at school was the most exciting thing that had happened all year.

The thought of the Wolfe family lingered even after the smell of homemade tomato sauce washed over me when I entered my house.

"Alessia? *Sei in ritardo*," my mother called out. Even though she had been in this country for fifteen years, she spoke a hybrid of Italian and English.

"Sorry, Mom." I hung my jacket and scarf on the peg by the door and found Lidia in the heartbeat of the house, the kitchen, her hands covered with bits of mozzarella. "Smells amazing."

"*Grazie, cara mia.*" My mother wiped her hands on her apron and gave me a tight hug. I breathed in the scents that always seemed to cling to her: grass, cheese, and fresh-baked bread. "Be a lamb, and get me a jar of pumpkin *mostarda* from downstairs, will you? I thought we could have it with some fresh cheese for dessert."

"Americans eat chocolate for dessert, not cheese." It was an old argument. She gave me a playful push, and I headed for the basement. The wooden stairs creaked as I stepped down to the concrete floor and faced the shelves that lined the walls. The *mostarda*, an Italian specialty made of candied fruit and mustard, filled the uppermost shelves in all different flavors: fig, pear, citrus, and pumpkin.

I dragged the rickety step stool over and climbed up. The pumpkin *mostarda* was farther back, behind the citrus, and as I reached for it my elbow bumped an empty jar at the edge of the shelf. It spiraled to the floor and shattered with a loud clatter. "Crap."

"Alessia? *Voi bene?*"

"Fine. I just broke an empty jar." I clunked down off the step stool and pulled the broom and dustpan from the corner. I swept all the big pieces into a pile and did a once-over on the entire floor, jabbing at the corners and edges along the wall. Lidia had a habit of padding around the house barefoot, and I didn't want her to wind up with glass in her toes.

As I swept along the wall by the shelves, the broom dislodged a loose brick right where the floor met the wall. I tried to push it back in with the stiff bristles, but something prevented it from going into place. Leaning the broom against the wall, I crouched down. Something blue was caught on the inside of the brick. I pulled it all the way out of the wall, and with it came a little pouch of bright blue cloth, tied up in string with a card attached. It looked like it had been inside the wall for a long time.

I placed the little bundle in the palm of my hand and held it in front of my face. The fabric was soft and silken, and even though it was faded, I could tell it had once been brilliantly iridescent.

The card attached to it was slightly larger than a playing card, with a red back. The face was splotchy with dirt and age. I peered at it closely. It was an old-fashioned painting of a woman in flowing robes with the words *La Empressa* underneath it. Light, spidery handwriting scrawled around the edge of the card. I brought it up close to my face, almost to my nose. *This house is under the protection of the Benandanti.*

# Chapter Two

*The Birthday*

Italians are superstitious. I had been raised with my mother's superstitions all my life, her constant crossing of herself if something unlucky strayed into her path and whispered prayers in the face of misfortune.

We had a long braid of garlic hanging in our kitchen, and though she plucked cloves from it to use in her cooking, I knew the real reason it was there. A crucifix and an icon of Saint Francis of Assisi, patron saint of animals, hung in the barn. And carved into the hillside behind the farmhouse was an altar to the Virgin Mary: a little white statue of the Blessed Mother nestled into a blue ceramic alcove, a weathered wreath of plastic roses around her feet. I had seen my mother kneel at the statue's feet and bow her head, her lips moving in silent prayer. And even though I teased Lidia about all these things, I couldn't help crossing myself whenever I passed the shrine too.

I sat back on my heels and turned the card over and over in my fingers. *This house is under the protection of the*

*Benandanti.* I had never heard that word before, even though I spoke fluent Italian. I ran it through my internal translator. *Good walkers.* The amulet had to be yet another manifestation of Lidia's superstition. Were the Benandanti one more entity for Lidia to pray to? If so, they hadn't been protecting us much lately.

"Alessia? *Dove sei*? Did you get lost down there?"

"Coming." I clutched the amulet in one hand, carried the *mostarda* in the other, and headed upstairs. The garlic braid was one thing; at least it had a double purpose. But amulets hidden in the basement? It was time for a superstition intervention.

But when I got upstairs, Lidia wasn't alone. Seated at the kitchen table was our neighbor. "Hey, Mr. Salter. Slumming?"

Lidia shot me an annoyed look.

But Mr. Salter laughed. "I don't think Twin Willows is big enough to have a slum." He jerked his chin toward the living room. "Brought you some firewood. Thought you could use it now that the weather's turning. We—I—got an extra shipment at the store today." Mr. Salter owned the hardware store in town. I worked there sometimes when he needed help.

"I just put my bathing suit away, and it's already cold enough for a fire." I set the *mostarda* on the table, but I tucked the amulet deep into my front pocket. It didn't seem right to bring it up in front of Mr. Salter. "Gotta love Maine."

"Yeah, well . . ." He toyed with the fork in front of him on the table. "I also thought you two could use some company today. Because—you know."

I stared at him, my face scrunched up.

He looked down at the fork. "The first birthday is always hard," he said quietly.

My heart slammed against my chest once and lay still. I couldn't breathe. How could I have forgotten? What kind of a daughter was I?

Lidia came over to the table and rested a hand on his shoulder. "It was very thoughtful of you to come over, Ed. You know Tom thought the world of you. You'll stay for dinner, of course."

I swallowed, the lump in my throat breaking into sawdust. "Mom?" It came out like a croak. "How long till we eat?"

"About twenty minutes."

"I need to go . . ." I paused in the doorway of the kitchen. "To check on the hens. One of them didn't look so good this morning."

"Now, *cara*?"

But I was already halfway up the stairs to my room. It took me less than ten seconds to grab what I needed and fly back downstairs.

"Take the flashlight," Lidia called after me, but I didn't need it. I could find my way blindfolded.

I ran past the barn, over the hill, and into the woods that bordered our farm. How, how had I gone through the whole day without realizing what this day was? It was unforgivable that Mr. Salter had remembered before I did. *I'm sorry, so sorry—*

But the only answer was the wind through the changing leaves.

The stone wall that marked the end of our property line loomed in the darkness. I climbed over its crumbling rocks without slowing down. Just beyond, I found the path. The little bundle I had grabbed from my room burned in my jacket pocket, its presence like a firebrand against my side.

Within minutes I heard the sound of water, growing louder with every footfall. I swerved through a copse of birch trees, their bark pale and shimmery. Once past them, I skidded to a stop at the edge of a wide stream and panted, my lungs on fire.

The water at my feet burbled over rocks until it reached a steep edge, where it tumbled into a waterfall and landed in a glassy pool below. I stepped onto a rocky overhang and dropped to my knees. Clouds shifted over the moon, fracturing light over every surface like a blessing.

I pulled the leather pouch from my pocket and held it in the palm of my hand. It was just a fraction of the ashes from the cremation, a handful I had stolen before the memorial. I tugged the drawstring and turned the pouch upside down, scattering the ashes in the stream. Heat tightened my throat, stung my eyes. "Happy birthday, Dad," I whispered.

I watched the little clump of ashes separate and swirl away until they disappeared over the waterfall.

Ten months ago at the memorial, I had bent my head during the prayers and promised my father we would celebrate his birthday one last time here at the waterfall, like we used to when he was alive. The waterfall had always been our secret, special place. Not even my mother knew about it.

But I had almost broken my promise. Every day for ten months I had felt the ache of his absence, and yet . . . today . . . what had distracted me? Bree and Jonah Wolfe? I shook my head. *Stupid, stupid girl.*

I rocked back on my heels and braced myself with my hand to stand up. White moonlight broke through the clouds and illuminated the opposite bank of the stream. And out of the brush, black as the night around it, a panther crept forward and paused, its bright eyes fixed on me.

Before I could stop myself, I scrambled backward, wincing as my hand scraped against the rock. A panther in these woods? I had seen wildcats before, but a panther sighting was rare. I inched off the rock, keeping my gaze on the panther. It was safely on the other side of the stream, but I knew if it wanted to reach me, it could—and fast.

Once down from the rock, I sidestepped along the streambed until I reached the edge of the waterfall. The panther didn't move, but its eyes followed me.

We watched each other. The wind rippled the stream between us. I had been in the presence of wild animals before—even dangerous ones—but never had I felt so . . . scrutinized.

A throb started in my palm where I had cut it on the rock. Breaking eye contact with the panther, I held my hand up in the moonlight. Blood and dirt dappled my skin. I glanced again across the water. The panther was utterly still, the only movement the rustle of the breeze in its sleek fur. I squatted down and dipped my hand into the flow of the waterfall. As the cold water rushed over my skin, I realized that in all the years I'd come here, I had never touched the water.

When my hand grew numb, I stood up and tucked both my hands into my pockets to warm them. I tiptoed away from the water's edge, back toward the birch trees.

The panther rose out of its crouch and stepped into the stream, its paws splashing lightly. I froze, my heartbeat shallow. The panther cocked its head. Its breath misted the air. I took a tiny step backward. The panther stayed where it was, its gaze more curious than predatory. I stepped back again and again until I bumped into one of the birch trees. The panther never moved, just stood ankle-deep in the stream, its eyes on me like two burning torches. Finally, when I ducked inside the copse, the stream—and the panther—disappeared from view.

I sagged against the tree and gulped in breath, suddenly aware that I'd practically been holding it since the moment the panther appeared. I couldn't get the image of the panther's eyes out of my head. The back of my neck prickled with the sensation of being watched. I turned in a wild circle, but there was nothing.

I fled out of the birch trees, wanting to put more distance between myself and the waterfall, but after several paces, I stopped. The waterfall was still audible through the forest. I clutched my hand at my throat. *I miss you, Dad. Every day.*

And yet, it had taken Mr. Salter to remind me of the date. I turned away from the sound of water and headed toward home. It wasn't surprising that Mr. Salter had remembered; his wife had died only a few months before my dad. He and Lidia had bonded over their mutual grief. I broke into a run again. Branches slapped my face, stinging my skin, but the tears that came to my eyes weren't from pain.

I reached the stone wall and clambered over to the other side. My vision was blurred with tears, the trees around me fuzzy, and before I could take a step I smacked into something warm and solid. I gasped and fell backward against the wall. "What the—?"

"Alessia?"

I blinked to clear my sight.

Heath, the farmhand my mother had hired a month earlier, stood in the path in front of me. The edge of his mouth curled up, crinkling the corner of his blue eyes. Though he was barely out of his midtwenties, he had little wrinkles there. "Sorry—didn't mean to scare you."

"You—you—didn't." I straightened. "What are you

doing out here?"

"Your mom sent me to find you." He searched my face. "But she seemed to think you would be at the hen-houses, not in the woods."

"I—" I tried to think of an excuse. I clamped my lips together. I didn't need to; I didn't owe Heath anything. He hardly knew me. "I was just heading back now."

"Great. I'll go with you." He brushed a lock of sandy hair off his forehead. "Lidia invited me to dinner too."

"Yeah, well, she likes to feed everyone." It was true. She had once invited a perfect stranger she'd met in a bookstore over to dinner.

We walked in silence for several minutes, emerging out of the woods and climbing over the fence at the edge of our pasture.

As we started up the hill, Heath glanced over his shoulder at the forest. "You should be careful in there, you know. There are wildcats."

"Next time I'll bring the shotgun."

Heath raised an eyebrow, unsure whether I was joking.

I wasn't. I knew how to take care of myself. My father had taught me that. He'd taught me many things, sitting on the rock at the edge of the waterfall. As I'd sat there tonight, watching his ashes disappear, I'd finally realized he was really gone. He'd never teach me anything ever again.

And I would never return to the waterfall ever again, either.

# CHAPTER THREE

*The Vision*

Before the sun rose the next morning, I was on my way to the henhouses, which were actually fifties-era trailers set at the edge of the pasture. Our farm was mostly a goat farm, although we sold our fresh eggs along with our cheeses at local farmers' markets and gourmet stores. It was a small operation, smaller since my dad had died, but we did okay. Collecting eggs had been my chore since I was seven, and while other kids might complain about the early hour, I loved watching the day rub the sleep from its eyes and come awake.

When my basket was full, I headed back across the pasture. I felt lighter this morning; it was actually a relief to have Dad's birthday over. I hoped Mr. Salter was right, that the first one was the hardest. The scene at the waterfall last night haunted me—the ashes swirling in the water, the moonlight shifting over the treetops, the panther watching me. I shivered and pushed it out of my mind. I tucked my basket in the crook of my elbow and buried my hands in my pockets.

My fingers met a lump inside my jeans; it was the amulet I had found. Mr. Salter had stayed late last night, so I hadn't asked Lidia about it yet, but the light in the kitchen spilled into the dawn-darkened pasture, telling me she was awake now. I cut through the barn, where the goats were starting to stir and bleat. Inside, blue dawn light illuminated a lean shape. "Hey, Heath."

He looked up and smiled, those little wrinkles appearing again. "Morning, Alessia." His voice was quiet and low; he said that loud noises upset the goats and spoiled their milk. Heath was always saying weird stuff like that.

I watched as he pitched a bale of hay into an empty stall. As reluctant as I'd been to let a stranger onto our farm, I had to admit that Lidia had made the right choice. The barn was cleaner than it had ever been in my lifetime. Not to mention that Heath made a crème fraîche that could make you cry.

"How's your French coming along?"

I made a face. Heath had lived in France for a few years and helped me with my French homework sometimes. "It's much easier to learn a language when you have a native speaker at home."

He snorted and dumped a forkful of hay into the stall. "I guess that's true."

"But you know," I said, "my teacher applied for a grant to take us to Paris next spring. So if we get to go you'll have to tell me all the cool places to visit."

He kept baling without looking at me. "I didn't spend much time in Paris. I lived in Provence."

"Oh." I leaned against the door. "What's Provence like?"

Heath paused. He closed his eyes and smiled, seeing something that I could not. "Purple."

"What?"

He opened his eyes. "Purple. With all the fields of lavender." He went back to his baling. "Have a good day."

That was Heath. More interested in hay and goats than human beings.

I slipped out of the barn and headed across the yard to the back door. Once inside the kitchen, I set the basket of eggs carefully on the counter. "Morning."

"*Buongiorno, cara mia*," Lidia sang out and snagged two eggs from the basket. She cracked them into the hot pan on the stove and scrambled them into the beginnings of an omelet. "Would you like spinach in yours?" she continued in Italian.

"No, just cheese," I answered her in Italian. Lidia always spoke Italian in the mornings, as though her brain didn't awaken to English until later in the day, and it was a good chance for me to practice.

"A growing girl needs her spinach. Come on, just a little bit. For the vitamins."

"Okay. Just a little." I slid into a chair at the table. Truth be told, I hated spinach, but it wasn't worth arguing. Lidia was stubborn. "Hey, Mom, I found something weird in the basement when I was down there last night."

"Oh?" She tossed the spinach into the omelet, along with a sprinkling of goat cheese, and folded it in half. "*Che*?"

"I'm not sure—some kind of amulet or something."

A sharp intake of breath made me look up from the table. Lidia's gaze hardened on the frying pan.

I narrowed my eyes at her. "It had a card attached."

"What kind of card?" She had switched to English.

"Like a tarot card." I bit my lip and watched her slide a spatula beneath the omelet, then deposit it on a plate next to the stove.

She kept her head turned away until she brought the plate to the table. By then her features had been rearranged into a placid smile. "It was probably something your father or his parents put there," she said and sat in the chair next to me. "*Mangia*."

"The card was in Italian," I said. I didn't touch my fork.

"Your father spoke Italian," Lidia said and became interested in a pull in the tablecloth.

"But why would he write on the card in Italian?"

Lidia pushed away from the table, went to the counter, and picked up the basket of eggs I had brought in. "Then maybe it was something I put there when I first moved into the house."

"That's what I thought," I said, picking up my fork. I shoveled a big bite of omelet into my mouth, chewed, and swallowed. "So what are the Benandanti?"

The crash shook me so violently that I almost fell off my chair. All the eggs I had gathered lay smashed on the floor around Lidia's feet, and she stood with one crushed in her hand, its broken yolk dribbling down her forearm. I met her eyes for an instant before she looked away, and I saw a darkness there that I had not seen since the night at the hospital when my father died.

I grabbed the roll of paper towels off its stand and knelt on the floor next to the yolky mess. The eggs seeped through the paper instantly. I laid another layer of towels down.

"I cannot believe I did that," Lidia said and crossed to the sink. "No, leave it; I don't want you to be late for school."

I rocked back onto my heels, the ball of sodden paper towels dripping in my hands. "But what are the Benandanti?"

Lidia slammed her palms against the edge of the sink. "Dammit, Alessia, I don't have time. This house was built two hundred years ago, so who knows who put it there? And now I have this mess to deal with—and . . . just get to school. *Bene*?"

I stared at her. Lidia rarely lost her temper. "*Bene*. Sorry," I muttered and tossed the towels in the trash.

Lidia cleaned up the mess in silence while I ate the rest of my omelet.

I still didn't know what the Benandanti were, but I was certain Lidia did and that she was determined to keep me in the dark.

I met Jenny on the walk to school. The high school was about a mile away at the edge of town, but I liked to walk, even when the weather grew cold. The fresh air, tinged with the scents of salt and sea, was so much better than the smelly bus.

"What happened to you last night?" Jenny asked as soon as she saw me. "You totally disappeared."

I told her about the scene with Bree and Jonah outside the coffee shop. "It sounds like their father moves them around the country every few months. That can't be fun."

"Yeah, but it's no excuse to act the way she did." Jenny grinned and poked me with her elbow. "But forget her—tell me about Jonah."

I shrugged, trying to ignore the flip-flop my belly did when she said his name. "There's nothing to tell. We said about five words to each other."

"Come on, Lessi," Jenny whined. "Now's your chance to get back at me for going on about boys for years and years. And all you can come up with is five words?"

I laughed. "I promise, if something more happens, I'll get my revenge."

We turned up Main Street; the school was in sight from here.

"Maybe he'll be in some of my classes today."

"One can only hope." Jenny sighed and linked her arm through mine as we approached the school.

Outside the shabby brick building that served as

Twin Willows High, grades eight through twelve, kids sat at the low cement wall that bordered the lawn, soaking up the morning sunshine before we were forced indoors for the greater part of the day. Students poured out of the buses in the parking lot and congregated into the usual groups: the band and drama geeks, the Goth crowd with their hairstyles that Lidia would never consent to, the cheerleaders and their jock boyfriends.

Jenny and I met up with Carly and our other good friend Melissa. We weren't the most popular kids in school, but we weren't the least, either. Soon a group of boys surrounded us, and I pressed my back against the large oak tree that shaded the grass. I wasn't half bad looking, but next to Jenny with her long legs and mass of golden hair, pixie-cute Carly, and curvy Melissa, my wild brown hair and overactive eyebrows paled in comparison.

It suddenly occurred to me that since I worked in the office first period, I might get to catch the Wolfes when they registered for classes. I said good-bye to the girls and headed to the office.

Sure enough, two dark-haired figures were clearly visible through the large office windows, alongside their red-haired mother. I tucked my flyaway hair behind my ears and opened the office door. "Good morning," I called out, and the secretaries answered in a choral return.

Principal Morrissey looked over Mrs. Wolfe's shoulder at me. "Ah, good. Alessia, you can help me register the Wolfes."

Bree turned and narrowed her eyes at me.

I gave her a wide smile as I edged my way around the counter, keeping my face turned away from Jonah until I stood next to Principal Morrissey. My neck ached with the effort of not looking at him.

"Good morning," I said to Mrs. Wolfe. "It's nice to see you again."

"Yes, lovely to see you too," Mrs. Wolfe said mechanically. Her eyes sunk into the shadows that ringed them, and there were little cuts on her lips, as if she bit them too often.

"Alessia is one of our top students," Principal Morrissey said with his trademark toothy smile. "She's won almost every award for creative writing in the county. She's a junior, the same as Bree and Jonah."

I usually hated it when Morrissey used me as the poster girl for the school, but when I slid my gaze down the counter to Jonah, I didn't mind so much. A little butterfly lodged itself in my chest. He was just as gorgeous as he had been last night. Our eyes met for the shortest of seconds.

"How can I help?" I murmured to Principal Morrissey.

"Copy out their schedules," he instructed, setting two blank schedule sheets in front of me. "Our printer still isn't working," he added apologetically to the Wolfes, then left me to deal with the paperwork.

I massaged my breastbone to quell the fluttery feeling and adjusted the glowing green screen of the computer at the edge of the counter so I could read Bree Wolfe's schedule clearly. My stomach dropped when I saw that we had virtually the same schedule.

An idea popped into my head. I glanced around; Mr. Morrissey was talking to one of the secretaries, and no one could see my computer screen. I swallowed and tapped on the keys, pulling up Jonah's schedule. It was completely different than Bree's; I'd dealt with twins before, and their parents usually liked to keep them separated. My fingers flew over the keyboard. In less than a minute, Bree's schedule had become Jonah's, and Jonah . . . was now in almost every one of my classes.

Heart thumping, I copied out Bree's new (and improved, in my opinion) schedule and handed it to her.

She snatched it and stomped out of the office.

I cracked my knuckles in an attempt to stop my fingers from shaking and clicked back to Jonah's schedule, although I could have written it out from memory. "You're in a lot of my classes," I said without looking at him, afraid my eyes would give away what I had done. "I can help you catch up, if you want."

"Fortune favors the brave."

I raised my gaze, expecting to see sarcasm written on his face, but he was just staring at me, his eyes hooded.

"That might be very helpful."

I swallowed and slid the schedule across the counter.

Mrs. Wolfe laid a hand on Jonah's arm. "Honey, do you—?"

"No, Mom. I'll see you after school." He barely acknowledged her as she squeezed his arm and turned to the door. A faint whiff of her sickly sweet perfume wafted into my nostrils as she left the office.

Jonah drummed his fingers on the counter, a thick silver chain bracelet just visible beneath his cuff. He searched my face, like a lost wanderer. I felt a flush creep from the base of my throat to my cheeks. "So what's our first class together?"

"Um, French. Second period." I tapped a finger on his schedule, brushing the side of his hand. I flattened my palm against the counter, but our pinkies were still touching, just barely. "But you have history first period."

The bell rang.

"And you're late."

He shrugged, his lips curving. "I'm sure they'll forgive me." He leaned forward a little. "How'd you land this office gig?"

I propped my elbow on the counter and rested my chin in my hand. "They had a big pageant. There was a swimsuit competition and everything."

Jonah grinned. "And of course you won."

"No, I was first runner-up. But the girl who won had a sudden unfortunate accident."

He laughed, his green eyes flashing. "You're funny. I like that."

A little squiggle of pleasure shot through me. It was the first time a boy had ever been so openly appreciative of me; usually I was in the background behind Jenny. "Thanks," I said, sure that my face was red as a strawberry.

"Mr. Wolfe, do you have a class to go to?"

I whirled around.

Mr. Morrissey stood in the doorway of his office, flipping through a sheaf of papers.

"Yes, sir." Jonah winked at me. "See you in French. *Au revoir*." And with that, he sauntered out of the office.

I watched him go. The little butterfly in my chest multiplied into a thousand. I took a deep breath and turned back to the computer. As I tapped the keys, my hands started to shake. *Don't be an idiot. He's just a boy.*

But the trembling intensified, ran down my legs so that I could barely stand. I gripped the edge of the counter to keep from falling. This wasn't the aftereffect of talking to a cute boy. This was something different, something unnatural . . . My mind darkened, closing out thought. I bent over the counter, my forehead pressed to its cool surface, but the trembles took over my whole body.

My knees buckled and I hit the floor. The lights went out. Pain seared across my chest. I tried to breathe, but my lungs sealed shut. Panicked, I squeezed my eyes closed, hoping everything would return to normal, but when I opened them the floor of the office was far below me.

I hovered in the air, gazing down at the scene below. Everyone in the office was frozen, the secretaries' fingers poised above their keyboards as though someone had hit the Pause button on them. What was happening? Everything was in razor-sharp focus, my vision crystalline.

I spun in the air to face the windows. Reflected in the glass was a magnificent falcon, its wings outstretched several feet across, its snowy breast in gleaming contrast with the blue-black feathers that covered its back. I blinked. So did the falcon. My heart in my throat, I turned my head as the falcon in the glass did the same.

The falcon was me.

I screamed, but instead of my voice a terrifying bird-cry ripped out of my throat. I dropped in the air, shock vibrating through me. Had I fallen asleep? Was this a dream? The last thing I remembered was leaning over the counter. Had I hit my head? Whatever was happening, it felt so real. I raised my wings and shot upward with dizzying speed. The top of my head hit the ceiling. I brought my wings down to level myself out. The floor below looked very far away, and my head spun with vertigo. *Wake up*, I told myself. *Wake up! Wake up!*

But I didn't—I couldn't—wake up. I circled above the secretaries' desks, the beat of those impossibly strong wings like thunder in my ears. I shut my eyes. Thunder *was* rumbling. I listened, every other sound in the world disappearing beneath the rumble. It was not thunder. It was . . . growling.

My eyes flew open. A huge black panther slunk in through the office door, its belly low to the ground, its fierce emerald eyes fixed on me. With its back paw, it knocked the door closed. I spun around; the door to Mr.

Morrissey's office was shut too. My gut twisted. I was trapped.

I faced the panther again. A jolt thudded through me. It looked exactly like the panther I had seen last night at the waterfall. *What the hell is going on?*

The panther sprang onto the counter, scattering papers. In one swift motion, it rose onto its hind legs and swiped the air.

I buffeted backward just in time; its long claws missed my feathered belly by less than an inch. A tiny cry escaped from me.

I flew back and forth above the panther while it paced the length of the counter beneath me. My biology teacher had once talked about the fight or flight instinct, but now that I was literally in flight, the panther blocked every move I made. I took refuge by the ceiling panels, my wings fluttering. With nowhere to go, I had to fight.

My mind whirled, but somehow this strange new body knew what to do. I tucked my wings in and dove, my eyes fixed on the panther's neck. In less than an instant, I was there. I turned, trying to understand how fast I'd flown, but in that moment of hesitation the panther pounced. It pinned me to the counter, its claws over my throat. I looked into its glowing eyes as it lowered its head, its jaws wide, its long teeth reaching for my throat . . .

Screaming filled my ears. It was my own voice.

"Alessia! What's the matter?"

I blinked, the fluorescent lights blinding. The office was normal again.

One of the secretaries bent over me, her face flooded

with concern. "Are you all right?"

I sat up, gulping in air. I held my hand in front of my face, flexing my fingers. It was only my hand, no wings, no feathers. "I don't—I don't know." I looked around. Principal Morrissey and the other secretaries stood in a semicircle around me, their faces perplexed. "Everything went dark for a minute. Was that just me?"

"You should see the nurse," Principal Morrissey said. "Has this ever happened before?"

My legs wobbled as I pulled myself up to stand. Other than the rapid pounding of my heart, I seemed to be okay. "No, I'm fine. I'm sorry—I think I fell asleep for a minute." I tried to smile. "Didn't sleep too well last night, I guess."

"Are you sure?" The secretaries clustered around me. Their motherly concern was smothering.

"Yeah. Yeah. Maybe I'll—" I glanced at the clock. The bell for second period would ring in ten minutes. "Maybe I'll just get some fresh air before my next class."

"Okay, dear. But see the nurse if you feel sick at all."

"I will." I pushed my way through them and out of the office, breaking into a run until I hit the front door of the school.

Outside, the air was cold and bracing. In the sharp, clear morning, it was easier to see that it had simply been a dream. A vivid, nightmarish dream but a dream nonetheless.

*That's all it was*, I thought and hurried inside as the bell clanged.

On the way to second period, I met Jenny in the hall. "You will not believe what Melissa said to me during homeroom," she started, then squinted at me. "Are you okay? You look weird."

I swallowed hard. "I'm okay." She looked unconvinced so I decided to distract her. "I registered the Wolfes."

"Oooh," she squealed, her eyes wide.

Several people near us turned their heads, but once they saw it was Jenny they lost interest. A day didn't pass without Jenny squealing in the hallway.

"I did something really wrong," I whispered. We were almost at the door of the French classroom. I leaned in close to her ear and told her about switching Bree's and Jonah's schedules.

She laughed. "Oh, Lessi, that wasn't wrong. That was so *right*." Still hooting, she opened the door.

I pressed two fingers to my temple, which still throbbed a little from the whatever it was in the office. I took a deep breath and followed Jenny into the classroom. As I walked to my usual seat between Jenny and Carly, I scanned the desks. Jonah wasn't here yet.

Carly leaned over her desk toward me, her perfectly plucked eyebrows arched high. "Bree Wolfe was in my first-period English, and Mr. Tanner almost sent her to the principal's office. In her first class!"

"What did she do?" I asked.

My desk nearly tipped over sideways as Jenny leaned her entire upper body onto it, joining the conversation.

"Well, first she—" Carly pulled back, sat up straight, and coughed.

I turned. Jonah Wolfe stood in the doorway, his broad shoulders nearly as wide as the frame. He marched over to Madame Dubois's desk and laid the transfer slip on it for her to sign.

"There's a free seat in the back," Madame Dubois said.

I darted my gaze around the room. The only free seat was behind me.

Jonah grinned and plunked down in the chair.

I took a deep breath and turned around. "Hey," I said.

"Hey, yourself." His voice made the hairs on my arms stand up.

"How was history?"

He leveled his gaze at me. The shadows across his face hid any kind of depth from me. "Oh, you know. You've seen one revolution, you've seen them all."

"Yeah, so many coups, so little time."

The second bell rang. I spun forward in my seat as Madame Dubois called the class to order. Out of the corner of my eye I saw Jenny scribbling fiercely in her notebook, no doubt a note to me. I cleared my throat and flipped open my French book.

"Now, class, settle down, or I won't tell you the exciting news." Madame Dubois stood in front of the blackboard and bounced on her toes, her hands clasped in front of her.

I shot a look at Jenny, who slid forward to the edge of her chair.

The noise level dropped a decibel.

"The grant I applied for from the Board of Ed has come through. We're going to Paris!"

"Ooooh!" squealed Jenny, and she wasn't the only one.

I twisted in my seat to meet Jenny's smiling face and clapped. Carly bounded out of her chair and joined us.

"We're going to Paris!" Jenny crowed, and we all laughed.

The whole class was in an uproar, shouting and whistling.

I glanced over my shoulder at Jonah, who doodled absently in his notebook with a bemused grin.

"Okay, quiet, everyone," Madame Dubois called out, but it took a few minutes for everyone to return to their seats.

I could barely sit still. Finally, here was the escape I longed for, the chance to see the places I had always dreamed about. I thought about what Heath said; now I would get to see those purple fields for myself.

"You will have to pay a little something—some fees and of course whatever souvenirs you might want to buy," Madame Dubois shouted over the hubbub. "But airfare, hotel, and meals will all be covered by the grant." She handed a stack of papers to the first student in the front row. "These are the permission slips that I'll need signed by your parents. And there's a spot on the slip for your parents to check off if they want to be a chaperone—we need at least five."

"Melissa is going to be so pissed that she took Spanish," Jenny whispered when the permission slips reached her. She handed the pile to me.

I took one and passed the stack to Jonah, who handed it to Carly without taking one.

"Aren't you going to go?" I asked him. An image of the two of us sitting on the Champs-Élysées, eating bread and cheese, popped into my head.

Jonah snorted without looking up from his notebook. "Like that'll happen."

"Why not?" I stayed turned in my chair, facing him, while Madame Dubois told us to start conjugating the verbs on page seventy-three in our books.

"By the time spring break rolls around, we'll probably be in a different state."

My ribs tightened at the thought of him moving away. "You never know. You could at least ask your dad."

Jonah shrugged, his gaze still on his doodles.

"What's going on back there? Mademoiselle Jacobs?"

I faced front so fast that a crick shot through my neck. "Nothing, Madame Dubois."

"Monsieur Wolfe?" Madame Dubois made her way through the chairs and stopped in between mine and Jonah's. "What do you have there?" she asked, nodding to his open notebook.

I expected him to flip it closed, like any normal kid would do, but instead he tilted it up and displayed his drawing. It was a highly detailed caricature of Madame Dubois lying on her desk in her underwear with the words *Voulez vous coucher avec moi?* in a bubble over her head.

I inhaled sharply through my nose, my face burning, and looked up at Madame Dubois. She was red to the roots of her hair, her nostrils white.

The other kids close enough to see the drawing wolf whistled and laughed.

Madame Dubois flushed even brighter. After a deep breath, she said, "Well, since you seem to have such a knack for art, perhaps you should visit Mr. Morrissey to see about getting into an art class," and pointed to the door.

"*Oui*, Madame," Jonah said without a trace of apology. He stood and gathered his things. As he moved to the door, I heard him whisper to Carly, "I beat Bree," and then he was gone.

# CHAPTER FOUR
*The Escape*

·

When I got home that afternoon, I dropped my backpack onto a kitchen chair and went out the back door to find Lidia. Goats dotted the hillside, grazing in the last few hours of daylight before we corralled them for the night. The whole scene was peaceful, in total contrast to my swirling thoughts.

I kept reliving the events of the day. Registering Jonah. His behavior in French class. And the incident in the office. What *was* that? *A hallucination*, I told myself. Lidia was always saying I had an overactive imagination; it had just gotten the better of me. That was all.

Meanwhile, the permission slip for the Paris trip burned a hole in my backpack. I jogged along the gravel path past the barn and around the curve of the hill to the Cave. That was what we called the cheese cave my father had built into the hillside years ago. He'd modeled it on the cheese caves in Europe, and we were one of the only farms in the northeast to have one. Once upon a time I'd find my parents in here, laughing together as they worked with the cheese molds, but now when I opened the door I saw Lidia and Heath, their backs to each other.

Lidia looked up when I came in, but Heath's concentration never broke. He went through the motions like a ballet dancer.

"How was school, *cara*?" Lidia asked as she ladled curd into a mold.

"Fine." I hugged myself. It was never more than fifty degrees in the Cave to allow the cheese to age properly. "Guess what?"

"What?"

I leaned against the knobby edge of the long table that dominated the center of the Cave. "Madame Dubois got a grant from the government to send our whole class to Paris for spring break. Isn't that awesome?"

Lidia froze for an instant before she half turned away from me. "That sounds very exciting," she said in a flat, guarded tone.

I tilted to the side, trying to see her expression, but she kept her face hidden, her hair falling in front of it as she returned to her cheese mold. "I need you to sign a permission slip. Oh, shoot, I forgot it in the house."

"That's all right; we'll talk more about it when I come in." She pushed her hair off her face.

I looked past Lidia. "I'll get to see those lavender fields. Right, Heath?"

He glanced up. "Right."

Lidia gave me a salty little smile. "Go do your homework. I'll be done in a little while."

I trudged back up to the house, my feet heavy with the gnawing feeling that Lidia was not doing cartwheels over the trip to Paris. As I sat at the kitchen table with my books spread around me, my mind spun in all different directions. None of them included biology, math, or *Wuthering Heights*, although I was thinking about French class. Okay, so Jonah's drawing of Madame Dubois had been pretty obnoxious. I twirled my pen in between my fingers. But there was more to him than that . . . something softer . . . I had seen it in the office and last night outside Joe's. I stared out the window, replaying those conversations with him.

By the time Lidia came into the house, I had barely made a chip in the mountain of homework before me. She laid out four chicken breasts on the kitchen island and seasoned them without a word.

I decided not to read into her silence and pulled the slip out of my French folder. "Hey, Mom, here's the permission slip you need to sign for the Paris trip."

Lidia set down the pepper mill in a deliberate motion and pressed her palms flat to the counter. "*Cara*, I can't sign that paper."

"What?" I twisted around in my chair to face her. "Why not?"

"Because I can't let you go."

"Why?" It came out much louder than I intended.

"You're too young to be traipsing off to Europe."

"But—but I'll be with the class. And there'll be chaperones. You could even chaperone if you want. Madame Dubois said—"

"No. I'm sorry. I know you want to go, but I can't allow it." Lidia turned her attention to the chicken as if the discussion were over.

I got to my feet and came to the other side of the island. "Is it the money? Because it's all paid for by the grant, and Mr. Salter is always willing to throw me some work at the hardware store."

"It's not the money." Lidia didn't look up. She sprinkled a pinch of Italian seasoning over each of the breasts. "I just don't think you're ready to travel overseas."

"Not ready? What does that mean? I'm sixteen. I'm not a baby."

"*Cara*—" A note of pleading crept into the pet name.

"It's so unfair! You never let me do anything!" I shoved the island with my full weight, and it trembled enough to knock over the pepper mill. "You think I don't have a mind of my own, but I do. I know you lied about that amulet thingy this morning—"

"Alessia." There was a warning tone in her voice, but I ignored it.

"Dad would let me go."

Lidia snapped her head up. She stared at me, her eyes full of tears.

I knew I had crossed a line, but I was too angry to

apologize. I flung open the door and ran out into the chilly night, pretending I couldn't hear her call my name.

The air tinged my throat with the cold smell of salt from the distant sea. I rounded the side of the house and climbed over the hill, came to the fence that marked our property, and hoisted myself onto the top rail. Heat cramped my chest, and I dug my knuckles into my breastbone as I looked over this tiny corner of the world.

Twin Willows was named for the two matching willow trees that marked the north and south ends of town. When I was a child I used to climb them, inching out along their bended boughs until I could see what lay beyond the "Welcome to Twin Willows" sign. In the last fifteen years I had discovered everything there was to know about the town. I wanted to see what lay on the other side of the two trees. I had never been anywhere except Nova Scotia on a family vacation. And even though I'd been born in Italy, I had never been back there. I was suffocating in this town, and I needed to escape, even if only for a week. Why wouldn't Lidia let me go? Why was she so overprotective?

I dug my elbows into my knees and took several deep breaths. I had to get out of here before I went crazy. I looked at the farmhouse, its windows yellow with light. I might not be able to go to Paris, but there were other ways I could get out of Twin Willows, with or without Lidia's permission.

I met Jenny on the way to school the next morning as usual, but when we got to the edge of town, I stopped and turned to her. "I'm going to Bangor for the day. Wanna come?"

Jenny dropped her book bag onto the ground and stared at me, jaw open. "Who are you, and what have you done with Lessi?"

I laughed and grabbed her wrist. "I'm not *that* much of a goody-goody. Come on—we'll miss the bus if we don't hurry."

Jenny jogged along next to me to keep up. "Seriously? What brought this on?"

I didn't answer. We walked to the opposite side of the street, and when we reached the corner where we would turn off to go to school, we continued down the block to the bus stop in the center of town in front of Joe's. The coffee shop bustled with activity. I peeked in through the windows, hoping no one inside would snitch on me.

In the far corner, I spotted Mr. Wolfe in a booth with his assistant, the man in the too-expensive suit. Mr. Wolfe sat with his head bowed, his hands clasped on the table in front of him. I watched his face as the assistant talked and gestured wildly. Mr. Wolfe's pale skin and downcast eyes seemed at total odds to the cold, confident businessman I'd met at the town hall meeting. I leaned in close to the glass to see better.

"They're going to call Lidia the minute you don't show up in the office," Jenny said, pulling my attention away from the window.

I peered down the road. The bus was nowhere to be seen yet. "I don't care," I said, and part of me really didn't.

"And she's going to send a search team out if you don't cover. Let me handle this." Jenny took her cell phone out of her bag and dialed a number from her contacts, waited a moment while it rang on the other line. "Yeah, hi, this is Jenny Sands. I was just walking with Alessia Jacobs to school, and she totally threw up in the middle of the road."

"Jenny!"

She flapped her hand in front of my face to shush me. "Yeah, she doesn't look so good. I'm going to take her home, so I just wanted you to know that she won't be there today. And could you let Mrs. Guilano know that I'll probably miss first period while I get her home? . . . Thanks . . . Uh-huh . . . Okay, I'll tell her. Bye." She snapped her phone shut and grinned at me. "They hope you feel better."

"I can't believe you did that." I shot a glance down the road. In the distance, the bus lumbered toward us, a cloud of smoke and exhaust billowing in its wake. "You know, they're going to call your mom as soon as you don't show up second period."

"Nah, it'll take them a while before they figure it

out." Jenny linked her arm through mine and rested her chin on my shoulder. "We're having an adventure! How fun!"

I snorted, but a little jolt ignited my insides.

The bus wheezed to a stop in front of us. After we paid our fare and found seats in the back, Jenny turned to me. "So, seriously. What's going on?"

I wanted to tell her about the weird daydream, but I knew it would sound crazy, so instead I settled for something believable. "Lidia won't let me go to Paris."

Jenny pressed her lips together and nodded. "I'm not surprised."

"Well, I'm pissed."

"Clearly." Jenny waved a hand, encompassing the bus, the world outside the grimy windows, and the fact that we were ditching school, which I had never done before.

"But I guess I wasn't really surprised, either," I said, tucking my feet up onto the seat and resting my chin on my knees. "I mean, she doesn't let me do anything. She's so freaking overprotective. Why is that?"

"I don't know," Jenny said, rolling the words around on her tongue like they were marbles. "But she's always been like that, right? It's not just since your dad . . ."

"No, I think it's gotten worse since he died. Maybe he kept her chill, and now that he's . . . not around . . . there's no buffer."

"Maybe."

I waved my hand. I didn't want to drag myself down so early in our adventure. "Whatever. Let's just have fun today. What do you want to do in Bangor?"

"Shop," Jenny said without hesitation, and we both laughed.

We spent the rest of the trip planning which stores to hit, where to eat lunch, and how late we could stay before suspicions were raised at home. I breathed a sigh of relief; Jenny never failed to cheer me up. I knew this day would come back to bite me in the ass, but I shoved all those cares aside and followed Jenny off the bus into downtown Bangor with an extra bounce in my step.

We bought lattes and headed toward West Market Square where a number of boutiques dotted the street. They were still closed, so Jenny and I slid onto a sidewalk bench and sipped our coffee.

Jenny balanced her cup on her knees and looked at me. "So what else is bothering you?"

My heart skittered. I shrugged but didn't meet her eyes. "Nothing."

"Oh, really? This new and adventurous Lessi wouldn't have anything to do with a certain tall, dark, and mysterious new guy, would it?"

I coughed on the hot coffee that burned the tip of my tongue. It was only half the truth but still. "That obvious, huh?"

"Well, probably not to anyone but me. I'm your best friend, remember? You can't hide anything from me." My face flamed, but Jenny didn't notice as she took another sip of her coffee. "Seriously. What's up with you two?"

"Uh, *nothing*. I've known him for a day. What could possibly be 'up' with us?"

"You had quite the conversation in French class."

"Yeah, and that got him sent to detention. *Please.* Like he would look twice at me." I buried my nose in the steam from my latte, let the delicious bittersweet aroma fill my nostrils.

"He did look twice. He looked more than that." Jenny's voice softened. "Just be careful, okay? I mean, I know I'm always going on about the bad boys, but Jonah—I don't know—he seems like he might be a badder boy than most."

I peered down the street, away from Jenny. "Stores are opening."

"Lessi? Did you hear me?" She tugged my elbow, forcing me to look at her.

"Yeah, I heard you. Don't worry. Nothing's gonna happen." But even as I said it, every fiber of my being wished the words untrue.

The sun dipped precariously low in the sky by the time Jenny and I climbed on the bus that would take us back to Twin Willows. We had already called our moms, told them we'd be hanging out at Joe's for a few hours and we'd be home in time for dinner. As long as there wasn't too much traffic heading out of Bangor, we would make it.

The urban landscape dissolved into suburbs as we sped along.

I turned to Jenny. "Are you sure that yellow sweater looks good on me?"

"For the millionth time, yes," Jenny said. "You have the perfect coloring for it. And it's mustard, not yellow."

"I love that bracelet you got," I said. "You have to let me borrow it."

"I will, if I can borrow that red jacket."

"Deal." I stuffed all the day's finds into my backpack, so Lidia wouldn't see the bags and start asking questions.

Outside, the headlights of the other cars flickered and shone against the glass. The bus slowed and curved down the exit ramp to the back roads. Soon we were driving past farms with barns and long fences. I turned to Jenny; she was dozing, her head tilted back against the seat. I smiled and looked out the window again. The outlines of trees loomed tall in the darkness, and above their tops the stars began to appear.

Jenny slept through all the stops the bus made while I read the novel I had picked up at the bookstore that afternoon.

"Twin Willows next," the driver called.

I glanced out the window. We were just heading onto the bridge over an inlet several miles from town; I could let Jenny sleep a few minutes longer.

Traffic whizzed by in the opposite direction on the bridge. I stared down at the steel pillars that seemed to grow out of the water. A flash of movement at the base of one of them caught my eye. I pressed my nose to the window and focused my vision. Everything around me darkened, and all I could see was an enormous wildcat, its edges shimmering against the black night around it.

My whole body trembled, and the world blackened, just like it had in the office. *No, no, this can't be happening again . . .*

An instant later, an inhuman shriek of straining metal and broken glass pierced the air, so loud and horrible that I had to cover my ears. The sound echoed inside me, filling my chest and throat and throbbing against my eardrums. I turned my head toward the window, but it was not where it was supposed to be. With a sickening smack my head hit the side of the bus, and the upside-down world went dark.

# CHAPTER FIVE
*The Bridge*

Pain crisscrossed my body, slicing me in two. Red spots exploded on the backs of my closed eyelids. I fought for air, grappling for one tiny, lifesaving breath . . .

Then the pain was gone, and I was floating. I opened my eyes, and the world was far below me. But in place of my arms were those great wide wings, the same as in the office. What was going on? Why was this happening again? A screeching cry escaped from inside me and was carried away by the wind.

I flew in a small circle. Despite my confusion, a small thrill of exhilaration shot through me. I was *flying*. And it was so real . . . like I had been born to it . . . I nose-dived and halted in midair a few feet above the water. Reflected in the moonlit water was the same falcon I had seen mirrored in the window of the office. A sharp, pointed beak curved out from what should be my mouth. Black feathers framed my own deep hazel eyes, and a ghostly blue glow haloed my entire body. I blinked and fluttered my wings up and down, mesmerized by the image.

Wind rippled the water, disturbing my reflection. I glided away, toward the bridge, and stopped. What I saw in front of me didn't make any sense.

The bridge was broken in half.

One of the pillars that supported the bridge had snapped, the steel cables dangling over the expanse between the two sides of the bridge. Cars piled up on both sides and in the water below the bridge. I scanned the length of the catastrophe until I found the bus. It lay on its side, the back end hanging over the hole in the bridge. My heart jolted. Jenny!

I plunged toward the bus. But something was off; there was no movement, no sound, on the bridge. I pulled up level with one of the stopped cars and peeked in the window. A driver and a passenger sat motionless, their heads turned to each other, their mouths open as though they were about to speak. It was just like it had been in the office, with the secretaries frozen in place. Someone had paused the entire scene. I flew from car to car, but they were all the same. I was the only thing moving in this entire disaster.

When I reached the bus, I peered through the windshield, the only glass that wasn't tinted. Halfway down the aisle I saw Jenny, clinging to one of the seat backs. She too was frozen in place but looked unhurt. Then my eyes were drawn to the figure lying next to her.

It was me.

I nearly collided with the windshield. How could I

be out here and inside the bus at the same time? I flew to the door, but the aluminum frame barely rattled when I knocked into it. I tried again and again, using my side, my wings, my talons, but it wouldn't budge.

*Alessia.* It was not my own voice that rang through my head but someone else's.

I whirled in the air. *Who are you?*
*We're coming. We'll be there soon—*
*What's going—?*
*Be careful!*

Something growled behind me.

I spun around. An enormous bobcat crouched on the pavement below me, its entire body haloed in a silvery aura. I stared, frozen. The bobcat sprang at me. I didn't react fast enough. Claws snagged my leg and ripped a deep cut in my feathers. I screeched and buffeted up, just out of reach. Eyes fixed on me, the bobcat let out a roar that shook me.

I flew higher and turned toward the water. The bobcat couldn't follow me that way. I glanced down at the bus. What would happen to my body if I went too far away?

A huge shape loomed over me. Long, sharp talons bore down on me. I wheeled away, but the other bird was faster; it caught my legs and plummeted, dragging me with it. I shrieked and thrashed, trying to break free of the ironclad grip, but I was held fast.

The bird—a raven, also glowing with that same silver aura—halted several feet above the ground and dangled me just out of reach of the bobcat. In the depths of its amber eyes I saw its hunger for me. I twisted against the raven's grasp, snapped my beak at its wings, and flexed my talons, but it would not let me go. It dipped lower, inch by inch, until it was at a height that if it dropped me, the bobcat could seize me before I could fly away.

*Help!* I screamed at the voice that had gone silent, and the sound tore across the still night like a knife.

The raven—I could swear it was laughing—let go.

But if this was a dream or a hallucination, I couldn't die, could I? My gaze fixed on the face of the bobcat as I fell. The spit dripping from its teeth was so real, so real . . .

A desperate howl pierced the air. A ferocious white wolf rammed into the bobcat's side, knocking it off-balance. My path clear, I shot upward and circled away. On the bridge below me, a group of animals gathered, including the white wolf. I dropped lower to get a better look. These new animals were huge too, but their auras were shimmering blue, just like the aura I had seen around myself in the water.

The raven burst through the air to get to me, but a massive eagle descended and sliced the raven's wing with a long golden talon. The raven fell away, its silver aura crackling. The eagle soared upward until it was level with me. Its eyes shone with a kind of fierce protectiveness. *Stay with me.*

It was a new voice in my head and distinctly female. I blinked at the eagle. *Was that—you?*

*Yes. I'm on your side. Come on.* She veered down toward the bridge, and I followed her. The bobcat faced off against three blue-haloed animals—the wolf, a lynx, and a stag. Outnumbered, the bobcat tried to dodge in between the lynx and the stag, but it wasn't fast enough. The three animals pounced, and the bobcat disappeared beneath their looming figures.

*What are they doing?* I cried to the eagle.

She turned her head, her eyes serene. *What is necessary. The Bobcat and the Raven came here to kill you.*

*What? Why?*

Before she could answer, the raven appeared below us, cawing loudly. The eagle dropped. I copied her motions, letting her guide me in this unreal reality. The raven reached the bridge before us and struck the lynx across the back. The lynx lurched to the side, enough to create a space for the bobcat to escape. It raced off the bridge, howling, with the raven barreling overhead.

The eagle hovered above the small group of animals, and I hung in the air next to her. *What is going on? Am I dreaming?*

*Are you all right?* The stag pranced over to the lynx.

*I'm fine. It's not deep.* The lynx's voice was deep and melodious, definitely male. He sat on his haunches and licked the wound on his back. *Damned Raven.*

The stag swept his gaze over the length of the bridge, his dark eyes shocked and sad. *Look what they did. To kill one of us, they've killed dozens.* He swung his head toward me. *At least they failed in their mission.*

*And we succeeded in ours,* the wolf said. It was the first voice I had heard, calm and masculine. He trotted toward me and lifted his head. *And now the Falcon has been Called, and our Clan is complete.*

*Hello?* I cried out as loud as I could in my head. *Will someone please tell me what—?*

A noise echoed nearby, pulling our attention. In one of the crashed cars, the driver was waking up, pulling at her seat belt.

*Their magic is lifting,* the wolf said. *We have to go.* I was low enough in the air to see his bright blue eyes, somehow familiar to me. *Welcome home,* he said, and everything turned black again.

Red spots danced on the backs of my eyelids. My lungs expanded and I gasped in air.

"Lessi? Lessi!" It was Jenny's voice.

I opened my eyes. I lay curled up against the side of the bus, my head on the window. "What—what happened?"

"The bus flipped. Oh, my God, you weren't breathing, and I thought—I thought—"

I sat up. My ribs ached and my head pounded, but nothing seemed to be broken. I held my hand up in front of my face, expecting to see a feathered wing, but it was just my hand. "I'm okay." I looked around, trying to get my bearings. At last I located the glowing red sign of the emergency exit. It was now on the side of the bus.

Jenny and I climbed over the seats and headed toward the open door. Every muscle in my body ached as I moved, and I had to stop a couple of times to catch my breath. The bus creaked and wobbled. I grabbed a seat back to steady myself.

"We have to get out of here," one of the other passengers, a man in a flannel shirt, said. "This whole thing could fall at any second."

"Come on." Jenny grabbed my arm and pulled me toward the emergency door.

The man in the flannel shirt pushed Jenny and me through the door, then climbed out himself. We scrambled over the side of the bus and slid down to the ground.

I gulped in deep lungfuls of cold night air. "Is everyone else off the bus?" I asked Flannel Shirt.

"Yeah." He pressed his hand to a small gash on his cheek. "Christ."

I followed his gaze to the center of the bridge where a ragged hole gaped, separating the two sides of the bridge. My stomach churned, but I was looking for something else: a bobcat, a white wolf, a stag, an eagle. They were nowhere to be seen.

The earth trembled, knocking me sideways. Directly in front of me, at the edge of the empty space where the bridge had dropped away, one of the other pillars wavered, threatening to tip over at any second and take the rest of the bridge with it.

"Move!" Flannel Shirt yelled.

I grabbed Jenny's hand, and we fled toward solid ground. My eardrum ached with the sound of breaking metal. I risked a glimpse behind me. The steel cables that held the pillar in place snapped. The pillar split from the bridge. With a sickening crash, it smashed into the water below, and the overstressed bridge tumbled into the sea. The ground shook, shifting beneath our feet as we raced away from the bridge. I ran faster, holding Jenny's hand tight in mine.

Only when we reached the safety of the ground beyond the bridge did I turn back to look at the wreckage.

Screams and cries rose from the water below.

I jerked away from Jenny, but she stopped me. "What are you doing?"

"Those people—someone has to help them—"

"Lessi, don't leave me!" She hugged me, burying her face in my shoulder.

I put my hands over my ears to block out the screaming. Within seconds it was replaced by the sound of sirens. An ambulance pulled to a stop next to us, and a group of paramedics jumped out. One of them handed us a blanket and told us to keep warm before rushing into the wreckage.

Jenny and I huddled under the scratchy wool blanket, trying not to watch the rescue teams as they hauled up one black body bag after another from the water. I rested my head on Jenny's shoulder, which shook beneath my cheek, and thought about my dream. Jenny had said I wasn't breathing. If I had blacked out, then the dream was simply that—a dream. It couldn't have been real. But why was I having different versions of the same dream over and over?

Jenny sniffled. "I need to call my mom." She wiped her nose with the back of her hand. "My cell phone—it was on the bus."

I looked out to where the bus still lay on its side, tottering at the edge of the broken bridge. I shivered. We could have lost so much more than a cell phone on that bus.

"I have mine," I said and dug my phone out of my pocket. The fact that I had cut school seemed insignificant now. I dialed home, suddenly wanting nothing more than to hear my mother's voice.

# CHAPTER SIX
*The Gift*

Lidia and Barb, Jenny's mom, arrived together. My heart skipped as Jenny and I walked toward the car. The passenger side door swung open, and Lidia tumbled out. "*Mi Dio! Grazie, Santa Maria, grazie, grazie, mi figlia bella, grazie, mi Dio*," she cried as she ran toward me.

I dropped my arm from Jenny's shoulders just in time to be scooped into my mother's warm and bone-crunching embrace. She kept up a steady stream of Italian prayers while she stroked my hair and patted me down to make sure I was all right.

Finally, I caught her hands in mine and held her still. "Mom, I'm okay."

Her eyes welled up again, and fresh tears spilled out to cover her already-stained cheeks.

I lifted a hand to her face. "I'm so sorry," I said and crumpled into her arms. "I'm so sorry I cut school and made you worry. I'm so sorry—"

"Shh, *cara*, shhh. All that matters is that you're all right." She was speaking English again, a sign she had calmed down. She held me as I sobbed, cradling me against her in a way she hadn't done since my father died.

When I stopped crying, we joined Barb and Jenny, who were having a tearful reunion of their own.

After another round of hugs, we all piled into the car and headed home. I let Jenny tell the story of what had happened and leaned my head on the back of the seat. Images flashed through my brain: the reflection of that otherworldly falcon in the water, the bobcat lunging at me, the eagle battling the raven. My hands shook, and I clasped them tight in my lap to keep Jenny from seeing.

I breathed a sigh of relief when we pulled into our driveway.

Lidia ushered me into the kitchen and sat me down at the table. "What do you want for dinner? I'll make you anything you want."

"I'm not hungry." I pressed my fingers into my temples. My brain hurt as memories of the bridge tumbled one on top of the other. "I-I think I'll just go to bed."

"Okay, *cara*." She kissed my forehead and cupped my chin in her hand. "When I think what could have happened . . ."

My eyes grew hot. I hugged her quickly and hurried upstairs before I started crying again. In the sanctuary of my room, I curled up under the covers and pulled apart what had happened on the bridge, separating images out like puzzle pieces. But when I tried to put them back together, nothing made sense. Moonlight crept in through my window, and a heated and fitful sleep, full of feverish dreams, stole over me.

When at last I woke up, sunlight dappled my comforter. I glanced at the clock. Almost noon. Rubbing a hand over my face, I slid out of bed and jogged downstairs.

Lidia sat at the kitchen table, looking over some papers. "How do you feel?"

"Why didn't you wake me to go to school?" I padded over to the coffeemaker to pour myself what was left in the pot.

"They cancelled school today." She flexed and unflexed her fingers on the surface of the table.

"What? Why?"

Lidia swallowed. "Because of what happened last night."

The coffeepot trembled in my hand. I set it down on the counter with a clatter. "Was there—anyone we knew?"

Lidia pushed back from the table. "How about I make you something to eat? Eggs and toast?"

I nodded, my neck stiff, hyperaware that she hadn't answered my question. I leaned forward and switched on the little television on the island counter.

But before an image had time to appear, Lidia clicked it off.

"Hey!"

Lidia looked at her hands. "You don't want to put that on."

"Why not?"

She sighed. "Because it's all over the news, and I don't think you need to see that right now."

It was so like her, trying to shield me from something that I couldn't be shielded from. As if I couldn't find out every last detail behind her back. I cleared my throat. "How many?"

Lidia turned back to the frying pan where the eggs had started to crackle. "Twenty-two."

I dropped into a chair at the table and laid my head down. I heard Lidia take a plate from the cupboard, but I didn't raise my head. Twenty-two people dead. I remembered what the stag had said, *To kill one of us, they've killed dozens*. But that wasn't real. Was it?

Lidia set my plate in front of me. "Come, *cara*. Eat. You'll feel better."

The Italian antidote for everything was food. It usually worked, but my stomach felt like lead. I knew that Lidia wouldn't leave me alone unless I ate something, though, so I raised my head and picked up my fork.

Lidia brushed a loose hair away from my face. "Every day is a gift," she said softly.

I met her eyes. "I know."

She gave me a small smile. Across the kitchen, my toast popped out of the toaster, and Lidia went to fetch it. "Butter for your toast?" she asked, trying to bring us back to our everyday life. "Or I have an open jar of *mostarda*, if you want."

"The *mostarda* sounds good."

She set the jar in front of me. As I dipped my knife into it, I suddenly remembered the little amulet I had found in the basement. It seemed like forever ago. I bit into the toast and let my curiosity about the Benandanti take my attention away from the recurring images of the bridge.

I finished my breakfast quickly and turned around in my chair. "I think I'll do some work in my room. For my creative writing class. Unless you need my help."

"No, you rest today. I'll be in the Cave if you need me."

Up in my room, I settled on the bed with my laptop balanced across my knees. When the browser opened up to Google I squinted, trying to remember the correct spelling, then typed in *Benendanti*.

*Did you mean Benandanti?* Google asked me.

"I guess so," I murmured and clicked on the link. Apparently the Benandanti had its own website. If I had just done this two days ago, we could have avoided losing a basketful of eggs.

The page loaded, and I pulled the laptop closer to read.

*The Benandanti is an ancient order of warriors who have the power to separate their souls from their bodies. While in this transformed state, their physical form remains as though dead, and their spiritual self takes on the shape of an animal.*

My throat felt dry. On the bridge my body had laid in the bus like a corpse while something else—my spiritual self?—had become a falcon. I swallowed several

**71**

times and told myself to stop being ridiculous. It couldn't have been real. I read the next paragraph.

*The origins of the Benandanti are believed to be rooted in the Friuli region of northern Italy.*

I sucked my breath in. Friuli was where Lidia—where I—came from. Before my nerves failed, I read the next sentence.

*Benandanti are born, not made; only those born with the caul are fated to join the ranks of the Benandanti.*

I scrambled backward on the bed. The laptop fell onto the mattress with a single bounce. Heart pounding fast, I leaned over and opened the top drawer of my nightstand. I drew out the locket inside and held it up to the light, the silver casing glinting under the lamp.

My mother had given me the locket when I was a baby. It was fragile with age; there was a mark on the back from a silversmith in Venice dating to the sixteenth century. I turned the locket over in my hand, feeling the light etching of a girl's face on the front with the pad of my thumb. Lidia told me that the necklace had been in her family for generations, and I liked to imagine the other girls who might have worn it—maybe my grandmother, whom I had never met, and her mother before her.

I never opened the locket; I didn't need to, because I knew what was inside. Not a picture of anyone, like normal people would have. No, the gift inside from my superstitious Italian mother was a leathery, dried-up piece of skin.

Some people might think that was gross, but it wasn't, really. The skin was part of the amniotic sac I was born in. My mother said that when I was born, the amniotic sac didn't break completely, and I came out of her womb with this thin membrane, light and sheer as a veil, covering my face. Old midwives, Lidia told me, called this being born with the caul, and it was considered a sign of great fortune.

I stared at the locket swinging hypnotically from my clenched hand. On the bed, my upside-down laptop dropped into sleep mode. I looked back and forth from the computer to the locket. I had a connection to all three things that I had just read about the Benandanti. I came from Friuli. I was born with the caul. And last night—not for the first time—I had felt my soul separate from my body and take on the form of a falcon. Not to mention the amulet I had found. *This house is under the protection of the Benandanti.* Who had put the amulet there?

"This is ridiculous," I said. The words seemed to echo off the walls of my room. I shook my head, my hair tousling in front of my eyes. The Benandanti couldn't be real. They were like Bigfoot or the Loch Ness monster. Maybe some people believed in them, but I lived in the real world.

And yet . . . I tucked the loosened strands of hair behind my ears. The memory of what happened on the bridge flooded my mind. The larger-than-life animals that glowed with an otherworldly aura . . .

Taking a few deep breaths, I tried to steady my beating heart, but the room suddenly felt too small and close to contain me. I fastened the locket around my throat, slid off the bed, and grabbed my boots from the closet.

The house was quiet when I got downstairs; Lidia was still in the Cave. I slipped out through the kitchen door and headed for the hen trailers. I thought the normalcy of chores would calm my nerves, but everything inside me was still jumpy. I felt like I was going crazy. Nothing that had happened over the last few days made any sense.

The rickety stairs shifted under my weight as I climbed into the first trailer.

Inside, the hens rustled and squawked, flapping their wings in agitation.

"What's wrong, ladies?" I cooed and worked my way through each nest. Pink sunlight streamed in through the tiny window in the center of the trailer. I glanced out through the grimy glass. In the low brush that lined the adjacent forest, I saw what was upsetting the hens.

A huge white wolf, its blue eyes fixed on me, crouched beneath the brown and bare branches. The edges of its figure shimmered deep blue, as though it were enveloped in a halo made out of sky.

Just like the white wolf on the bridge last night.

Goose bumps rippled my skin.

The wolf turned and walked a few feet away from me, stopped, and tilted its head. Although it seemed insane, I knew it wanted me to follow. I came out of the trailer and fell into step behind the wolf as it trotted into the woods.

After a minute, the wolf stopped, lifted its head toward the sky, and let out a long, low cry.

I clutched the front of my jacket, my knuckles white. I had heard the same cry the other night on my way home from the town meeting.

The wolf lay down on the ground, and I saw what it had led me to. A familiar figure lay motionless in the shelter of an oak tree.

I rushed forward and dropped down next to the body. "Heath? Heath!"

I reached out to touch him, but quick as lightning, the wolf leapt onto his chest and faced me.

"Get away from him," I screamed, waving my arms at the wolf. The air glimmered all around me. I put one hand up to shield my eyes. The light was so brilliant I thought I would go blind.

And then it was gone, and the world was normal again. Next to me, Heath gasped and sat up.

"Are you okay?" I looked around wildly. "There— there was a wolf—what was that?"

Heath gripped my hand, forcing me to look into his blue eyes. "That," he said, "is the gift of the Benandanti."

# CHAPTER SEVEN
*The White Wolf*

Wind blew through the trees, scattering red and gold leaves. I stared at Heath. "The Benandanti? I was just—"

Heath's fingers tightened on mine. "Alessia, listen. We don't have a lot of time before your mother comes looking for you. Last night on the bridge, you had what you probably thought was a dream. A dream about turning into a falcon."

I felt like someone was pressing on my chest with a very heavy stone. "How did you—?"

"Because it wasn't a dream." He leaned in, his eyes searching my face. "I was there with you."

I shook my head as though to get rid of the memory.

"Don't you remember? The white wolf?"

The memory was still there, clear and vivid. I couldn't deny it. *Their physical form remains as though dead, and their spiritual self takes on the shape of an animal . . .* "The wolf. That was you?"

Heath nodded. "I am a Benandante. And so are you."

The bare branches above us clacked against one

another in the chilly breeze. I squeezed my eyes shut, but when I opened them again, Heath was still there, his hand still clutching mine. "But that's impossible. People's souls can't turn into animals."

"How did you know that's what we do?" Heath asked, his voice sharp.

I squinted, trying to organize my thoughts. "I looked it up. The Benandanti. After I found the amulet."

"What amulet?"

"The amulet I found in the basement. I asked Lidia about it."

Heath stiffened. "What did she say?"

"Nothing. So I looked it up on the Internet—"

"The what?"

Despite myself, I snorted. "The Internet, Heath." I made a face. "What, they don't have computers in Provence?"

"Someone wrote about us *online*?" Heath exhaled hard, air whistling between his teeth. He tapped his finger against his lips. "That's not good."

"Why not?"

Heath grimaced. "It's not like we walk around saying, 'Look what I can do' to everyone we meet."

I yanked my hand away from him. "What *can* we do? What are the Benandanti? Would you please start explaining things before I scream?"

Heath looked around in all directions, but there was only the wind and the distant clucking of the hens to keep us company. "I'll show you." He closed his eyes, his lips moving silently.

My chest tightened, pain radiating around my heart. It was the same pain I had felt twice before, and now I knew that I was indeed being split in two. I gasped as my soul left my body and I became a falcon once again, my enormous wings lifting me high into the air.

Down below, light beamed out from Heath. He fell backward, his body limp as the wolf appeared beside him. I stared at our two bodies lying next to each other on the ground, two empty shells now without our souls.

Heath raised his wolf's head to me. *You see now? That's what we can do. That's our gift.*

I blinked. *How are you talking to me?*

*The Benandanti communicate telepathically.* He trotted toward the woods, checking over his shoulder to make sure I was following.

*So that's how I heard the other animals last night? They could read my mind?* I glided from tree to tree, rising higher and higher through the branches.

*Sort of. We can't 'listen in' on each other's thoughts, but if we need to communicate something, you'll hear it.* He disappeared beneath thick brush, then reappeared an instant later.

I dipped low, skimming through bare branches in order to keep him in sight. *Where are you taking me?*

*To the place that is at the center of all this.*

I could feel his nervousness in my mind. It was an

odd sensation, feeling someone else's thoughts and emotions inside my head.

*The reason the Benandanti are in Twin Willows. There's magic here—*

*Magic?*

He must have heard the skepticism in my voice because he tilted his head up to look at me. *You just tore your soul out of your body and took the shape of a Falcon. I think you can stop wondering if magic is real or not.*

I fluttered my wings. If I said—or thought—it out loud it would make the fairy tale real. But I couldn't deny what was happening. *I guess.*

*Look, I know this is a lot to take in—*

*Understatement of the century.*

*—but I need you to listen and stay sharp.*

I took a deep mental breath. I could sort it all out later, after I had the facts and I was alone with my own thoughts. *Okay.*

*Good. As I was saying, there's magic all over the world, but there are seven sites in particular that contain extraordinary power.*

I soared through the thick branches of an oak tree. *There's one here, isn't there? In Twin Willows?*

*Yes.*

*Are you kidding? This dumb town where nothing happens?*

*Do I sound like I'm kidding? This dumb town is actually host to an ancient magic.* He leapt over a fallen tree, his long white form graceful as a ballerina. *And the*

*Benandanti are here to protect that magic. There are seven Benandanti Clans, one to protect each site. Each Clan has five members.*

*Who are you protecting the magic from?*

*The Malandanti.*

The word sent a cold wind through my feathers. I turned it over in my internal translator. *Bad Walkers?* In my mind's eye I saw the bobcat with its silvery aura. *That bobcat. And the raven. They were the Malandanti?*

*Yes, two of them. There are five members of each Malandanti Clan too.* In the shadows of the forest, Heath glowed more vibrantly through the brush.

I rose higher in the air, keeping his blue aura in sight as I stretched toward the sky.

*We're almost there. Fly low and as quietly as you can. We cannot alert the Malandanti to our presence.*

*What will happen if they see us?*

*They will kill us.*

The air around me shivered, as though the temperature had suddenly dropped. I glided down until I was just inches above Heath and followed him through the brush. As we emerged out into the open, a shaft of afternoon sunlight broke through the trees, and I recognized where we were.

The waterfall.

# CHAPTER EIGHT

*The Waterfall*

I spun in the air, my vision blurred. *Oh, my God.*

*Do you know this place?*

*I*— I stopped myself before I could answer. I didn't want Heath to know how I knew this place. I stared instead at the rock where I used to sit with my dad. It looked foreign to me now, like an alternate-universe version of the place I loved. Over the entire waterfall, a weird silvery black mist hung, like a veil made out of black diamonds. The water no longer looked crystalline; it looked dirty, mottled, and murky. *What happened?* I asked Heath. *It wasn't like this the other day when I was here.*

*It was*, Heath answered. *You just couldn't see it. Now that you've been Called, you can. Just like you can see my aura now too.*

Inside the veil, the Raven that had attacked me on the bridge sat perched in a tree. It launched into the air and descended to the water. Waves rippled outward to the shore as it dragged its talon across the surface.

Heath's fur bristled, his ears pinned back against his head. *It makes me sick, to see them using the magic like that.*

*That's the magic? The water?*

*Yes. Whoever touches the water inside the barrier will have visions of the future.*

I fell so fast out of the air that I barely had time to catch myself on a branch above Heath's head. *Are you serious?*

Heath lifted his head. *Deadly serious.*

I stared at the Raven as it drew lazy circles on the water's surface. The tip of my wing burned, as though it were my human hand, reminding me of something. *I touched the water. The other day when I was here.*

Heath blinked, his wide eyes soulful. *And less than a day later, you had a vision. Am I right?*

The vision in the office. *It was so real . . .*

*I wouldn't know. I have never touched the water.* He stepped out of the brush. Sunlight broke through the trees and illuminated his aura.

The Raven shot into the air, droplets of water falling from its talons. With a loud caw that echoed through the trees, the Raven barreled toward Heath. But when it reached the misty barrier, it stopped short.

Heath stepped right up to the barrier, raised his head to the sky, and let out a howl that filled all the crevices in the woods. His nose was practically touching the silvery mist.

On the other side of the barrier, the Raven beat its wings so hard that wind ruffled my feathers. The Raven struck the mist with its beak, and the barrier crackled, like a stone thrown against an electric fence.

Heath lowered his head and backed up until he was right under my branch. *Let's go.*

I followed his white form through the woods as he raced toward the clearing. *What was that all about?*

*There's always at least one Malandanti here, guarding the site. And as long as their magical barrier holds, we can't go in.*

The panther I had seen the other day wasn't just a panther. It was a guardian of the site, a Malandante. The enemy. I shook myself. I couldn't think like that yet.

We reached the spot where our bodies lay, and the sight of my helpless human self made me shudder. An instant later I lay on my back, staring at the deep blue sky. I gulped, trying to fill my lungs with air.

Heath grabbed my elbow and pulled me to my feet. "Come on. I didn't realize how late it was. Your mom's expecting me in the Cave."

"But why do the Malandanti control that site and not the Benandanti?" My breath came out in little gasps as I jogged to keep up with him.

"We used to. But then we lost a member, and that weakened the Clan enough for the Malandanti to take control." We reached the stone wall. I scrambled over it after Heath. When we neared the edge of the pasture, Heath rounded on me. "Come find me in the Cave in fifteen minutes. I'll figure out a way to get Lidia out of there."

"Wait—"

But he was already striding away.

I stumbled backward, feeling my way to the nearest

tree. I sank to the ground at the base of its trunk.

On the other side of the pasture, Heath disappeared into the Cave.

What was going on? Was this really my life now? All because of that stupid amulet. No, it started before that, when I had gone to the Waterfall to spread my dad's ashes. Briefly I wondered if he had known anything about the Waterfall's true purpose, but I shoved that thought away. I could only handle so much information overload in one day. I touched the locket around my neck. The metal was warm from my skin. This whole thing hadn't started that day at the Waterfall. It had started the day I was born with the caul.

The Cave door opened, and Lidia emerged, her shadow lengthening across the grass. She paused to say something to Heath and headed over the hill to the barn. At the Virgin Mary shrine she knelt and bowed her head for a few moments. I beat my hands against my thighs. Lidia rose, crossed herself, and continued to the house.

The instant she was out of sight I was on my feet and running for the Cave. The pungent smell of ripening cheese washed over me when I crossed the threshold.

Heath worked at the long table, folding various herbs into different piles of soft cheese. "Make yourself useful," he said. "And keep an ear out for your mother."

I folded my arms over my chest. "I'm not making myself useful until you answer some questions."

Heath glanced up. "Fine, but if your mother comes

in and asks why we're talking about the Benandanti, *you* can tell her."

I peeked out the door, but there was no sign of Lidia. "Why do we need to protect the magic? What's so bad about the Malandanti controlling it?"

Heath stared at me like I had just called North Korea misunderstood. "Every time the Malandanti use the magic, it weakens the earth a little bit more. That stuff you hear on the news—tons of fish washing up dead, bee colonies disappearing, birds dropping out of the sky—it's because of the Malandanti. It's all connected. And they'll stop at nothing to keep control of the magic." He slammed his hand down on the table, leaving a cheese handprint on the wood. "Don't you get it? They used the magic and saw that a new Benandante would be Called. They saw the Falcon on the bridge. So they went there to stop it. To stop you." He leaned into the table. "To kill you."

I remembered what the Stag had said at the bridge. *To kill one of us, they've killed dozens.* I clung to the door, feeling sick. "All those people . . . they're dead because of me . . ."

Heath's face softened. "No, Alessia. They're dead because the Malandanti have no conscience." He traced a groove in the table. "But you can honor their memory by helping us regain control of the Waterfall."

I swallowed, my mouth dry and scratchy. "What happens if we regain control?"

"Right now, the Malandanti control five of the seven sites," Heath said. "Once we control all seven, we can safeguard the magic forever."

Outside, the goats in the pasture bleated. I looked out into the twilight and spotted Lidia climbing the hill. "My mother's coming." I met Heath's eyes across the length of the table. "What do I do now?"

"You decide." He brushed a lock of sandy hair out of his eyes, leaving a trail of herbs on his forehead. "The Benandanti give you a choice. You can say no and pretend this never happened."

"Pretend?" I shook my head. He was insane. As if I could ever forget what it felt like to spread my wings and fly. "And if I say yes?"

Heath's mouth twisted into the shadow of a grin. "You have to say yes before I can answer that."

# CHAPTER NINE

*The Decision*

Until sundown. That was all the time Heath said I had to decide whether or not to accept the Call. All the time I had to decide the rest of my life. Even Ivy League schools gave you more time than that.

I met Jenny on the way to school as usual, but this morning she ran to me and gave me a tight hug. "I was really worried about you yesterday. I called you in the morning, but Lidia said you were asleep."

"I'm okay," I said. A little knot tightened in the pit of my stomach. I had always shared everything with Jenny, and now there was something I couldn't tell her. "How are you?"

Jenny hunched her shoulders. "Still kinda freaked out."

"I can't believe they cancelled school yesterday."

"I know." She tucked her arm through my elbow, and we headed down the road. "I went to Joe's in the afternoon, and everyone was all over me about what happened."

I didn't say anything. What could I possibly say, when the accident was my fault? However much Heath assured me it wasn't, I was still the cause of the bridge collapse. I swallowed several times to dispel the lump in my throat and watched our feet as we walked, my dirt-stained UGGs next to Jenny's pristine red cowboy boots. I wished there was some way I could ask her advice without telling her about the Benandanti. "Was there anyone we knew? Lidia wouldn't tell me."

Jenny clutched my arm tighter. "The guy who owns Pizza Plus. He was the only name I recognized."

My skin prickled, hot and cold all at once. Pizza Plus was in the next town over; we went there at least every other week. I could picture him, a rotund man with white hair and a mustache, red cheeks, always smiling. Gone. Because of me. "That's—that's—really sad," I managed to choke out.

"I know." Jenny leaned her head on my shoulder as we walked. "I keep thinking about those people. The ones, you know, who were in the middle of the bridge when it fell."

Tears pricked at my eyes. "It haunts me," I whispered.

Jenny threw her arm around me and squeezed hard. "Me too." We stood for a moment in the middle of the street, hugging and sniffling. Jenny pulled back and dried her eyes with the back of her hand. "My dad said when things like this happen it makes you stop and think about what's really important."

"He's right." We started walking again in silence. I turned her words over inside me. What *was* really important to me? Being a normal girl? Or protecting my home? I twisted my fingers into the plush sheepskin of Jenny's jacket, as if holding on to her would give me the answer I needed.

We walked into the schoolyard, still arm in arm. Kids bustled in through the front door, laughing and horsing around before the walls of the school confined them. I watched them as though they were inside a snow globe and I was outside, shaking it upside down. They had no idea how fragile the world was.

By the end of my first period in the office my head hurt from all the questions banging around inside it. I downed a bottle of water on my way to French. The chair behind me was empty, but I hoped it wouldn't be for long. At the thought of seeing Jonah, my headache eased a little. I tapped my foot against the leg of the desk, my gaze flitting from the door to Carly, who asked question after question about the bridge collapse.

I kicked the chair in front of me. "It was really scary, and the last thing I want to do is relive it. So stop asking me about it. Okay?"

Carly stared at me for a minute. "Fine. Sorry."

I rubbed my temples, ignoring the hurt look on her face.

Just before the bell rang, Jonah slouched into the room and sank into the chair behind me.

I ducked my head and pretended to be fascinated by my French textbook. As Madame Dubois called the class to order, I felt a poke on my shoulder and turned.

"Hey."

"Hey," I answered.

Jonah swallowed. "I heard about the bus crash." His face was pale. "Glad you're okay."

A small smile crept onto my face. He cared that I wasn't dead. That was something at least. "Thanks."

"And don't forget that your permission slips for our trip to Paris are due in just a few weeks."

The words pulled my attention to the front of the room and wiped the smile right off my face. I slumped over the desk, my chin pressed into my wrists. Sure, I could fly out my bedroom window, but I still couldn't go to Paris.

A note landed on my desk and skittered toward the edge. I caught it before it fell off and glanced up at the front of the room. Madame Dubois had her back to the class, writing out verb conjugations on the board. The note was folded in eighths; I opened it one fold at a time to minimize the noise, expecting to see Jenny's loopy handwriting scrawled across the page.

But instead, neat rows of block lettering met my eyes.

*Why so blue?*
*If it was up to you*
*What would you do*
*On this fine day*
*Wouldn't you say*
*A better way*

*To pass the time*
*It would be divine*
*To drink wine*
*And fly kites*
*In the City of Light*
*On starry nights?*

It was entirely in French. I had trouble with *kites* and had to flip through my French-to-English dictionary to find the translation. I read through the poem again, translating it in my head. Madame Dubois's voice became a distant buzz in my ear as I read the note over and over again. At last, I twisted slightly in my chair and looked behind me.

Jonah met my eyes and winked.

I faced forward so fast I got dizzy. What did it mean? Did he like me? Or was he just bored? I smoothed the paper out onto my desk. Whatever it meant, it deserved a response.

*If it was up to me*
*I'd be in gay Paree*
*Sitting under a tree*
*Eating Brie.*

I folded the note into eighths again and tossed it lightly over my shoulder.

In less than two minutes, the paper sailed back to my desk.

*So let us catch a breeze*
*To the land of wine and cheese*
*We'll stroll the Tuileries*
*And do just what we please.*

I felt myself smile, the first real one since the crash. The weight of my dilemma was a little lighter on my shoulders as I poised my pen over the paper and tried to think of a word to rhyme with *Versailles*.

By the time class ended, every inch of the paper was covered in our writing. I tucked the note into my backpack as the bell rang and stood up.

Jonah brushed past me, his hand touching mine for a fraction of a second.

When I looked up, he was halfway out the door.

Jenny waved to me from the cafeteria table where we usually sat with Melissa and Carly, but I ignored her for a moment and scanned each of the long tables, trying to find the figure in black amongst all the multicolor. Jonah was nowhere to be seen. With a sigh, I trudged over to where my friends sat and dropped into a chair. "Carly, I'm sorry I snapped at you in French."

"It's okay. I was probably being annoying."

"You?" I cocked my head. "Never."

She laughed, and I knew that all was forgiven. At

least that was one thing taken care of.

"All right, enough with the lovefest," Jenny said. She grinned at me. "You gonna cough up that note or what?"

Melissa and Carly leaned forward eagerly.

"You got sauce on your sleeve," I told Carly, and she pulled her elbow out of her plate of spaghetti with a grimace.

"Come on," Melissa said, elongating her vowels as if she were speaking to a disobedient five-year-old.

I hugged my backpack. "It doesn't say anything important. It's silly."

"Then why won't you show us?" Jenny said, sitting back in her chair with her arms folded across her chest.

"Because it's private." I swallowed. "Look, he didn't say anything about his weirdo family or anything. It's just a funny little note."

"If it's just—"

"Oh, my God, leave it alone." I stuck my tongue out at Jenny to show her I wasn't really mad but that the discussion was over. I wasn't sure why I didn't want them to see the note, but the thought of them reading it seemed wrong.

They all shrugged and dug into their lunches. I pulled my brown-bag lunch out of my backpack and emptied its contents onto the table. Melissa eyed my goat cheese and prosciutto sandwich on thick homemade bread. I pushed it toward her. "Go ahead."

"Really?" she asked, not waiting for further permission before snatching the sandwich up.

"Really," I said. "I'm not hungry." Against my will I

glanced toward the door to the cafeteria, but it framed a trio of giggling ninth graders. Well, at least I had found something to distract me from the life-altering decision I had to make. I glanced at the clock. It was just after noon. I had less than six hours left before I had to tell Heath yes or no. I gulped some bottled water and watched Melissa chomp on my sandwich. "Hey, can I ask you guys a hypothetical question?"

"Sure," said Carly as she dabbed at her stained sleeve with a wet napkin. She only succeeded in leaving little bits of paper clinging to the sauce stain. "Crap. I liked this shirt."

"You have another just like it," Jenny told her and turned to me. "What's up? You have your serious face on."

Carly dropped the napkin to focus on me and folded her hands on the table. "You're right; she does. What's wrong?"

Under the intensity of their combined gazes, my insides wilted. "Nothing—I—never mind."

Jenny cocked her head. "If you can't talk to us, who can you talk to?"

Who indeed? But I couldn't tell them this, not without sounding insane. I swallowed, my throat sticky despite the water I'd downed. "I just—" I took a deep breath and exhaled the words in a rush. "What would you guys do if you had the chance to do something really amazing, but it would change the rest of your life? Like, your life would never be normal again?"

"Who wants normal?" Jenny popped a fry into her

mouth. "I can't wait to get out of this town and find out what not normal is."

"I don't know," Carly said slowly, shaking her head. "There's a lot to be said for normal."

"Well, are we talking about going off on some awesome trip?" Melissa asked. "Or like, getting bit by a radioactive spider?"

I scrunched up my face. "More the latter."

"Oh. No way," Carly said. "You saw what a hard time Peter Parker had. I would never want to live like that."

"Even if you could save lives?" I asked.

"I'd leave the lifesaving to someone else," Carly said.

"Saving lives would be its own reward," Melissa said, picking at a chip in the table, "even if it meant giving up other things."

I gave her a little smile. I knew she was thinking of her mother, who suffered from an autoimmune disease that prevented her from doing things that all the other mothers did.

"I think it would be hard to pass up that kind of power if someone offered it to me," Jenny said. "Especially if it meant saving lives." A shadow fell across her eyes as she searched my face. "Is this about the bus crash?"

"No. Well, sort of, I guess. I'm reading this book, and I wondered what you guys would do."

"Oh, man," Melissa breathed. "Look who just walked in."

I glanced at the door to the cafeteria, let my gaze hang there. Bree stood in the doorway, her face pinched and tight. "I wonder where Jonah is," I murmured.

My three friends exchanged looks.

"What?" I said defensively. "I just figured they'd be together since they don't know anyone."

"He knows you," Carly said with a giggle and a nod toward my bag where the note lay hidden.

"Oh, shut up." As Bree approached our table, I caught her eye. "Hey, Bree. You can sit with us if you want."

She stopped and swept her gaze over the four of us. "Why would I want to do that?"

"Because you don't know anyone else."

"I don't know you, either." She hitched her bag higher up onto her shoulder.

"Look, I know it must suck having to move around so much, but your brother said—"

Bree slammed her palm down on the table, making Carly and Melissa jump. She leaned in close to me. "You leave my brother out of it." Her green eyes flashed, jewel bright against the paleness of her skin. "And if you know what's good for you, you'll stay away from him."

I fought the urge to back away from her. "Wow, overprotective much?"

"Save your breath, Lessi." Jenny's voice pitched louder than necessary, and several kids from the tables surrounding us turned around. "She's obviously got issues. Who needs that?"

Bree pushed away from the table. Without looking

at anyone, she walked straight to the only empty table in the cafeteria and sat down, her back like a steel rod.

"What *is* wrong with her?" I said to no one in particular.

"Nothing. She's just angling for Bitch of the Year," Jenny said.

"I think she'll blow the competition out of the water," Carly said.

I checked my watch. It was past noon, and I was no closer to an answer than I had been at the beginning of lunch. "I think I'll go to biology early and study," I said. It wasn't unusual for me to do this, and the girls waved good-bye as I stood and slung my backpack over my shoulder.

I didn't go to biology, though; I wandered around the school, unable to quiet my mind. *Only those born with the caul are fated to join the ranks of the Benandanti*, according to the website. What did that mean? Did my parents know about this? I remembered Lidia's reaction when I asked her about the amulet. She had to know something. But I couldn't ask her without losing another basketful of eggs.

A group of freshman girls spilled out of the bathroom, their laughter echoing off the walls.

I ducked down an empty hallway and leaned against the cool concrete wall. In my head, I kept seeing the Raven dragging its claws through the water and Heath's horrified reaction. How could I say no to protecting the beautiful place my father had loved? Then I remembered the Raven dangling me above the Bobcat, and I shivered. Saying yes didn't mean just protecting the Waterfall. The Malandanti wanted to *kill* us. Did I want to live with that kind of danger?

I launched myself off the wall and hurried past a long wall of windows that looked out onto the marshy grounds next to the athletic field. There, sitting under the bleachers, was the only thing that could distract me from my train of thought. Jonah.

He had a book open in his lap. The wind tousled loose strands of hair around his face.

I put my palm against the window, almost as if I could touch him through the distance between us. As I did so, he whipped his head in my direction. I saw something lighten in his face when he saw me. It was that something that kept me at the window, holding his gaze, my hand printing itself on the glass.

The loud shriek of the bell jolted me backward, and I dropped my hand.

Students poured into the hallway, their voices echoing around me.

I peered through the window again at Jonah. He was hunched over his book, making no motion to come back into the building and go to biology, which I knew he had next. I shook my head—what was wrong with him?—and headed up the hall toward the biology classroom.

When I got home that afternoon, Lidia's car was gone. The sun stretched itself thin across the sky, waning toward evening. I dumped my backpack at the bottom of the stairs and stared at the grandfather clock in the corner of the living room. Each tick seemed to echo in my rib cage.

I paced the border of the braided rug in the center of the living room for so long my feet started to hurt. Outside, the light began to fade. My insides twisted. At twilight, Heath would demand an answer, and I didn't have one.

Jenny, Carly, and Melissa had known me forever, but even they couldn't help me. Even though Jenny said power was hard to pass up, she had no idea the kind of power I was dealing with. What would they say if they ever found out? They'd think I was a freak of nature. And they would be right. I ran my hand over my face. Would they still be friends with me?

But what if Jenny found out I was the reason the bridge had collapsed and had given up the chance to make amends for that tragedy? Wasn't that just as bad? I didn't want to be branded a coward.

I stopped in mid-pace and bent over, digging my elbows into my knees and my hands into my hair. I was only sixteen. It wasn't fair to have this kind of responsibility thrust at me. I didn't know how long it would take to regain control of the Waterfall, but it didn't seem like it could be done in a week. What if it took years? How much of my life was I expected to give up?

My throat was tight and hot as I straightened. Time ticked away. I pressed the heels of my hands into my eyes and rubbed hard. In the months since my dad had died, I had never wanted to talk to him so badly. If he were alive now, I'd go to him in the Cave and lean against the door. "What's eating you?" he'd ask. If it was a big enough problem, he'd take me to our waterfall, and we would talk it out over doughnuts and a thermos of hot chocolate.

The Waterfall. It wasn't just my dad's special place anymore; it was one of the most powerful places in the world.

I whirled around and found the photo of my dad on the coffee table. His soft brown eyes gazed out at me. I knelt in front of the table as though it were an altar. "What should I do, Dad?" I whispered.

But he only stared back at me, silent and two-dimensional.

My vision blurred. I blinked to clear it, but the whole room was like a soft watercolor painting, its edges frayed. Deep down, I knew what my dad wanted me to do. He had loved this farm, this land, second only to my mom and me. He would want me to protect it.

The deepening blue light of dusk seeped in through the front window. I rose from the floor and walked straight through the back of the house, out the kitchen door, across the yard, and into the barn. Inside, Heath was putting the last of the goats in their pen for the night. I waited in the doorway until he was done.

He wiped a gloved hand across his forehead and turned to the door. "Jeez! Didn't see you there," he said, laughing at his jumpiness.

"Okay," I said before my nerve failed. "I'll do it."

A slow smile spread across his face, lighting up his blue eyes like candles. "Welcome home," he said, echoing the words he'd said to me on the bridge, and even though the balance of the world was still tipped against us, in that moment everything was perfectly aligned.

# CHAPTER TEN
*The Guide*

Stretching under the covers the next morning, I saw everything with new eyes. I felt grounded and free at the same time, like an oak tree whose roots go down for miles beneath the earth while its branches dance in the wind. I finally had a place in the world.

I rolled onto my side and picked up my locket from the nightstand. It dangled from my fingers, the silver surface shiny in the morning sunlight. I clasped the locket around my neck, the chain cool against my skin, and climbed out of bed.

On Saturdays, Lidia often spent half the day at a farmers' market in Bangor, selling our cheeses. I usually went to Joe's for breakfast with the girls. It was our weekend ritual, dishing everything that had happened during the week over plates of pancakes and cheese-covered eggs. But as I neared the coffee shop, I realized that the biggest thing I had to dish, I couldn't talk about.

Taking a deep breath, I opened the door. The place was packed, as it always was on the weekends. But I noticed it wasn't as loud as usual, and there was a large glass jar on the counter with a handmade sign next to it: For the Victims of the Atterbury Bridge Collapse.

Jenny waved to me from our corner booth.

I dug into my pocket and dropped a ten-dollar bill into the glass jar on my way to the table. I would have given a hundred dollars if I had it.

There was already a steaming cup of coffee, black and unsweetened just as I liked it, waiting for me. I slid into the booth next to Melissa. "Hey."

"You look weird." Jenny set her cup down hard on its saucer, sloshing coffee onto the table. "What's up?"

I touched my forehead. Did being a Benandante show on my face? "Nothing. I . . . didn't sleep well last night."

Jenny glanced across the diner at the counter with the glass jar. "I know what you mean," she murmured. She gave me a little smile.

Steam from my coffee tickled my nose as I raised the cup to my mouth. Listening to Carly's and Melissa's chatter was comforting, and for a moment I forgot all the other weird stuff going on in my life.

"I'm giving up on Seth Campbell," Carly said. "I've tried to get him to ask me out for eight months, and if he hasn't gotten the hint by now . . ."

"Then he's an idiot. Why give him the time of day?"

"Because he's superhot," Jenny interjected. "For a body like that, I think I'd put up with a little idiocy."

I laughed, spraying coffee.

"Ew! Lessi!"

I coughed. "Sorry."

Jenny flicked an imaginary drop of coffee off her shirt, but she winked at me.

I could always rely on her to bring me back to my life, the one filled with friends who loved me no matter what. *No matter what.* I hoped that included freaks who could turn into birds.

"Speaking of superhot." Melissa elbowed my side.

I grimaced at her, then followed her gaze to the door.

The entire Wolfe family stood on the threshold, looking around for an empty table.

I got that fluttery feeling in my chest again and downed some more coffee.

"Jonah can squeeze in here," Melissa said.

"Yeah, maybe you guys can pass more notes to each other," Jenny added.

"Ha-ha," I said, but I had to sit on my hand to keep from waving him over.

Mr. Wolfe led his family to a free table across the restaurant. A few people nodded to him, but most shot him suspicious glances and turned away when he passed.

I tried not to notice how Jonah's dark green T-shirt brought out his eyes, not to mention his biceps.

As though she could sense me looking at her brother, Bree turned and smirked at me. She tucked her arm through the crook of Jonah's elbow and whispered something in his ear, tossing her hair.

As they sat down, Mr. Salter walked by their table and shot Mr. Wolfe a scathing look that he didn't catch.

I squinted at Mr. Salter as he left the coffee shop. "What was that all about?"

"What?" asked Carly, pouring more cream into her coffee.

"That look Mr. Salter gave Jonah's dad. Like he just killed a puppy or something."

"It's probably about the power plant," Jenny said.

"*Hydroelectric* power plant," said Melissa.

"Whatever." Jenny flagged down one of the waitresses, and we ordered.

"I heard my mom and dad talking about it," Jenny continued after the waitress had left. "They're trying to get a bunch of people in town to protest it. They think it's going to ruin the environment."

"I thought water power was good for the environment," Carly said.

"Who knows?" Jenny dumped about a cup of sugar into her coffee. I curled my lip in disgust, and she grinned at me as she took a sip. "My parents are such hippies. They'll protest anything. Anyway, Mr. Salter was over the other night talking to them about it. They were going on and on about how we can't let corporate America take over Twin Willows." She rolled her eyes. "They're all planning to raise a bunch of questions after Mr. Wolfe gives his presentation on Monday."

I looked at the Wolfes. Jonah and Bree sat on one

side of the table, heads bent together, engaged in a conversation that seemed to block out the rest of the world. Their dad was oblivious, talking animatedly to their mom, who toyed with her silverware and stared off into space. I watched Bree doodle something on a napkin. She pushed the napkin to Jonah and handed him her pen. He added to the doodle and gave it back to her. I had once read an article about "twin speak," the private language that twins have with each other, and I wondered what secret things Jonah and Bree talked about.

"Earth to Lessi." Melissa snapped her fingers in front of my face, pulling my attention back to the girls. "Jeez, you really do have it bad, don't you?"

"I don't get it," I said, unable to keep my gaze from wandering to Jonah and Bree. "With him, she's like a real person. But with the rest of us, she's a—"

"Yeah, yeah, she's a bitch." Jenny drowned her pancakes with maple syrup. "Last week's news. Let's move on."

But I couldn't. I kept glancing over to the Wolfes. Bree and Jonah never spoke to their parents for the entire meal, and Mrs. Wolfe never said a word while her husband talked at her. Maybe I really was sheltered, because it was the oddest family dynamic I had ever seen.

After breakfast, I usually went over to Jenny's house, where her mom would try to get us to eat flaxseeds and mung bean sprouts. But I begged off, telling Jenny I had too much homework. It wasn't exactly a lie; I did have homework. It just wasn't for school.

I found Heath in the milking room adjacent to the barn, releasing the last goat from her harness. "There you are," he said, giving the goat a pat on her rump as she bolted through the gate. "We have work to do."

"Work?" I asked. "Don't I even get like a welcome to the Benandanti celebration?"

Heath raised an eyebrow.

I sighed. "Sense of humor, Heath. Look into it."

"I have a sense of humor," he said defensively. "I just use it on special occasions."

I laughed.

"I didn't mean that to be funny."

"So you have an accidental sense of humor," I said, following him out of the milking room. I jogged to keep up with his long strides. "What are we doing today?"

Heath grabbed his backpack from the ground by the barn door. "We start with the basics. I have a lot to teach you before we can even think about going up against the Malandanti."

We skirted along the edge of the pasture. The sun beat down, unusually strong for this time of year. At the edge of the forest we climbed over the fence and passed into the cool, quiet depths of the trees. A little ways in, we picked up an offshoot of the main trail that I knew ran well into the next county, because once when I was eleven I had followed it all the way there before the search party Lidia had sent out caught up with me.

I shoved a branch out of my way. "So, you're like the Obi-Wan to my Luke."

"What?"

"Please tell me you've seen *Star Wars*."

Heath glanced back at me. "Of course I have. Oh. Well, yeah, I guess."

We came to a small clearing in the woods. The path ran right through it, but Heath stopped and dropped his backpack to the ground. "Every new Benandante is given a Guide."

"Who's your Guide?"

Heath shook his head, his hair flopping onto his forehead. He pushed it away from his eyes. "I can't tell you. See, within each Clan, the only other member whose identity you will know is your Guide's. We keep it that way in case we're captured by the Malandanti and forced into giving information. Because, you know, we're easier to harm in our human form."

The thought that I now had enemies who wanted to harm me made me shudder. I folded my arms over my chest and hugged myself. "So, I could be sitting next to a fellow Benandante in biology for all I know." My insides chilled. "Or a Malandante. I could be sitting right next to a Malandante in Joe's and not know it."

Heath waggled a finger at me. "You gotta get over that. When I first joined the Benandanti, I thought that about everyone I met. It'll drive you nuts, so just let it go. Besides, you can't attack the Malandanti when you, or they, are in human form."

"Why not? You just said they do."

"Just because they do it doesn't mean we have to stoop to their level. That's what makes us good." He walked to the center of the clearing. "We're not here to talk about that. You need to learn to transform."

"I know how to transform," I said, planting a hand on my hip. "I did it the other night."

"Okay. Transform. Right now."

I squeezed my eyes shut and tried to summon up that feeling of being torn in two, of my soul breaking away from my body. After several minutes of trying to make it happen, I opened my eyes. "Why can't I do it?"

A smug smile tugged at his mouth. "The other night on the bridge, you were Called by the *Concilio Celeste*, as is the tradition when a Benandante is Called for the first time. And when we were in the woods, I Called you."

"Who are they?"

"The *Concilio Celeste* is a seven-member council that has power over all the Clans." He waved his hand. "Can we get back to the lesson?"

"Hey, it's just as important for me to learn about the hierarchy of the Benandanti, isn't it?"

Heath glared at me, his jaw clenched.

I stuck my hands in my pockets and gave him an I'm-paying-attention face. "Sorry. Go on."

"When you're Called, you have no choice. You have

to transform. But you can also transform at will, and that's an important skill to know. If you're attacked in your human form by a Malandante, you'll need to transform in order to defend yourself." Heath squatted and folded his hands under his chin. "Try focusing on something that ties you to your Benandante form—like how it feels to fly."

I blew out a big sigh and closed my eyes again. I tried to remember how I had felt as a Falcon. Confused. Scared. Disbelieving. I shook my head. That wasn't right. Those were human emotions. I dug a little deeper. That moment over the water, that thrill at being able to fly . . . A tingling, unnatural and startling, started at the base of my spine. My eyes flew open.

Heath pointed at me. "Something happened, right? What did you feel?"

"I wanted to fly."

"Good. Concentrate on that."

I thought again about what it was like to rise above the treetops and look down from that dizzying height to the ground below. For a moment the memory was so real that I was back in the air, my wings spread wide as I soared . . .

Something ripped through me, something sharp and piercing. I opened my mouth to scream, but instead a bird-cry came out. I looked down and found myself hovering in the air. Just below me lay my body, still and silent in the grass as Heath stood across from me.

The earth spun. This was not the way the world was supposed to be. Dizziness engulfed me, and the next thing I knew, I was lying faceup on the ground, staring at the cloudy afternoon sky.

Heath's head blocked my view of the sky as he bent over me. "Are you okay?"

I tried to nod, but the motion made me want to vomit. "I think so," I rasped.

"You had it." Heath sat back on his haunches, looking a little like his wolf-self. "It was just for a second, but you did it."

I struggled to prop myself up on my elbows. "Yeah," I said weakly, "I guess I did."

"Try again," Heath urged.

I lay on the ground and closed my eyes. This time I let the image of the Waterfall creep into my mind, the way I had seen it through my Falcon eyes. An ache spread through me, the need to protect my dad's secret place as strong as a grip on my heart. With a sear of pain, I felt my soul leave my body.

When I opened my eyes, I was in the air above my inert form again, but I wasn't confused now. In fact, the world seemed *right* this way.

An unearthly blue light filled the clearing below me. When it dimmed, the White Wolf sat next to Heath's unmoving body.

*You did it!* Heath the Wolf jogged beneath me as I stretched my wings and flew a little distance away. It was still so odd to hear his thoughts in my head.

*Is there a way to close off the thoughts of the other Benandanti? You know, in case I want some privacy?* I sped up in the air, my wings beating wildly.

*Just intend your mind to be closed off, and it will be.* Heath raced to keep up with me, a flash of pale fur as I swerved through the trees that ringed the clearing. *But you should always stay open when you're with the other Benandanti. That's the best way to hold your mind during a battle.*

I circled the top of a pine tree, then swooped down so I was flying between the trees. *So basically, if I'm thinking about French class right now, you won't know.*

Heath ran below me, his strides strong and loping. *No, but you shouldn't be thinking about French class. It'll break your concentration.*

The mention of French class brought the image of Jonah into my mind. I slowed, my wings suddenly heavy. There was no way he could like a freak like me . . .

I dropped in the air, the ground coming up fast. Letting out a screech, I wrenched my mind into the present and soared into the air. It was a relief when I was aloft again.

*See?*

*Yeah, I see.*

*No matter what's going on in your outside life, you have to keep your focus. You have to compartmentalize.*

*Easier said than done.*

*You'll get the hang of it.* Heath stopped. *Let's go back*

*to the clearing. I want you to practice shifting in and out of your Benandanti form until it's second nature.*

I swooped around the crown of a pine tree. *I want to go to the Waterfall.*

*No.*

*Why not?*

*It's too dangerous. There's always a Malandante there.*

*So? We went the other night.*

*Yeah, but only because I needed to show you what you were fighting for. You're not ready to return.*

*But—*

*Just drop it. We're not going to the Waterfall, and that's that.* Heath wheeled around and raced toward the clearing. *Don't be a brat.*

That stung. I flew above his head, silent.

When we reached the clearing, I shot up toward the sun, reluctant to go back to my body. No wonder man had been trying to fly since Icarus. This was the most amazing feeling in the world.

*Alessia, come down here.*

I sank slowly to earth and fluttered above my still body. *You're no fun.*

Heath tilted his black-nosed snout up to me. *Ha-ha. Don't you want to know how to transform back?*

*If I must.*

*Just as you thought about what you want as a Falcon, think about what you want as a human.*

The image of Jonah winking at me in French class

flashed in my mind, and the next thing I knew I was lying on the ground, staring at the sky. I sat up and caught myself on my hand as the dizziness knocked me sideways.

"Easy," Heath said. He was human again too. "The transformations can be a little overwhelming at first. Here." He dug into the backpack and handed me a bottle of water.

I gulped it down. "You said the Malandanti could attack our human forms. What happens if they attack your human body while you're transformed?"

"If your human body is killed, your soul can't return to it." Heath looked down at his hands. "Your soul will wander the earth, unable to find peace . . . It's a horrible fate." He took a deep breath and removed another bottle of water out of his pack. "It's not just the Malandanti who can kill you. If *anyone* turns your body while you're transformed, your soul cannot return."

The wind whistled in my ears. I lowered my water from my mouth. "Are you kidding?"

Heath reached into the collar of his flannel shirt and tugged at a silken cord that I had never noticed him wearing before. He pulled it out of his shirt, showing me the little leather bag that dangled from it like a charm. "This amulet contains the single most important thing we Benandanti own."

"What is it?" I asked.

"My caul." He nodded toward the locket around my

neck. "That's yours, right? It protects our human bodies while we're transformed. But you have to be wearing it, or it won't be any good to you."

"I guess I won't take it off," I said, giving the locket a squeeze before I dropped my hand.

"Good idea." Heath folded his long legs underneath him so he sat cross-legged like a Buddha. "Now, I want you to transform back and forth three times."

Even though I had just done it, I still had a hard time. By the third transformation, my head was pounding. I collapsed onto my knees next to Heath and rubbed my temples. "Does it always feel like this?"

"You'll get used to it." He took a protein bar out of his backpack and handed it to me. "Eat this."

After I gobbled the bar, Heath made me transform twice more.

Sweat prickled my skin despite the cold when I sat up after the second time. "No more," I gasped. "Please."

"Yeah, that's enough for today." Heath shouldered his backpack and helped me to my feet. "You did good."

I managed a weak smile and followed him onto the path back to the farm. My legs were wobbly, and I still had the sensation of flying, like the way you feel the sea even after you've left a boat.

When we reached the barn, I noticed the driveway was still empty; Lidia wasn't home yet.

Heath turned to me. "We need to figure out a way to train without your mom knowing. Do you think she suspects something? You said you asked her about that amulet."

"I don't think so," I said, toying with my locket. "Should I say something to her?"

"Absolutely not." He slid the barn door open. "Not only could it put her in danger, but you cannot—you must not—speak of the Benandanti to anyone. Understand?"

"I got it," I said. "The first rule of Fight Club is you do not talk about Fight Club."

Heath furrowed his brow.

I sighed. "Really, Heath. Get a DVD player."

When I stepped into school on Monday morning, I tried to look at everything as if it was the same, but nothing was. Everyone who walked past me was a potential Benandante or a possible enemy. I peered into the faces of the other students, wondering who was friend and who was foe.

By the end of first period, I was convinced that Principal Morrissey was a Malandante, because he gave me a three-inch stack of e-mails to file according to date. It was truly a diabolical task.

In the hall between classes, I leaned on my locker and watched kids jostle by. Heath had said it would drive me nuts, and he was right.

At least I had Jonah to distract me. I slid into my seat in French and watched the door, waiting for him to walk in. As I drummed my fingers on the desk, I finally had to admit it to myself. I had a crush on Jonah Wolfe.

Just before the bell rang, he sauntered in and took his seat behind me.

I turned around. "Hey."

His lips curved in a half smile. "Hey. Saw you at Joe's on Saturday."

"I saw you too."

"Is that the most happening hot spot in Twin Willows?"

"Pretty much." I traced a groove in the surface of his desk with my forefinger. "It's basically that and cow tipping."

"Or goat tipping in your case," Jonah said.

I raised an eyebrow.

"Because you have a goat farm. Right?"

"Oh, right." I faced front as Madame Dubois called the class to order, my face hot. He'd found out something about me. Maybe he *did* like me. The blackboard blurred as I pictured us snuggled into a back corner booth at Joe's, his arms around me as I fed him a French fry . . .

The classroom slammed back into sharpness as reality set in. I would never be that normal girl at Joe's. I would always have a secret—a deep, dark, and dangerous secret. I hunched over my desk and rested my chin on my folded arms. There had to be some way to make it work, balance it all out. The other Benandanti had to have normal lives too, right?

All I had to show for French and my next two classes were a bunch of bad doodles in the margins of my notebook. I spent lunch in the library, reading *Wuthering Heights* rather than endure Jenny's questions about where I had been all weekend. On my way to biology, I spotted Jonah under the bleachers again, the collar of his jacket turned up against the drizzle. By the time I took my seat in seventh-period government, my mind was a massive jumble of twisted cables and ropes.

This was my one class I had been unable to erase from Bree's schedule, and when she flounced in, Jenny rolled her eyes and jerked her chin at me. "Tell her," she said to Carly.

"Tell me what?"

Carly leaned across the aisle toward me. "Bree finally succeeded in getting sent to the principal's office today."

I glanced over at Bree. She was staring out the window, her fingers tapping some secret code on her desk. "What'd she do?"

Carly's eyes were wide. "She put up a flyer on the bulletin board in biology looking for human test subjects to replace the frogs we're dissecting this semester."

I laughed. Every year someone protested the frog dissection, but this was by far the cleverest form a protest had taken. "Simons sent her to the principal for that? Seems a little unreasonable."

"Yeah, well, they got into it in class, and rather than debate her, Simons just sent her to the office." Carly shot a glance at Bree, who was still drumming on her desk. "It's too bad. I think it could have been a lively discussion. More interesting than class, that's for sure."

The bell rang. I pulled my government textbook out of my bag while Mr. Clemens came around to the front of his desk and sat on it, his legs dangling. For some reason he thought this made him look cool, but really he looked like a dork. "So I thought we would do something a bit different for tonight's town hall meeting," he said.

I slumped down in my chair. I had forgotten about the meeting. Somehow I'd have to work it out with Heath; we had plans to train.

"At tonight's meeting, Mr. Wolfe is going to present the Guild's proposal for the hydroelectric power plant," Mr. Clemens continued with a little nod toward Bree.

She kept staring out the window and didn't even acknowledge him.

He pursed his lips before going on. "This is such a great opportunity for us to see corporate politics in action. So I'm going to put you in pairs, and each pair will debate a pro and con stance for the power plant. Doesn't that sound fun?"

It really did not.

Carly groaned and dropped her head to her desk. She hated public speaking.

Jenny turned to me. "Wanna pair up?"

Before I could answer, Mr. Clemens raised his voice above the low murmur that had broken out in the class. "*I* will assign the pairs—I want you working with people you haven't worked with before. When you've been assigned, please sit with your partner, and discuss your strategy for the rest of the class."

Jenny gave a dramatic sigh when her name was

called with Josh Baker, the most obnoxious jock in school. "Great. I'll have to do all the work." She pushed away from her desk with a violent shove and moved over to him.

I was happy to see Carly paired with an outspoken member of the debate team; maybe she'd get some help with her public-speaking phobia.

As the number of students left in the class began to dwindle, my stomach bottomed out. Soon there was only one other person left.

Bree Wolfe.

# CHAPTER ELEVEN

*The Presentation*

The town hall meeting was more packed than I had ever seen it. Apparently a lot of people had a lot to say about the power plant proposal. Carly had actually made it to this meeting; she waved to me, then turned back to the partner Clemens had assigned her. Jenny's parents were even here, talking to Mr. Salter at the front of the hall. I spotted Jenny in the back row next to Josh. He was talking loudly on his phone about the last Red Sox game. Jenny mimed blowing her brains out.

I scanned the hall but didn't see Bree. Great. Maybe she wasn't even going to show up. I slid into a seat toward the back so I could keep an eye on the door and chewed on my cuticles. Heath hadn't been happy to cut our training short and insisted on continuing our session after Lidia went to bed. I was in for a long night.

Mr. Wolfe appeared in the doorway, deep in conversation with his assistant. The sharp angles of his face were creased as the assistant whispered in his ear. Mrs. Wolfe trailed behind them with Bree. I craned my neck.

Jonah wasn't with them. He didn't have government this semester, but I thought he'd at least be here to support his dad.

Bree saw me, jabbed her mom's arm, and plunked down into the chair next to mine. She didn't say anything, just pulled her feet up and rested her chin on her knees.

I stared at her for a moment, trying to think of something friendly to say, but the only thing that came out was a strangled "Hey," which she didn't return. I blew a breath out through my lips and watched Mayor Lawson struggle with an ancient tripod screen at the front of the hall.

On a desk in the middle of the aisle, Mr. Wolfe set up a sleek laptop that looked like something from *Star Trek*.

Mayor Lawson approached the podium. "I think we're all excited to get this meeting started."

I rolled my eyes.

"I'm sure you all remember Mr. Wolfe from last week's meeting and his assistant, Pratt Webster." She nodded to Mr. Wolfe and bustled off the stage.

Pratt—nice name, I snorted—dimmed the lights. Mr. Wolfe plugged a flash drive into his computer, and the screen lit up with the glittering black-and-silver logo of the Guild.

"Welcome to the future," Mr. Wolfe boomed, his voice echoing in every corner of the hall. The slides changed rapidly, each an image of happy people in happy towns. They smiled at us as they drank fair-trade coffee or displayed cacao beans they had harvested themselves. "All with the help of the Guild," Mr. Wolfe told us.

I felt myself lulled by the brightness of the images; the edges of my mind dulled like an unused knife. I glanced over at Bree. She slinked low in her chair, headphones stuck in her ears. I clenched my jaw. She wasn't even freaking listening.

I stared back at the screen. Computer-generated images of the proposed power plant flashed before my eyes. The building was silver and modern, all sharp angles that felt wide awake, in complete contrast to the sleepiness of the rest of the town.

Mr. Wolfe listed how many jobs the plant would create and how much business the plant would bring to the town. He rattled off numbers and figures and percentages that got all jumbled in my head.

The final slide appeared on the screen, a Photoshopped image of the Twin Willows sign on the road just outside of town side by side with the Guild's logo. "Twin Willows and the Guild, working together to lead the race for clean energy." With a flourish, Mr. Wolfe shut the laptop. "Any questions?"

A couple of people raised their hands, but their questions were vague, and Mr. Wolfe projected a colorful chart that seemed to satisfy everyone. There was a general positive murmur in the hall. I could see why; there didn't seem to be anything bad about the power plant. Even Jenny's parents were nodding and smiling.

At the back of the hall, Pratt hit the lights. I blinked, trying to dispel the large spots that danced in front of my eyes.

As Mr. Wolfe came down from the podium, Mr. Salter shook his hand. That was quite a change from the attitude he'd had in Joe's the other day.

I furrowed my brow, watching them until I felt a nudge in my side. I turned to Bree.

Her earbuds draped around her like a necklace. "Let me guess," she said. "You want the pro position."

"I guess so," I said, "but how did you—?"

"Don't worry about it. I'll take the con stance." Bree stepped over me and left the hall.

I watched her go, the back of my neck prickling. My brain felt odd, like I'd just woken up from a long afternoon nap. I grabbed my bag and went over to Jenny.

She cast a dirty look at Josh, who was on his phone again, and pulled her jacket on. "Worst assignment *ever*."

"Hey, at least you're not stuck with Bree," I said. "I don't know why she has to be so difficult. I mean, she—"

Jenny elbowed me hard in the ribs, making me yelp. She jerked her chin at something over my shoulder.

I turned, rubbing my side. Mr. Wolfe strode toward me, his assistant in tow. "Thanks," I muttered to Jenny.

"Miss Jacobs," Mr. Wolfe called. "A word."

I hugged my backpack to my chest. Had he overheard me bad-mouthing his daughter? "Um, sure."

Mr. Wolfe tucked his little flash drive into his breast

pocket and smiled at me. It was an odd smile, with no warmth behind it. "Did you enjoy the presentation?" He straightened his cuffs. "What do you think of the plan?"

"It's good, I guess." He was asking *me*, of all the townspeople? "I mean, clean energy is always good, right?"

"Exactly." Mr. Wolfe narrowed his eyes. "By the way, your family owns the goat farm just outside of town."

I nodded even though he hadn't said it as a question.

"I'm having a second presentation in about a week for anyone who missed this one. It would be wonderful if your father could come."

"Her mother owns the farm," Pratt said. "Mr. Jacobs died last year."

My gut twisted as it did every time my father came up in conversation. I blinked. "How did you know that?"

Pratt shot Mr. Wolfe an annoyed look and started playing with his BlackBerry. "A good assistant is always one step ahead of his boss."

"Yes. Well. So sorry about your father," Mr. Wolfe said, although it was obvious he couldn't care less. He handed me a business card. "Would you make sure your mother knows about the presentation, then?"

"Um, sure." I stuffed the card into my jacket pocket. "She's usually pretty busy, though. I can just tell her about it."

Mr. Wolfe leaned in toward me, his mouth curved up but his eyes sharp. I smelled peppermint on his breath. "I'm sure you can, dear. But we're trying to reach out to all the town residents *personally*." He smoothed his lapel. "Have a nice night, girls."

Jenny and I watched him leave, Pratt right on his heels.

"Well, you gotta give them credit," Jenny said.

"For what?" I asked.

"For connecting so strongly with the community," Jenny replied.

The back of my mind itched, like I'd forgotten to do something. But I couldn't remember what it was, so I squashed the feeling.

When I got home, Lidia was cooking in the kitchen. I left Mr. Wolfe's business card on the coffee table in the living room and went up to my room.

A piece of paper peeked out from under my pillow.

**Training after Lidia goes to bed. Meet me in the clearing, transformed.**

**—H**

I crumpled the note and tossed it into the wastebasket. Now that I was home, away from the distractions of the meeting, Jenny, and the Wolfes, my body tingled with the desire to transform, to soar into the air and be free of everything on the earth below me. I pulled my books out of my bag to start my homework, but by the time Lidia called me to dinner, I had barely gotten anything done.

The clock seemed to tick forward three minutes and backward two as I counted the hours until Lidia kissed my forehead and wished me good night. I waited until the light under her bedroom door disappeared, then shut my own door and locked it. I opened my window to let in the night, and before I could even lay down on the bed, the shift overtook me and I flew out, over the hill and toward the stars.

Heath and I kept up our nighttime training for the rest of the week; it was easier to sneak out after Lidia had gone to bed. But by Friday morning I was sleepwalking through school. Despite the giant cup of coffee I snagged from the office kitchenette, I could hardly keep my eyes open and misfiled the entire stack of folders Principal Morrissey gave me.

At lunch Jenny swiveled in her chair and hissed at me, "What's wrong with you?"

I yawned. "What do you mean?"

"You barely said a word on the walk in this morning, you stared out the window all during French, and"—she leaned in, her eyes narrowed—"you forgot Carly's birthday."

"Oh, shoot." I glanced around the cafeteria, but Carly was nowhere to be seen. "Where is she, anyway?"

"She's at her music lesson—like she is every Friday. Honestly, where is your brain?" Jenny took a giant bite out of her burger, glaring at me over the soggy bun.

"I've had a lot on my mind," I said defensively. I dug into my paper bag and took out the tuna sandwich Lidia had made for me.

"Well, so have I, and I've managed not to piss off my friends." Jenny set her burger down. "Lessi, I think about it all the time too. What happened on the bridge. So, you know, if you want to talk about it . . ." Her face softened. "I'm here."

"I know. I just—" I ducked my head to hide my eyes. "I don't want to talk about it. But I'm sorry. For being distant all week."

"Forgiven. For now." Jenny picked up her burger and polished the rest of it off in three bites. "Anyway, don't forget about tonight."

I swallowed the lump of sandwich in my mouth. "What's tonight?"

Jenny sucked at her soda, making a gurgling sound through her straw, and slammed her cup down. "You're kidding, right?" When I didn't answer, she blew out a noisy, exasperated breath. "Pizza Plus, remember?"

"Oh yeah." I shoved the last of my sandwich into my mouth, so I wouldn't have to talk. A twinge of guilt flicked through me as I reached for my apple. In all that had happened, I had completely forgotten that Jenny, Melissa, and I had planned a little party for Carly's birthday.

"Oh, and I invited the Wolfe twins."

I coughed, spraying little bits of apple onto the table.

Jenny laughed and took a bite of her cookie. "I figured that would get a reaction."

"Why did you invite them?" Involuntarily, my gaze ricocheted around the cafeteria. Jonah wasn't here, but Bree sat alone at a corner table, scribbling furiously in a leather-bound journal. I stared at her for a moment, and she looked up. I turned quickly back to Jenny. "Trust me. She is not someone I want to get to know better."

"Yes, but don't you want to get to know Jonah better?" A wicked grin twisted her lips. "And they're kind of a package deal, seeing as they're twins and all." Jenny finished her cookie. "Really, I don't need any thanks. Just give me your firstborn, and we'll call it even."

"You didn't have to invite him," I mumbled, but my face flushed as I took another bite of apple.

The rest of my classes passed in a haze. My mind was foggy, caught in between two clouds—the one in which I spent the evening in a restaurant booth, pressed up against Jonah, and the other one high in the sky as I soared over the treetops in my Falcon-self. I barely listened on the walk home as Jenny debated what to wear to the party.

As we headed toward the end of Main Street, I heard footsteps and glanced over my shoulder. Bree and Jonah walked several paces behind us. I raised my hand. "See you tonight!"

He returned the wave with a nod and a lopsided

smile that set the butterflies in my stomach fluttering. They turned off onto a side street behind the town hall. Mrs. Wolfe stood at the foot of their driveway, a plate of cookies in her hands. When her children reached her, she held up the plate as if she was making an offering. I watched the twins each take a cookie and walk quickly into the house with their mother at their heels.

"That is really bizarre," Jenny said, startling me. I hadn't realized that I had come to a full stop to watch this little scenario with the Wolfes.

"I know, right? Who *does* that? Not even Lidia."

"My mom would never do that." She nudged me, and we started up the road again. "She's usually in a headstand when I get home." Jenny's mother was into yoga and generally greeted her daughter with an inversion in the afternoon.

"Lidia's usually up to her elbows in curd when I come home," I said. I glanced over my shoulder at the Wolfe house, which was now out of sight around the corner. "Looks like Mrs. Wolfe is pretty traditional."

"Looks like Mrs. Wolfe has nothing better to do," Jenny replied.

I snorted. With a last look backward, I fell into step with her.

A beautifully wrapped jewelry box with an enormous silver bow sat on the kitchen table next to the snack

Lidia had laid out for me. She poured me a glass of milk. "What time do you need me to drop you off at Pizza Plus?" Her lip curled a little as she said this; Lidia did not approve of any pizza that was not made by her own hands.

"Seven. Thanks for wrapping the gift."

"Well, if you had done it . . . ," she said, rolling her eyes with a grin. "Home by ten."

"Twelve."

"Ten thirty."

"Eleven thirty."

"Eleven."

"Okay. I'll call you if I need a ride, but Jenny will probably give me one." I was usually able to wrangle a later curfew out of Lidia, but considering I hadn't been punished for cutting school I wasn't going to push it.

My belly gave a little flip-flop when we pulled up to Pizza Plus. The front picture window had been covered with a giant poster of the owner with the words *We will miss you* below his smiling face. On the sidewalk below the window, dozens of white candles flickered, their wax dripping onto the pavement. And there was a sign on the front door that pledged to keep the restaurant open to honor the owner's memory. I swallowed hard and reached for the doorknob.

Inside, it was warm and crowded. The hostess directed me to the private back room, where a long table had been decorated with wine bottles stuck with candles and covered in old wax. A cluster of balloons adorned the chair at the head of the table, where Carly held court. I made a beeline for her after adding my gift to the pile on a small side table in the corner. "Happy birthday," I said, giving her a hug.

"Thanks!" Carly tugged my arm, and I squatted next to her chair. She leaned in close to my ear. "I think Jenny invited the entire school. You have got to keep her under control."

I laughed. "As if. You know how she is at parties." The last party we'd been at Jenny had hijacked the music and played disco all night. "But I'll keep an eye on her."

"Thanks. And, hey"—Carly nudged me—"I'm really glad you're here. I've barely seen you this week."

"Yeah, it's been . . ." I shrugged instead of finishing the sentence. I wasn't quite sure how to finish it, but Carly nodded as if she understood. Not that she could understand, but I smiled as if I didn't have the biggest secret in the world and went to find Jenny.

I spotted her in the corner by the gift table, surrounded by half a dozen boys. Glancing around, I realized there were far more boys at the party than girls. I shook my head and worked my way around the table to where Melissa sat, chatting with a couple of boys from our French class.

The door from the main part of the restaurant swung open and banged against the wall. I looked up, and my breath caught at the sight of Bree and Jonah framed in the doorway. With their black hair, pale skin, and bright green eyes, they resembled comic book characters. Despite my dislike of Bree, there was no disputing that she was stunning. She *was* Jonah's twin.

Jenny broke away from her pack of admirers and swaggered over to the Wolfes. "Thanks for coming," she sang out.

"What should I do with this?" Jonah asked, holding up a bright pink box. He shifted from one foot to the other, drumming his fingers against his thigh.

Jenny pointed to the gift table.

"Our mother picked it out, so it's probably pretty lame," Bree said. Jonah shot her a look that she ignored. She snatched the gift from his hand and flounced away after Jenny toward the head of the table.

Jonah hadn't moved from the doorway. I took a deep breath to calm the jitters inside me and walked up to him. "Hey."

"Hey." He smiled. "I'm glad you're here."

"Oh, really?" I said, my cheeks tingling with warmth.

"Yeah." Jonah glanced up and down the table. "You're the only person I know."

"I can introduce you to some people, if you want." I gestured at the full room. "I mean, this is the crème de la crème of Twin Willows High."

"I can see that," he said, but he wasn't looking at the room. He was looking at me.

I locked eyes with him, long enough to count the flecks of gold in his green irises.

He put a hand on my arm. The heat of his fingers sizzled through my sweater. "Actually, I'd love some fresh air. You want to go outside?"

I knew I should stay and help Jenny with the party, but I also knew that Jenny would be the first to shove me out the door with him. I nodded and followed him through the main restaurant to the front door and out onto the street. A few of the candles on the sidewalk went out as the door shut behind us. The air was cold and tinged with autumn dampness, and I had left my coat inside. I hugged myself against the chill. "So what do you have against a good party?"

"I hate crowds."

"Really?" I glanced at the brightly lit windows. "Is it like a clinical thing or an I-hate-people thing?"

"I don't hate people," he said quickly, stepping closer to me. "It's just—when I'm in a crowd, I can't hear my own thoughts. And I hate that feeling. You know?"

"Yeah," I answered slowly. "Yeah, I do know. You're like Thoreau."

He grinned. "Exactly."

"Why come at all if you're happier out here than in there?" I gestured back toward the front door of the restaurant.

He looked into my eyes. The light from the windows reflected in his eyes, deepening their green to almost black. "Because I knew you'd be here."

My heart banged against my ribs. I wanted to be coy and flirty, but every single clever thought left my brain.

"Twin Willows isn't as bad as you make it out to be," he added, taking pity on my speechlessness.

"So it's not the worst town you've ever lived in?" I said, finding my voice again even though my heartbeat was all over the place.

"Definitely not." Jonah leaned back against the brick side wall of the restaurant.

"What was? The worst, I mean."

"This town in Connecticut. Everyone wore khakis."

I laughed.

Jonah picked at a loose brick. "Dad swears Twin Willows is it—no more moving."

"Oh yeah?" I said, unable to keep the hope out of my voice.

Jonah cocked his head, the corner of his mouth turning up as he surveyed me.

I lifted one hand to smooth my hair down. *Stop being so easy to read*, I could hear Jenny advising me. *Play hard to get.* "I should get back inside." I turned to go.

Jonah caught my arm. "Don't go yet."

I moved closer to him and felt the heat emanating from his body. "Okay," I murmured, tilting my head back to look at him. I wondered briefly if he had had a girlfriend at each of his old schools, then realized I didn't care.

"Have you lived here your whole life?"

I nodded, then stopped myself. "No, actually. I was born in Italy."

"Wow. What was that like?"

"When I have regression therapy, I'll let you know." I waved a hand at his quizzical look. "I was a year old when we left there. I wish I could say I've been back, but alas I've been stuck here ever since."

"You don't remember Italy at all?"

"No." I closed my eyes. "Well, there is one thing."

"What?"

I opened my eyes and looked at the sky. "I have this weird memory of a stone angel on top of a church with green and brown hills behind it. I told my mom about it once, and she said that was the church in the town where I was born."

Jonah searched my face. "It's amazing what the mind holds on to, isn't it?"

I lifted my chin and took a baby step closer to him. "Yes," I whispered. "It is."

He touched my hand, not a brush like in French class but full-on hand holding. His silver chain bracelet rested against my wrist, the metal warm from his skin. "Hey, what are you doing tomorrow night?"

My breath felt shallow. "Nothing."

"You want to go out or something?"

Warmth flooded my face, my neck, my whole body. "I—"

"There you are," growled a familiar voice.

I jumped away from Jonah, and he let go of my hand.

Heath stood on the sidewalk, arms crossed. He glared at me. "You need to go home."

Jonah launched himself off the brick wall and moved next to me. "Who is this guy?"

His tone held a little bite that made me flush. "Uh, he works for us. On our farm." I squinted at Heath. "Did my mom send you?"

"Yeah." Heath reached for me, but I twisted away from him.

"She said I could stay out until eleven."

Heath closed the distance between us and took my elbow. "Well, she changed her mind." He narrowed his eyes and I understood. Lidia had not sent him.

Jonah grabbed my hand. "Don't go. Call your mom, and tell her you'll be late."

For a moment I stood between the two of them. Jonah's palm pressed into mine, his skin rough and warm. But Heath's grip was tight on my arm, and I knew which way I had to go. "I'm sorry," I murmured to Jonah. "She's been a little overprotective since the bus crash."

Jonah dropped my hand and stepped back, his jaw clenched. "Whatever."

"Hey." I shrugged away from Heath and put myself directly in front of Jonah, forcing him to look at me. "I'd stay if I could but I can't. Please don't be mad."

His face softened. "You didn't answer my question.

About tomorrow."

"Alessia, *come on.*"

I glanced over my shoulder at Heath. "*Coming.* I'll call you," I told Jonah.

"You don't have my number. I'll get yours from Carly and text you."

Heath cleared his throat.

"I need to get my coat," I said and dashed into the restaurant. The party was in full swing in the back room, with music blaring and kids dancing. I found Carly, apologized for leaving, and tried to ignore the hurt look on her face as I made my way outside. As I climbed into Heath's truck, I glanced at the spot where Jonah and I had just been, but he was gone.

Heath started the ignition and revved the engine as he spun out into the street. "I waited for you in the barn for an hour. What were you thinking?"

I stared at him. "What? Oh. Shoot, Heath, I'm sorry. But the party—"

"Don't make excuses. You forgot."

"Well, yes, but it would have been really hard for me to get out of—"

Heath expelled a long, loud breath. "Look, I know it's important to keep up appearances. But the Benandanti have to come first. I spend every waking moment—and sleeping moment, for that matter—thinking about our mission. You need to learn to have the same kind of devotion." He shifted gears and the truck jerked forward. "Did you see that picture in the window of the restaurant? Do I need to remind you what you're fighting for?"

I twisted in the seat. "You don't need to remind me. I see reminders everywhere."

He glanced at me, then back at the road.

"It isn't just keeping up appearances for me. I care about school, about my friends. I'm not just hanging out with them so they won't suspect I have a double life."

"I know but—"

"But nothing!" I looked out the window as we passed the school, dark and weekend-empty. "I have a life, and I intend to keep it."

"Good luck," Heath muttered.

"What is that supposed to mean?"

"I had a life. In Italy. And the Benandanti made me come here to babysit you."

"Sorry to inconvenience you," I snapped. I raised an eyebrow. "Wait. I thought you said you lived in Provence."

"I did. Then I moved to Italy, and that's where I was Called. I was part of the Clan in Friuli before they sent me here." Shadows moved across Heath's face from the reflection of moonlight.

"If they sent you here, then someone must have been sent there to take your place, right?"

Heath nodded, his eyes on the road.

"So the Benandanti aren't necessarily trapped in one place?"

Heath slowed the truck as we approached the farm. "Not necessarily but that's not what you should be thinking about right now."

"I just need to know I won't be stuck here forever—"

"You need to be thinking about the mission here and now in Twin Willows. That's your priority." Heath talked right over me as though I hadn't said anything. "And you can't let yourself be distracted." His tone was pointed.

I clenched the hand that Jonah had touched. As I climbed out of the truck after we pulled into the driveway, I felt my phone vibrate.

Heath started toward the barn. "We have until eleven when Lidia expects you home. Let's not let this night be a total waste."

"Fine," I said. I followed a few paces behind him, so I could pull my phone out without him noticing. *New text message.*

*So . . . tomorrow? I never got an answer.*

Heath opened the barn door and disappeared inside. I hit Reply.

*Tell me where. Tell me when. I'm there.*

# CHAPTER TWELVE
*The Graveyard*

The ancient wrought-iron gate creaked when I pushed it open. The wind blew it shut as I stepped into the graveyard. I shuddered and pulled my scarf tighter around my throat. Dead leaves skittered across the ground, and the night wind gusted through the graves, making it sound as if the souls beneath were whispering. Every hair on my body stood at attention, every nerve alive and tingling, as I walked quickly through the headstones. I hadn't gone on many dates before, but I was pretty sure that a first date in a cemetery was not normal.

I threaded through the aisles of old and new graves. Alexander Smith died 1790. And just beyond it, Dolly Salter. I stopped. Someone—it must have been Mr. Salter—had left a bouquet of daisies recently. I touched the cold marble that covered Dolly and wondered if she could see me standing at her grave. Did she know I was here?

"Did you know her?"

I shrieked and jumped about a foot in the air, my heart in my throat. I whirled around to see Jonah standing a few steps away from me, his black coat buttoned all the way up his neck, hands shoved deep into his pockets.

"I'm sorry." He grinned. "Didn't mean to scare you."

"You can't sneak up on people like that in a graveyard," I said, trying to steady my breath. "Yes, I did know her. She was Mr. Salter's wife. He owns the hardware store in town."

Jonah looked at the grave, his eyes boring into the stone. "Oh yeah. There's a picture of her over the register. My dad and I were in there the other day."

"Somehow I don't see your dad as the hardware store type."

"He's not." Jonah brushed a lock of hair out of his eyes. "But he pretends that he is, you know, to get in touch with the 'common man.'"

"What about you? Are you the hardware store type?"

"I can hammer a nail when necessary," Jonah said, miming a hammer with his hands. "You must be pretty handy, living on a farm and all."

"Oh, I can milk a goat," I said, "but when I was eleven I accidentally nailed the barn door shut, and I haven't been allowed to hold a hammer since."

Jonah laughed. "So no power tools for you."

"Nary a screwdriver. My mom even wrote a note to get me out of shop class."

"You're lucky. My dad made me take an *after school* shop class. Three schools ago."

"Ugh."

"And he made Bree join a home ec club. One day we decided to switch. When my dad found out I'd been baking pies all afternoon and Bree had been building a bird feeder, he flipped out."

"He's really into those traditional roles, isn't he?"

"I'm thinking of becoming a ballet dancer just to piss him off." He smiled at me. The fluttery feeling I usually got with him was replaced with a warm content-edness. He closed the distance between us and offered his elbow. "Want to take a stroll?"

"Okay." I tucked my hand through his arm. We turned away from Mrs. Salter's grave. "So, um, when I said 'tell me where,' I didn't think that would mean a graveyard."

"Well, I like to be different." Jonah didn't elaborate.

There was a fine line between different and weird. *Says the girl who turns into a Falcon*, I reminded myself.

We meandered to the older, more historic head-stones. I pointed out the oldest one from 1765. "I'm thinking they all died of boredom from living here," I said, gesturing to the row of ancient graves.

"Oh, come on." Jonah touched a moss-covered cherub that sat atop one of the headstones. "*Something* inter-esting must have happened in three hundred-odd years."

"Well, actually . . ." I looked up into his face, edged in shadow. "When my dad brought us back from Italy. That caused a ruckus."

"Oh yeah?" Jonah grinned, his teeth flashing white in the dark. "Don't keep me in suspense."

"Apparently my dad was the catch of the county. Every girl from here to Bangor wanted him. So when he returned from Italy with a wife and kid, he got a lot of crap from some very disappointed girls."

"What kind of crap?"

I bit back the giggles that always seemed to bubble up whenever I told this story. "Literally. A flaming bag of pooh. On our front step. My mother still overcleans the spot."

Jonah stopped in his tracks and doubled over with laughter. When he straightened, he said, "Your dad must be one good-looking guy."

I swallowed. "Yeah," I said, staring at the stars that had come out from behind the clouds. "He was."

"Was?"

I kept my eyes fixed on the sky. "He died. Last year. Of a heart attack."

Jonah slid his hand into mine. His palm was rough and calloused. "I'm sorry," he murmured. "Is he buried here?"

"No," I said. "He was cremated. We scattered his ashes over the sea. He loved the sea," I whispered and swallowed again, blinking rapidly. I didn't want to cry on a first date. I shook my head a little to get rid of my thoughts about my dad. I just wanted to be normal tonight.

We stood there and gazed at the stars for a long time. I tried to find Orion's Belt but couldn't until Jonah pointed it out to me. We sat down side by side on the bench under the willow tree near the older graves. The wind blasted through the branches and blew leaves into our laps. I moved a little closer to Jonah for warmth and liked how it felt to be pressed up against his side. I hooked my elbow around his and buried my hand in the folds of his coat to keep warm.

"I know it's weird to have a date in a graveyard," he said, breaking the silence that had stretched comfortably between us. "But I've always liked them." He looked down at me. "Remember how I said I didn't like crowds because I couldn't hear my own thoughts?"

I nodded.

"In a graveyard, you're surrounded by people, but they're all quiet. So I can be alone without being alone."

"It's like being in a meditation room," I said.

Jonah's face lit up at my understanding.

I leaned into him. "Is that why you skip so many of your classes?" I asked softly. "Because you can't hear your own thoughts in school?"

"Yeah. Ironic, isn't it? Not being able to think in school? By the afternoon it gets to be too much for me."

"That's why you always eat lunch outside," I said, more to myself than to him.

"Yeah." He locked his eyes on mine. "But you could come out there with me. Being with you—actually—makes my thoughts clearer."

I barely breathed. We held each other's eyes for a

moment, and then, quickly as if he didn't want to over-think it, he lowered his head and pressed his lips to mine. His mouth was cold from the wintry air, but his breath was warm. After a moment, I was no longer cold. I put my free hand on the back of his head, curling his hair around my fingers. Jonah wrapped his arm around me and held me to him.

We sat like that for a long while, alternating between talking and kissing. He told me about how Bree used to make him dress like a girl when they were little because she wanted an identical twin. I told him about how over the summer I had left the pasture gate open one night and all the goats had escaped and Lidia and I spent two days chasing them back into the barn. "That's when my mom realized we couldn't run the farm by ourselves."

"So she hired that guy."

"What guy?" My senses were filled with the spicy smell and taste of Jonah, and it made my brain fuzzy.

"The guy who picked you up last night."

I blinked, my mind suddenly clear. "Heath?" I tight-ened my arms around Jonah's neck. "I don't want to talk about him."

"I don't want to talk," Jonah murmured and bent his head toward my throat.

The night clouds parted to reveal the moon directly over our heads. "Oh, shit!" I scrambled off the bench, freed my cell phone from my pocket, and flipped it open. I had five missed calls from home, and it was just past midnight. "Shit, shit, shit! My mother is going to kill me!"

"What's wrong?" Jonah got to his feet and shoved his hands into his pockets again.

"I was supposed to be home at ten, and it's after midnight. Shit!" I dashed through the gravestones, dodging in and out of the macabre aisles.

Jonah caught up to me and grabbed my elbow. "Hang on. I'll walk you home and apologize to her."

"Uh, no. Trust me. You do not want to be subjected to my mother's wrath." I rushed toward the entrance gate to the cemetery.

Jonah fell into step with me. "No, I don't mind. I could tell her that I took you to a late movie or my car broke down on our way home from the restaurant or we ran into some other friends and lost track of time or—"

"Wow, you really have a treasure trove of excuses, don't you?" We reached the gate, and I pushed it open. The loud, rusty creaking was a thousand times creepier at midnight than it had been when I'd come in earlier. "Don't you have to get home, too? What's your curfew?"

"They don't care," Jonah said and took my hand as we turned in the direction of my house. He was walking far too slow, and I tried to pick up our pace, almost dragging him down the deserted street. "They'll be in my dad's office, fighting. They always fight after they think we've gone to bed." His tone bit through the still air.

Despite my desperation to get home, I stopped and stared at him. He swallowed and looked away, but I still saw the pain that flashed through his eyes. "I'm sorry, Jonah," I said and touched his arm. "That must be really tough."

He stiffened. "It is what it is."

"What do they fight about?"

He met my eyes again.

"I'm sorry. You don't have to tell me. It's none of my business."

Jonah talked fast, like he wanted to get rid of something. "My mom used to be the breadwinner, and she put my dad through school to get his MBA and PhD and all that."

I held still while he talked, afraid that if I moved he would stop.

"Then when my dad got the job with the Guild he made my mom quit her career and become the perfect housewife. And she hates it." He took a deep breath. "Whatever. As long as he's happy, right?"

"So he gets to be happy, and everyone else is miserable?" I shook my head. "No wonder they fight."

"Yeah, it sucks," Jonah said in a tone that told me he didn't want to talk about it anymore. He tugged on my hand. "Come on. Let's get you home."

"Listen," I said, "you don't have to walk me home. You'll just have to backtrack to your house. And I-I kinda lied to my mom about where I was tonight. So it'll probably be better if I deal with her alone."

"Whatever," he said again and pulled his hand out of mine.

I reached out and grabbed his wrist. He tried to pull away, but I held fast. "Hey, I didn't mean that I wanted our date to be over. I don't. I'm just thinking of your own best interest. You don't want to meet my mom when she's angry."

He smiled and slid his hand back into mine. "I don't want this night to be over, either." Moonlight moved over his face, shadows shape-shifting in his eyes.

I stepped into him and stood on tiptoe to kiss his lips. He snaked an arm around my waist and held me close. Thoughts of my mother and curfew flew from my mind. I was already late; what did a few more minutes matter?

"Alessia Maria Jacobs!"

I sprang away from Jonah and whirled toward the sound of my mother's voice.

Lidia emerged from the darkness like a flash of brilliant white light, her eyes blazing, her face flaming with anger.

"Mom?" I took a step toward her, caught a better look at the expression on her face, and stepped back toward Jonah. "What are you doing here? I was just coming home."

"I'm very sorry I kept her out so late," Jonah said.

I glanced at him; how could he talk like silk and chocolate under such duress?

My mother stalked toward us, her gaze fixed on Jonah like she was thinking about which knife in her collection would do the job best.

He held out his hand. "I'm Jonah—"

She halted and cocked her head. "Does your mother allow you to be out this late?"

"Of course," Jonah said with a shrug.

Lidia took hold of my wrist, her fingers like the iron manacles I was certain she would have me in from now on. "Well, in my house we do things a bit differently. Alessia has a curfew. And she knows better than to defy me." She tightened her fingers, and I winced as my skin pinched under her grasp. She gave Jonah a curt nod. "*Buonanotte.*"

"Good night," Jonah said. "And again, sorry."

I tried to smile at him, and he lifted his shoulders a little, then let them go with a sigh. As my mother turned away and pulled me with her, I stretched my free arm back and felt Jonah's fingers brush mine. My fingertips tingled after we'd let go.

I jogged behind Lidia, my wrist still in her fierce grasp. She muttered under her breath in Italian—not a good sign. I gave up trying to follow her words until she burst out in English, "Two hours late! I think, she must be dead in a ditch somewhere, so I go out to look for you, and instead you're kissing a boy in the middle of the street like a *puttana*!"

"Mom!" I stopped. It was the worst thing she had ever said to me. Shame and hurt roiled inside me.

Lidia let go of my wrist and turned. Her eyes glistened in the darkness, and she put her hand up to her mouth, pulling at her lips. "*Mi scusi*, Alessia," she whispered and rubbed her face. "I just don't know what's gotten into you lately. Cutting school, staying out late . . . this isn't like you."

"Maybe it is." My voice echoed down the empty street. "Maybe this is who I really am, okay?"

"No. It's not."

"How do you know?" I yelled. "You know nothing about who I really am. Nothing!"

Lidia sighed, her shoulders slumping. "Let's just go home. *Bene?*"

"*Bene*," I muttered.

The house was ablaze with light when we returned. Lidia had left the front door ajar. She kept up a steady stream of Italian, asking God for the strength to deal with such a willful daughter, as we turned off the lights and locked the doors. When I reached the top of the stairs she switched to English. "You're grounded."

"Are you kidding?" I had never been grounded before. Never, ever.

Lidia crossed the landing and cupped my face with her hand. "You've always been such a good girl." She stroked my temple with her thumb, her eyes boring into mine. "If there is something going on, you can tell me. I hope you know that you can tell me . . . *anything*."

I blinked several times, but her eyes never left mine. All the pieces I knew came rushing back—the amulet in the basement, Lidia's reaction to the mention of the

Benandanti, Friuli. What did she know? And was she the one person for whom I could break the cardinal rule? *You must not speak of the Benandanti.* "There's nothing going on," I whispered, my mouth dry.

She searched my face for another moment, then sighed and dropped her hand. "Good night, *cara.*"

I watched her disappear into her room before dodging into mine and locking the door. My eyes adjusted to the darkness in an instant, my vision clear as my Falcon's. I freed the locket from inside my sweater and clutched it in one hand. By the time I crossed the room and opened the window, my body was already tingling.

*Grounded my ass,* I thought as I soared out into the night.

# CHAPTER THIRTEEN
*The Plan*

The dawn light crested the horizon as I rose over the treetops. My wings ached from the exhausting pace Heath had set for the last couple of weeks.

*One more time*, Heath commanded.

*It's nearly morning.*

*You've got to get this. One more time and then we'll go home.*

I choked back a screech, circled a tall pine tree, and hovered in midair. My speed as a Falcon was so fast that sometimes I overshot a target, and that was what today's lesson was all about. I plunged straight down at breakneck speed, my talons stretched out in front of me. The ground gained alarmingly fast, but I didn't slow down. Just before I hit the earth, I slowed enough to snatch a pinecone that Heath had placed as a target.

I shot upward and came to rest on one of the upper branches of the pine tree. *Happy?*

*Very. That was great. Okay, let's go home.*

I flew low to the ground and kept pace with Heath

as we raced back to the farm. We'd been training every night for two weeks, which was easier to get away with as far as Lidia was concerned, but it left me drained. Sometimes I skipped working in the office first period, instead finding a quiet corner in the auditorium to catch up on sleep.

Heath broke into my thoughts. *You're doing well. Of course you have your awesome and amazing Guide to thank for that—*

*Oh, shut up.*

I heard his laughter in my mind and decided to jump on his good mood. *Do you think I'm ready now? Can we retake the Waterfall?*

*It's not up to me to make that decision. It's up to the Stag—he's the head of our Clan. And I don't know if he'll throw you into battle so soon.* He tossed his head, white fur glistening in the darkness. *Patience, young Padawan.*

I almost fell out of the air. *Heath! Did you finally get a DVD player?*

*Better than that—Blu-ray.*

So many kids in my government class had a hard time finding any con to argue about the Guild's plan that Mr. Clemens had to postpone the debates so everyone could do some research. He gave over class time for us to meet with our partners, but when I sat down opposite Bree, she didn't even look up from the journal she was scribbling in.

I cleared my throat.

Nothing.

"Um, hello?"

With an exaggerated sigh, she flung her pen down. "What?"

I gritted my teeth and leaned toward her. "Look around you. Everyone else is working with their partner. Can we please go over what we're going to do when we get up in front of the class, so we don't make fools of ourselves?"

Bree glared at me for a moment. "Fine." She shoved her journal into her bag and pulled out a purple spiral-bound notebook. "Tell me what you're going to say."

"Well . . ." I fumbled in my bag for my notebook and a pen. "I was going to talk about how many jobs it would create—"

"So is everyone else."

"—and the positive environmental impact it would have on the county."

"Oh, please." Bree waved her hand in a circle. "Everyone else in this room is going to say the exact same things. Find something original."

Heat crept up my throat and into my face. I took a deep breath. "What do you suggest?"

She shrugged and studied her notebook. "That's your problem. I've already written mine."

"Oh yeah?" I folded my arms over my chest. "Can I see it?"

"Nope." She flashed me a humorless grin, and for

an instant she looked so much like Jonah that my heart jumped. "It's better if it's a surprise."

"Okay, that's it." My voice rose above the low din in the classroom, and the people nearby looked at us. "What is your problem? I have been nothing but nice despite your crappy attitude, and you continue to be a total bitch to me."

"You think because you're dating my brother you deserve special treatment?"

"Why is it such a big deal to you if I date him, anyway? It's none of your business."

Bree's nostrils flared, and the edges of her mouth turned white. "It is," she hissed. Her green eyes glowed like emerald coals against her pale skin.

I jerked away from her, the back of my neck prickling.

Bree launched out of her chair and bent over me. "Trust me," she whispered in my ear. "My brother is not someone you want to get involved with." She whirled away, her long black hair fanning out behind her, while I stared openmouthed at her back.

"Why does your sister hate me?" I asked Jonah at lunchtime. I had taken to spending almost every lunch with him outdoors under the bleachers. I had smuggled a blanket to school, and we ate with it spread across our laps to keep our legs warm. When we were done eating, we would tuck it around us and snuggle until the bell rang.

"*Hate* is a very strong word." Jonah fished in my

paper lunch bag for one of my mom's homemade cookies. "I'd say *strongly dislike* is more accurate."

"Oh, like that's so much better." I took the bag away from him, took out the last cookie, and broke it in half. "Seriously. What is her problem?"

Jonah popped his half of the cookie into his mouth. He looked out into the woods, his profile shadowed by the bleachers so that I couldn't see his eyes. "Bree is—I don't know—she's overprotective for some reason. It's like, she's nine minutes older than me, but sometimes she acts like it's nine years."

"Why does she feel the need to protect you from me?"

He turned to me, grinning. "Because you're obviously a bad influence," he said, reaching under the blanket to grab my waist. He pulled me into him and nipped at my neck. "With your shockingly good grades and disturbing habit of never cutting class—"

I shrieked with laughter and swatted at him, but he held me fast. "I cut class *once*—"

"—and your life like an open book—"

I stopped breathing and wriggled away from him. "What do you mean?"

"You don't have anything to hide. And that just *kills* Bree. She doesn't have anything to bargain with."

My ribs tightened and clamped around my heart like a torture device. If Bree only knew . . . I ducked my head and busied myself with cleaning up our trash. It never failed. Sitting here under the bleachers with Jonah every day, I felt like a normal girl with a normal life, but somehow the Benandanti always seemed to intrude.

"Hey." Jonah brushed my hair away from my eyes and tilted my face up toward his. "What's wrong?"

"Nothing."

He leaned in and kissed me. "You just hate it when someone doesn't like you."

I swallowed and managed a smile. "Yeah. That's it."

The bell clanged.

I pulled away and hopped to my feet. "Are you coming to biology today?" Most of the time Jonah stayed outside. I'd given him my locker combination, and at the end of the day I'd find the blanket in my locker with a pretty leaf or a note in French or a page torn from a book with a sentence underlined.

"Nah." He grabbed my hand and kissed my palm. "Take notes for me?"

I cupped my hand around his cheek, then ran my fingers through his hair. "Sure."

"Oh, and don't worry about Bree. She'll come around." He smiled at me, but his eyes stayed cloaked.

At the end of the day, I waved good-bye to Carly and Melissa and joined Jonah on the sidewalk in front of the school. I usually walked home with him until the turn-off to his house, but today as we crossed Main Street he said, "Do you want to come over?"

I stared at him. "Um, really?" Even though I had

come within steps of his house every other day, he had never invited me in.

"Yeah, my mom wants to meet you."

"You told her about me?" From what I gathered, Jonah barely spoke to his parents.

"You might've come up in conversation." Two little spots of color appeared high on his cheeks. It was the first time I'd ever seen him blush.

A slow grin spread across my face. "You told your *mom* about me."

Jonah kicked me lightly on the shin. "Don't gloat. Are you coming over or not?"

"Sure." I was technically still grounded, but I could usually get away with coming home a little late from school since Lidia was so busy on the farm. I glanced over my shoulder at Jenny, who always followed at a distance to give us privacy before joining me on the rest of the walk home. "Just let me tell Jenny."

"I want details," Jenny said as we stood a few feet away from Jonah at the bend in the road. "Which, by the way, you have been very bad about. I don't have a boyfriend right now. I need to live vicariously through you."

"Okay, okay," I said with a laugh. "I'll call you tonight."

"You better," Jenny yelled as she bounced down the street.

I rejoined Jonah at the corner. He held my hand as we walked, but when we came within sight of his house he wriggled his fingers out of mine.

Mrs. Wolfe descended from the porch and met us halfway down the driveway. Bree disappeared into the house. I hoped she would stay out of the way during this social call.

"Hi, Mrs. Wolfe."

"Hello, dear. I'm so glad Jonah brought you over." She held up the plate in her hands. "Peanut butter cookie?"

"Sure." I took one and bit into it.

Jonah followed suit with an air of forced cheerfulness. I got the sense they ate a lot of cookies.

"Well, come inside."

I followed Mrs. Wolfe with a glance over my shoulder at Jonah, who shook his head a little and shrugged. I swallowed the rest of my cookie (it was too dry) and jogged up the steps to the front door.

The house was warm. I hung my jacket by the door and veered into the kitchen. Jonah plunked onto one of the stools that surrounded the island in the middle. I climbed atop the one next to him. Mrs. Wolfe set the plate of cookies in front of me and gestured that I should have another one. I thought it would be rude to refuse, so I reached for one. To my enormous relief, Bree was nowhere to be seen or heard.

Mrs. Wolfe moved between the stove, where something was stewing in a large pot, the island, the fridge, and the sink. She seemed to know exactly when something needed to be stirred or salted. "Jonah tells me you and he are lab partners in biology, Alessia."

I shot Jonah a look that simultaneously conveyed my annoyance at being part of his lie and admiration for the ease with which he was able to lie to his mother. I needed to learn that. "Um, yeah," I said and shoved an entire cookie in my mouth, so I had time to gather my thoughts. I chewed slowly and swallowed. "We dissected frogs last week."

Mrs. Wolfe gave a delicate shudder, smiling tightly. Her smile, like her husband's, didn't reach her eyes. A hot feeling of pity shot through me. I tried to imagine what her life was like, being bounced from place to place by her husband's work. As if she could read my mind, she asked, "You've lived here all your life, haven't you?"

"Since I was a baby," I said.

Jonah rolled his eyes at me, silently asking me to humor his mother.

I took another cookie.

"It must be nice to have roots," Mrs. Wolfe murmured as she carried a cutting board with diced pepper and carrots to her pot, slid the vegetables in, and stirred the contents for a few minutes.

Silence stretched across the kitchen. Jonah and I looked at each other, our feet tangling between our two stools.

Buzzing broke the silence.

"I think that's my phone," I said and slid off the stool to retrieve it from my backpack. It was Lidia. "Hi, Mom."

"Where are you?"

I glanced at Mrs. Wolfe, who was clearly listening. "At Jonah's. His *mom* invited me over for an after-school snack." I figured it couldn't hurt to emphasize it was his mother's idea, not mine.

"You're still grounded, young lady."

"I know but I won't be long. Please?"

Lidia mumbled something in Italian, then said, "Be home by dark."

"I will."

"*Ciao.*"

"*Ciao.*" I hung up and slid the phone back into my bag. "Sorry about that."

Jonah sprang off his stool. "Do you need to go home?" There was a hopeful look in his eyes.

I almost lied, but some part of me was oddly fascinated with his weird home life so I shook my head.

"Let's go upstairs," he muttered, and while his mother's back was still turned, he pulled me into the hall.

I followed him up the stairs. On the landing there were a few boxes piled against the wall. I peeked inside one: family photos that had yet to go on the wall. The photo on top was Jonah and Bree when they were about four, both sitting on the same glittery carousel horse. I took it out of the box to look closer. A thick layer of dust coated the frame.

"Those almost never make it out of the box before we have to move again," Jonah said. "But my dad says he's putting them up this weekend."

I traced my finger along four-year-old Jonah's jaw. "You were a cute kid."

"Oh yeah?" Jonah stepped close to me, and I felt his breath on my cheek. "How 'bout now?"

I put the photo back in the box. "Obviously something went wrong." I ducked under his arm, laughing, and he caught me around the waist. He lifted me and growled while he bit my neck lightly. I shrieked and kicked at him as he carried me down the hall.

A door flew open with a clatter. "Can you two keep it down, please?" Bree stood in the doorway, her lip curled as she took in the sight of us mock wrestling. "I'm trying to study."

"Give it a rest." Jonah didn't let go of me, but I lowered my head to avoid Bree's piercing gaze. "I don't think your straight-B average is in jeopardy."

"Not all of us have girlfriends to cover for us in class," Bree said and slammed her door. Angry-girl rock music seeped out into the hall.

I fought the urge to stick my tongue out at the closed door.

Jonah carried me to his room at the end of the hall and set me down.

A huge black-and-white poster of Jack Kerouac took up half the door. The walls were painted grey and covered with all sorts of things I had never seen in a teenager's room before: African masks, South American baskets, a framed poster of Machiavelli. I took it all in for a moment. "Cool room."

He smiled. "Thanks."

I pointed to the African masks. "So when your dad said the Guild worked in the Congo . . . Did you guys actually go there?"

Jonah nodded. "Just for a few months. It's not the safest place. Plus, we had to be homeschooled while we were there and my mom . . ." He shrugged, leaving the sentence undone, but I gathered that Mrs. Wolfe was not the homeschooling type.

Jonah closed the door and sat down on the edge of the bed.

I dawdled by the desk, fingering the stack of paperbacks, and suddenly realized that this was the first time I'd been alone with a boy in his room since I was twelve. On the rare occasions I had boys over to my house, Lidia was adamant about keeping us downstairs, where she could watch us.

"You like to read," I said, motioning toward the books.

"Yeah." Jonah leaned back on his hands, watching me. "Just not the crap they make us read in school."

I peered at the spines of the books. *Slaughterhouse-Five*, *A Clockwork Orange*, *A Portrait of the Artist as a Young Man*, *On the Road*. I picked up *The Prince*. "Machiavelli, huh?"

Jonah grinned. "I have grand plans to be a tyrant."

I laughed and set the book back on the desk.

"Hand me the Joyce—I want to read you something."

I brought him *A Portrait of the Artist as a Young Man* and then, because it seemed obvious not to, sat beside him on the bed. Our thighs touched as he flipped through the early pages of the book. Many of the passages had been underlined.

Jonah stopped at a folded-down page and read, "'He would fade into something impalpable under her eyes and then in a moment, he would be transfigured. Weakness and timidity and inexperience would fall from him in that magic moment.'" He closed the book and ran a finger down the cover. "I underlined that quote the night I met you."

My breath stopped in my throat.

Jonah dropped the book to the floor and kissed me. I tangled my fingers in his hair and pulled him closer until we both toppled backward onto the bed. He pressed his hand to the back of my neck, and I moved my hand under his shirt, the heat of his skin burning my palm.

His bedroom door banged open, and my heart nearly leapt out of my chest. We pulled apart like taffy, parts of us still stuck together, and sprang off the bed.

Bree stood inside the doorway, hands on her hips.

Jonah rearranged his shirt. "God, Bree, don't you freaking *knock*?"

"Sorry," she said with a smirk. "Mom wants you downstairs."

"Tell her we're studying."

Bree pressed a hand to her chest. "Are you asking me

to *lie*?" She narrowed her eyes at me, and though I didn't want to flush, I couldn't help it. "Besides, I'm pretty sure she knows what's really going on up here." She spun on her heel and left the room. A few seconds later her door slammed, and the angry-girl music started up again.

Jonah looked at me. "Sorry."

"It's okay." I glanced out the window; orange and pink light streaked the sky and lengthened shadows in the backyard. "I should probably get going soon anyway." I headed for the doorway.

But Jonah grabbed my hand and pulled me to him. He kissed me, one hand in my hair, the other at my waist, and I didn't care who walked in on us. For an instant I forgot where I was, who I was, and everything complicated in my life smoothed itself out. I clung to him, not wanting to return to that other life. I wanted this world, where it was just me and Jonah and nothing else.

When he finally released me, my whole body trembled. I had fallen hard for Jonah Wolfe, and there was no going back. I could only hope he felt the same way about me and that his family really was staying in Twin Willows. Because if they picked up and left . . . I drew a shaky breath. "Let's go downstairs."

Mrs. Wolfe was still cooking in the kitchen.

"I should head home," I said when we reached the counter. "Thanks for the cookies, Mrs. Wolfe."

She looked up from the onion she was dicing. Her face was streaked with tears, but her mouth held a bland smile.

A shiver ran down my spine. "Are you okay?"

"What? Oh." She swiped her cheek with the back of her hand, but it only succeeded in smearing the make-up that was caked on her face. "Cutting onions always makes me cry," she said with a shrill laugh.

A door creaked open from down the hall, and for the first time all afternoon I saw Mrs. Wolfe's mask come down.

"Your father's coming in from his office," she whispered to no one in particular. She pulled a paper towel off the roll by the sink and blotted her face. She used the reflection in the knife's blade to check her makeup, rearranged her features into pleasant blandness, and went back to calmly dicing the onion.

I turned to Jonah. "Your dad works from home? Doesn't the Guild have a big office in Bangor?"

"Yeah, but he needs to be close to the actual site."

A shadow darkened the entrance to the kitchen. Mr. Wolfe straightened his tie as he strode past Jonah and stole an apple from the bowl on the counter. He sniffed the air. "Beef bourguignon again?" With a frown he took a bite of the apple, then spotted me and swallowed quickly. "I didn't know we had company." He peered at me. "Alexis, right?"

"Alessia," I corrected him.

"Of course." He took another bite of apple. "Well, I'm in the middle of a conference call. Nice to see you again, Alison."

Jonah let out a loud sigh as Mr. Wolfe headed back

down the hallway. "Sorry," he mumbled to me.

"Don't worry about it." I touched his hand lightly. "Before I go, where's the bathroom?"

"On the left." Jonah pointed down the hallway where Mr. Wolfe had disappeared.

"Be right back."

More boxes were stacked against the wall, including a bunch of empty ones outside a door across from the bathroom. A sign read Private below the mottled glass window that took up half the door. I could only assume it was Mr. Wolfe's office.

The murmur of voices leaked into the hallway after I came out of the bathroom. ". . . that goat farm . . ."

I stopped.

". . . don't need her permission . . ."

I pressed myself against the wall next to the office and leaned my head toward the door hinge.

"It's outside the boundary of the farm's property." It wasn't Mr. Wolfe's voice.

I peeked in through the murky glass for a split second, withdrawing quickly before they could see me. The assistant—Pratt, I remembered—sat at the side of an enormous desk. Mr. Wolfe stood behind it, palms flat on the wood as he leaned over a grey teleconference phone.

"Are you certain?" asked a disembodied voice from the speaker. The voice had an accent; I could swear it was Italian.

"I'm sure," Pratt said. "I checked the town, county, and state records. Her property ends at a stone wall marker in the woods, and it's past that."

"Who owns the land?"

"The town," Mr. Wolfe answered.

"So we are *bene*." Definitely Italian.

"Not quite," Pratt said. "She could still cause some trouble."

"Wasn't she at the meeting?" There was something about the steel-edged voice on the phone that made my skin itchy.

"No," Pratt said. "She wasn't there."

"Take care of it, gentlemen," said the unseen voice, followed by a click and then a dial tone.

I risked another peek through the window. Pratt hit a button on the phone and got to his feet. I backed away from the door and ducked into the bathroom, my temples throbbing. Why were they talking about my mother and the farm?

I heard the office door creak open. "Coffee at Joe's?" Pratt asked.

"Sounds good," Mr. Wolfe said.

I waited until their footsteps disappeared before stepping back into the hall. My heart was shaky, like I'd just run a fast mile in cold weather. I glanced toward the kitchen. With a deep breath, I slipped into the office.

The desk sprawled out in the center of the room, and surrounding it were shelves and bookcases crammed with folders and papers and documents rolled up into long tubes. The walls were covered with tacked-up index cards and blueprints. I turned in a slow circle, trying to find something that would give me a clue as to why they'd been talking about my farm.

I walked over to one of the walls where sets of blueprints hung so close together that some of them overlapped. TWIN WILLOWS FACILITY—FOUNDATION, read the label on the bottom of the blueprint. I tried to make sense of the plan, but the silvery lines swam in my vision.

A dry-erase board hung beside the blueprint, its surface divided into two columns. One column was labeled AGREE. It listed many of the town's small business owners, like Mr. Salter and Joe Burns of Joe's Coffee Shop. The other column was titled POSSIBLE PROBLEMS. My mother was first on that list. I touched her name in red marker. What was going on here?

I moved down the wall, past a plan labeled TWIN WILLOWS FACILITY—SECOND FLOOR and stopped at the blueprint next to it. This one was titled TWIN WILLOWS FACILITY—EXTERIOR and showed the landscape surrounding the imaginary plant.

The black-and-silver graphics of the plan blurred in front of me. I blinked to clear my vision, to make sure I was reading the plan right. My hand shook as I touched the blueprint. I walked my fingers until they struck the exact center of where the plant would be. I didn't need a blueprint to tell me where it was; I could find this spot with my eyes closed if I had to.

The Guild's hydroelectric power plant sat directly on top of the Waterfall.

# CHAPTER FOURTEEN
*The Clan*

"What are you doing in here?"

I whirled around.

Jonah stood just outside the doorway as though an invisible barrier prevented him from going in.

I backed away from the wall, still burning with the knowledge I had just discovered from the blueprint. "S-sorry." I hurried toward him, my brain spinning to come up with a good excuse. "I thought—" I swallowed. "Maybe there was something in here that might help my presentation. You know, the one for government class."

Jonah reached out to me without stepping inside the room. I took his hand, and he pulled me into the hallway. His hand was cold. "We're not allowed in that room."

"I'm sorry. I shouldn't have gone in there."

"*I* don't care," Jonah said. "It's just a good thing I found you and not my dad."

"I'm sorry," I said again. "I was just curious."

He leaned in so close to me that our noses touched. "You know what they say about curiosity." He nibbled my lips.

I pulled back.

"What's wrong?"

"N-nothing. I should really be getting home."

"I'll walk you."

"No."

Jonah looked at me, his brow creased.

I took a deep breath, hoping he wouldn't notice how shaky it was. "I mean, my mom is probably the last person you want to see, and it smells like dinner is almost ready."

"Okay, but don't complain to me that chivalry is dead." He raised my hand to his mouth and kissed it. "My lady."

"You're a nerd," I said.

He laughed and led me to the kitchen.

I thanked his mom and grabbed my jacket from the coatrack by the door, my nerves fighting to stay inside my skin.

Jonah walked me out onto the front porch. As soon as we were out of his mom's sight, he pulled me against him, one hand under my jacket, the other buried deep in my hair. "Meet me tonight. At the graveyard on our bench."

"I'll try." My brain was on fire to get home and find Heath, tell him what I had found. But my body melted into Jonah as he kissed the breath out of me.

At last he drew back. "Sure you don't want me to walk you home?"

"I'm sure." I gave him a watery smile and one last quick kiss. "I'll call you later," I said and ran to the top of the driveway before he could stall me again. When I turned around, he was still on the porch, watching me.

At the end of his street, I bolted into a run. My backpack flopped painfully against my spine, but I didn't slow down. By the time I reached the farm I was sure I could give the track team a run for their money.

Heath's truck was in the driveway. *Don't be in the Cave*, I prayed; there was no way I could ask to talk to him privately in front of Lidia without raising her suspicion. But just as I skidded around the back of the house, the barn door banged open, and Heath walked out into the dying sunlight.

"I have to talk to you—it's really important," I gasped, bending over a little to ease a crick in my side.

"It's too risky now," he said. I traced his gaze to the Cave where Lidia could emerge at any moment. "Let's meet tonight in the clearing at eleven."

"But . . ." I straightened up and sighed. "Okay." My insides danced between hot and cold as I struggled not to spill what I knew about Mr. Wolfe and the Guild then and there. We needed a quiet place to talk it out, but I wanted Heath to make sense of it for me now, to tell me that the Benandanti knew all about it already and had a plan, that what I had seen meant something else. That the Guild didn't intend to destroy the Waterfall . . .

I trudged to the house and squinted at the sky just before I went inside. Daylight was weakening into greying dusk, and eleven felt decades away. I took out my cell phone and sent a text to Jonah. *Can't tonight. Tomorrow?*

He responded less than a minute later. *OK*.

At ten thirty, I stood in the doorway to my room, waiting for the light that seeped out into the hall from under Lidia's door to disappear. Finally, at ten to eleven, the light went out.

Carrying my boots in my arms, I tiptoed down to the kitchen in my socks. Moonlight skittered over the table and counters, turning them the color of bone. I put on my boots and slipped out the door. It felt strange to leave the house in my human form; I was more used to soaring out my second-story window, the ground like a toy map beneath me.

Heath was already at the clearing when I emerged from the dark woods. "What's going on?"

I swallowed hard, my throat suddenly sticky. "I was at the Wolfes' house today—you know, that new family that moved to town?"

"What were you doing there?"

"I—" I pressed my lips together. "Nothing. But when I was there—"

"You were with that boy, weren't you? The one from the party. Jonah."

"Well, yes, but that's not the point." I folded my arms over my chest. "Wait a minute. How do you know his name?"

"I live in this town too, you know."

"Yeah, but you're—" I threw my hands up in the air.

"Never mind. It doesn't matter *why* I was there or with who. The point is, I was there, and I was in Mr. Wolfe's office, and I saw a blueprint of where they're planning to build that power plant."

Heath straightened, his whole body tense. "Where?"

I pointed into the dark forest. "Right over the Waterfall."

"Shit." Heath bent over, digging his elbows into his thighs. "They've done it."

"Done what?" I grabbed his shoulder and heaved him upright. "How did we not know this before? The Guild is a huge company. Are they a front for the Malandanti?"

"Something like that." Heath ran his hands through his hair. "We're not sure how exactly the Malandanti and the Guild are entwined. We know they are some-how, but every spy the Benandanti has ever sent into the Guild hasn't come out alive."

I drew back. Even though I had seen firsthand what the Malandanti were capable of, reminders of it always pierced my gut. "So that's why they're here. To destroy the Waterfall."

"No, they don't want to destroy all that magic. They want to control it." Heath blew out a hard breath. "But this is the first time they've ever tried to build over one of the sites."

"What does *that* mean?"

Heath paced in a little circle. "It means they're

stepping up their game. Once that power plant is built we'll never break through the barrier. We'll never get control back." He looked off into the forest. "We've got to take this information to the rest of the Clan."

"You think?" I said.

But Heath's mouth was already moving, already uttering secret words to Call the Clan.

Pain pierced my heart, tearing me in two. I gripped Heath's arm for support, but his knees buckled at the same time as mine, and we both fell on the ground. The clearing filled with blue and white light, brighter than moonlight and daylight mixed together. My insides gave one last twist, and my soul left my body.

I shot up out of the clearing.

*Our meeting place is the birch trees near the Waterfall,* Heath told me.

I stretched my wings and soared over the treetops. In the forest below I glimpsed patches of starry-blue auras—the rest of the Clan racing to join us.

Below me, I spied the copse of birch trees, their bark silvery in the moonlight. I glided lower and landed on one of their branches.

The Eagle took a perch above me while the rest gathered below.

*Tell them what you told me,* Heath said.

Careful to keep out any details that could give away my identity, I related what I had seen.

*You're sure you didn't misread the blueprint?* asked the

Stag. I recognized his deep, authoritative voice from the bridge.

*I'm sure*, I said.

*But how did this get past us?* It was the Lynx. *I was at the town meeting when the plan was proposed. The location of the plant must have been part of the presentation. How come we didn't realize it then?*

*I was there too*, said the Eagle.

*Me too*, I said, echoed by the Stag.

*I wasn't there*, Heath said. *What do you remember of the presentation?*

No one answered.

I tried to dredge up specific details of the presentation, but all I could remember were bright photographs of smiling people and the sense of compliance I had when the presentation was over. *It's kind of a jumble*, I said. *All I can say is that I didn't think anything bad about it.*

Heath's ears pricked forward. *Did any of you think anything bad about it?*

The silence that followed answered his question.

The Stag pranced in place. *Are you thinking what I'm thinking?*

*If you're thinking the Congo, then yes.*

The Eagle burst upward from her perch a few inches, her wings beating wildly. *Of course! How could we not have seen it?*

*I can't believe I was so dumb*, the Lynx said, sitting back on his haunches.

*Hello?* I cocked my head. *Newbie here. What are you talking about?*

Heath turned his head up toward me. *One of the magical sites is in the Congo. It holds the power of mind control.*

*It's not really mind control*, the Eagle clarified. *It's more like an influence.*

*Okay, fine. Mind influence. Regardless, the Malandanti control that site. They must have used the magic on the town.*

The conversation dimmed in my mind as I realized that we weren't just talking about the Malandanti or the Guild. We were talking about Jonah's father. What did Mr. Wolfe know? How far deep was he? Was he—a little needle stabbed my heart—a Malandante?

*—can't let this happen.* The Stag's stout voice snapped me back to the here and now. *We have a complete Clan now. We can retake the Waterfall.*

*When?* asked the Lynx.

*Tonight. Now. We're all here—*

*No way.* Heath's fur bristled. *She's not ready.*

*Well, she has to be. Here's the plan—*

*Wait—what?* I fluttered off my branch and hovered in the air. *Are we attacking the Malandanti?*

*Yes*, answered the Stag.

At the same time Heath said, *No.*

They stared at each other, the air crackling between them.

The Stag raised his head, and his antlers caught

the moonlight, casting a long, pointed shadow on the ground. *I know you're her Guide, but I'm the head of this Clan. I have the final say.* There was no ego in his voice, just a quiet authority. He actually sounded a little weary. *Who knows how much more damage the Guild could do if we wait any longer? We're going in tonight.*

# CHAPTER FIFTEEN
*The Attempt*

As the Stag laid out the plan, I tried to keep the fear out of my mind.

Heath sensed it anyway and blocked out the rest of the Clan from his thoughts. *It's okay. Just remember your training, and you'll be fine.*

*The minute we come out of hiding, the Malandanti on patrol will see our auras and call for backup,* finished the Stag. *So be ready. And everyone keep a lookout for our newbie,* he added with a nod to me. *All right. Here we go.* In bocca al lupo.

*In bocca al lupo . . .* may the wolf hold you in its mouth. An Italian blessing I had heard Lidia say many times before a big test or a writing contest.

If I were my human self, my hands would be trembling, my stomach a mess of butterflies. But in my Falcon form, my wings stretched wide and caught the wind, my sharp eyes spotted an insect clinging to a leaf, and the quietest sound from the smallest creature rang like surround sound in my ears. I was so awake to every tiny thing in the world when I was a Falcon that I felt like I spent the rest of my life sleeping. The only other time I felt this alive was with Jonah.

My aura flickered. I pushed thoughts of Jonah from my mind and focused on the training exercises I had done with Heath. Keeping low to the ground, I followed the Eagle through the trees. How many times had I walked this path with my dad? I blinked; now wasn't the time to think of him, either. Just ahead, the trees thinned out. The sound of the Waterfall filled the air.

*Get ready*, the Stag told us.

I took a deep mental breath.

As soon as we broke through the trees, we fanned out. The Eagle and I flew down to the pool below the Waterfall. Inside the sparkly black barrier, the Malandanti Bobcat sat on a rock beside the water. The Stag was right. When it spotted the five Benandanti, it howled.

The plan was that when the other Malandanti showed up, we would overpower them, and the Bobcat would have to come outside the barrier to help. I had expected that we would have several minutes between the Bobcat's alert and the arrival of the rest of its Clan. But the instant the Bobcat howled, bursts of movement exploded on all sides.

They had been waiting for us.

Before I could move, before I could think, the Raven was on me, its talons ripping into my feathers. I screeched and flailed, unable to get free until the Eagle knocked the Raven away. We soared over the Waterfall, the Raven close on our tails.

Above the Waterfall, it was chaos. I had thought the Raven and the Bobcat were bad enough on the bridge, but the Malandanti Clan in its entirety was a hundred times worse. An enormous Boar faced off with the Stag. Heath was locked in battle with a huge grey Coyote. And the Lynx grappled with a massive Panther.

I pulled up short. It was the same Panther I had seen on my father's birthday, the same Panther from my vision in the office.

*Watch out!*

I tore my gaze off the Panther. The Raven, talons outstretched, came right at me. I shot upward. The Eagle met the Raven head-on. In a shower of feathers, they spiraled away, a fiery ball of blue and silver light.

On the ground below, the Malandanti fanned out and surrounded the Benandanti. I pitched downward, glancing inside the barrier. The Bobcat still sat on the rock, watching us. Obviously it had its orders: remain inside the barrier, no matter what.

The Malandanti closed in. With one fluid, swift motion, they pounced on Heath and dragged him away. His pale form disappeared beneath their silvery auras.

I screamed, the sound ripping through the air, and plummeted toward the fight.

The Malandanti Panther turned and met my gaze, those fierce green eyes boring into me.

I landed on the Panther's back, my talons digging deep into its flesh. The Panther bucked beneath me and stumbled away from the pack. The other Benandanti followed my lead. One by one, we hauled the Malandanti away from Heath. He lay on the ground, his white fur stained dark with blood, his chest heaving.

With a cry of relief, I released the Panther. It jabbed at me with its claws, but I dodged out of reach and landed next to Heath. *Are you all right?*

He struggled to find his footing. *I'm okay. Let's go.*

We took off into the forest, and the rest of the Benandanti followed.

The Malandanti did not give chase.

Several miles from the Waterfall in the heart of the dark forest, we stopped and gathered in a small circle. The Eagle landed on the Stag's antlers, but I kept close to Heath. His breathing was labored, and he was favoring his left side a lot. *Are you sure you're all right?*

*Yeah, I'm okay.* He lay down, resting his head on his paws.

The Stag stamped his hooves like thunder on the cold earth. *They were waiting for us. How the hell did they know we would be there?*

*They could've had a spy at the birch trees,* said the Lynx. He had a wound on his paw and sat down to lick it.

*What a miserable failure.* The Stag lowered his head. *We need a better plan for next time.*

At the thought of "next time" my heart sped up. *That Bobcat didn't even blink,* I said. *We need something to lure them outside the barrier. Something they can't resist. And I don't think seeing their Clan mates in danger is it.*

*We weren't ready,* rasped Heath. He looked at the Stag. *I don't want to say I told you so—*

*Then don't,* snapped the Stag. *I made a decision, and it was a bad one. We need to regroup and figure out our next move. But we can't wait too long.* He tilted his head toward me. *How reliable is your source to the Guild?*

*My what?*

*Your source,* he said impatiently. *However you found out the information about the plant. Can you keep pumping that source?*

*Um, I guess so.* I'd have to finagle another invite to Jonah's house and sneak into his dad's office without raising any suspicion—yeah, that wouldn't be too hard or anything. I kept my doubts to myself, but there was one thought I couldn't keep inside. *Do you think that Mr. Wolfe is a Malandante?*

Heath hauled himself up and shot me a dark look. *Are you crazy?* he said to me alone. *This is not the time—*

*I need to know.*

*It's possible,* the Eagle said, cutting into our private conversation. *Did everyone notice the Panther tonight? That's a new member of their Clan.*

*But it could be anyone,* argued the Lynx, *not necessarily Mr. Wolfe. The Malandanti are known to have several* allies who don't actually have the ability to transform, people they've bribed with promises of money and power in order to do their bidding, and Wolfe could very well be playing that role.

*But it* could *be him—*

*Finding out their identities is less important than retaking the Waterfall,* the Stag interrupted, silencing all of us. *And given what we know now, that's more important than ever.*

*You see?* Heath told me privately. *I told you the secret identity thing would drive you nuts. You need to listen to me.*

*Okay, okay.*

*And I think it's time to add you to the patrol,* the Stag said, pulling our attention back to him.

*Patrol?* I asked.

*Every night one of us patrols the Waterfall.*

*How is that possible? With the Malandanti there?*

*We don't confront the Malandanti,* the Lynx said. *We stay hidden and observe.*

*And then you share your observations with the rest of us,* the Stag said. He tossed his head, shadows catching on his antlers. *Rule number one of warfare: know your enemy.*

The air felt cold on my feathers. The realization that this was indeed a war had been brought home to me tonight.

*Time to go,* the Stag said. *I don't want the Malandanti to find us here.*

After working out the patrol schedule, the Clan

took off in different directions. I flew low to the ground, just above Heath, as we headed toward the clearing. It was slow going; he had to stop several times to catch his breath. Just as well. My mind was jumpy as a newborn goat, and there was no way I was going to sleep when I got home.

When we had transformed back into our bodies, I helped Heath along the path through the trees.

At the edge of the woods, he looked down at me and squeezed my arm. "I know I'm hard on you sometimes, but you did good tonight. I'm proud of you."

"Thanks, Heath."

"Get some rest. And don't make yourself crazy."

"I'll try." I watched him limp across the pasture and didn't move until I saw the lights in his cabin click on. I went over the hill to the house, hugging myself against the cold. The stars above were clear and bright. I wished my life were the same. Instead everything was murky and unknown.

I knew when I accepted the Call that I was expected to lay down my life for the Benandanti if it came to that. But that had seemed like such an unreal possibility. Now that I had been in a battle, it didn't seem so unlikely anymore.

Wind swept over the grass, chilling me to the bone. And now I was expected to patrol and spy on Jonah's father . . . Just what *did* he know? *Was* he the Malandanti Panther that was brand-new to their Clan? Even if he wasn't, he wasn't totally innocent, either. He worked for the Guild. I thought about the conference call I had overheard, the unseen Italian on the other end of the line. If Mr. Wolfe was a puppet, who was controlling his strings?

My shoulders ached with all the responsibility piled on top of them. I rubbed the back of my neck, trying to ease the pain that crept in there. There was only so much weight I could handle before I snapped.

# CHAPTER SIXTEEN

*The Debate*

My body was still sore from the battle when I woke up on Monday, and the frigid morning air didn't help. I gathered the eggs as fast as I could and was thankful for the warmth of the kitchen when I burst in through the back door.

Lidia set a plate of scrambled eggs and toast on the table.

I gave her a tired smile as I sat down. "Eat with me, Mom."

She sat across from me, her hands curled around a mug of coffee. "Did you finish all your homework from the weekend?"

"Yeah, I didn't have a lot." Which had been a blessing. I'd spent most of the weekend taking surreptitious baths to soothe my aching muscles.

"Mmmm." Lidia nodded and took a sip of her coffee. She reached over and brushed a lock of hair off my face. "You look tired, *cara*. Did you sleep?"

"Not well."

"Why not?" She grasped my chin gently and made

me look at her. "What's the matter?"

"Nothing," I said as I pulled away from her. "I just have a lot on my mind."

"Is it this boy? Jonah?" She peeked at me over the rim of her mug. "I don't want him affecting your schoolwork."

I sighed. "He's not. He's—well, he's a good thing. Stop worrying."

"A good thing doesn't keep you out until midnight."

"That happened once."

"And if I let you out with him at night, who's to say it wouldn't happen again?"

"You don't even know him, so stop judging him, okay?" I shoveled a forkful of eggs into my mouth.

Lidia cocked her head. "Maybe I should get to know him."

I swallowed too quickly, making myself cough. "What do you mean?"

"Well, his mother had you over to their house. I should do the same. Why don't you invite him over for dinner?"

I set my fork down. "Do you mean over to *eat* dinner or have *him* for dinner?"

Lidia laughed and tousled my hair. "Silly girl."

"I'll ask him." I picked up my fork. "And, Mom? Thanks."

"*Niente*," she muttered and went to the stove.

As I gobbled down the rest of my breakfast, I thought about how unfair fate was to my mother. She had lost her husband too young, and now her daughter was leading a dangerous double life.

The feeling of melancholy stayed with me as I left the house. The morning air smelled of salt and autumn. I shrugged my face deep in the cocoon of my wooly scarf. It was odd that it hadn't snowed yet, but it would soon. I could taste it.

"Where were you yesterday?" Jenny asked as soon as I met up with her.

"And good morning to you too." I stuck my tongue out at her.

"Don't pull that." She planted her hands on her hips and glared at me. "You missed the memorial for the bridge collapse."

"Oh, crap." I pressed my hand to my forehead. I'd seen the flyer for it in the school office, but the battle on Friday night completely wiped it from my mind. "I'm so sorry. I was sick all weekend."

"Is that why you weren't answering your phone?" She didn't budge from her stance.

"Yeah." I touched her arm. "I'm really sorry, Jenny. I should've been there."

"Yeah, you should've." Her voice softened. "It was really sad."

I bit my lip. I *was* sorry I had missed the memorial . . . but deep down, I was relieved. I didn't know if I could sit with all those people who had lost loved ones, knowing they had died because of me. "I'm sure it was," I whispered and slid my arm through hers. She didn't pull away.

We walked for a bit in silence.

"So my mom invited Jonah over for dinner," I said finally.

Jenny snorted. "Hide the knives."

I laughed, and after a moment, she joined in. I figured I was forgiven then. Still, it pulled at me, like a loose thread. I had allowed the Benandanti to preoccupy me so much that I had hurt my best friend. I needed to work harder to keep them separate.

Jenny nudged me with her elbow. "By the way, Seth Campbell asked me out."

"About time."

"But don't say anything to Carly," Jenny said. "You know she's had a crush on him for months. I want to talk to her first before I say yes."

I squeezed her arm. "You're such a good friend." *Not like me.*

Jenny shrugged. "I know the Girl Code." We crested the hill into town, and in the distance I spotted Jonah and his sister, waiting on the corner for us. "But I think you need a little reminder."

"What?" I pressed my hand to my chest in mock offense, but when I saw the seriousness on her face, I dropped my arm to my side. So she wasn't totally over it yet. "Okay. Remind me."

"The number one rule of the Girl Code is that you don't forsake your girlfriends for a guy. And you have been doing just that."

"I have not," I said, even though it was a lie.

"Oh, come on. You could spend at least one lunch period with us a week instead of always going outside with Monsieur Wolfe."

I leaned my head on her shoulder. "You're right." I blinked up at her and she laughed. "Forgive me?"

"Yeah, yeah. Now get off before your boyfriend gets suspicious." She punched at me playfully.

I exhaled; we were back to our old selves again.

"Hey, Wolfe!" Jenny yelled when we were several yards away from Jonah. "I hear you're going into the lion's den."

"What?" Jonah asked when we reached them.

"My mom wants you to come over for dinner tonight," I said.

"Uh-oh," he said, but he was grinning.

"Just don't bring up the Mafia, Mussolini, or the Vatican," Jenny said.

Jonah raised an eyebrow at me.

I shrugged. "The cardinal rule when talking to an Italian." He took my hand, and we all sauntered toward school. Bree marched ahead of us, her long black pony-tail swinging like a pendulum. I tore my gaze away from it. "So you'll come to dinner?"

"I dragged you over to my house," he said. "It's only

fair that you return the favor."

"Oh, crap," said Jenny. I turned to her; she was digging through her bag. "I forgot my notes for our debate in government today."

I sucked in a sharp breath.

Jenny looked at me. "What?"

"I totally forgot the debates were today."

"Oh, good, I won't be the only one standing up there like an idiot," Jenny said, hoisting her bag onto her shoulder.

"No, my notes are in my locker. I did it last week." My insides twisted, and I clenched Jonah's hand harder to stop mine from shaking. How could I argue for the power plant now when I knew its real purpose?

"Great." Jenny sighed. "I guess I'll have to redo mine during lunch."

I pulled away from Jonah and jogged to catch up with Bree. "Hey."

She didn't look at me. "What?"

"Um, I was wondering if you wanted to switch sides in the debate today."

She stopped short and peered at me, her brows drawn together. "You're against the plan now?"

"Well, I did some more research and, yeah, I am." I rocked back and forth.

Bree stared at me, chewing her lip. When she finally answered, her voice held an odd note. "Sorry. I've already done the work on the con stance." She picked up her pace again. "Can't you just fake it?"

"I guess so." I let her walk ahead, and when Jonah reached me I took his hand. "I'm screwed."

"Nah, she'll come through," Jonah said.

I stayed quiet. It wasn't Bree I was worried about.

When government class rolled around, my palms were sweating in anticipation of the debate. Mr. Clemens made us sit with our partners as we watched the other debaters. By the third pair, I started to notice a pattern.

"Hold up," Mr. Clemens said when Jenny and Josh had finished. "That wasn't much of a con stance, Ms. Sands. In fact"—he waved his arm in the air—"none of you have presented a decent con stance. What's going on?"

*Mr. Wolfe used magic to make everyone agree with him*, I thought but didn't think it was entirely appropriate to say out loud.

Bree's arm shot up into the air, making me jump. She had been as still as marble throughout the other debates. "Mr. Clemens, I think I have a good con stance."

He blinked as though noticing her presence for the first time. "Really? Well, then, let's hear it. Ms. Wolfe, Ms. Jacobs, the floor is yours."

We traded places with Jenny and Josh at the front of the room. I looked at Bree to give her the go-ahead, but she didn't even acknowledge me as she faced the class. "The Guild is nothing more than a front for a small group of people who want to conquer the world," she started.

Everyone laughed, but Bree's straight face told me she wasn't making a joke. I stared at her. Without naming the Malandanti, Bree had just described the Guild exactly.

"Look at their track record. Their so-called good works projects in Venezuela and the Congo have done nothing but devastate those regions. They hide this fact behind pretty pictures of shiny happy people and promises of a 'new tomorrow.'"

My breath caught. *The Congo.*

The laughter in the classroom died down as everyone fixed their attention on Bree and her tone of contempt for her own father's company.

"They tore down homes in order to build their coffee plantation in the Congo, and then they left before setting up any kind of infrastructure to keep the plantation running." Bree swung her gaze over the class. "I know. I saw it firsthand."

How had I not made that connection before? The Wolfes had been to the Congo. That was where Mr. Wolfe had harvested the magic he'd used at the presentation. It had cast its spell over everyone in the hall. I started, dropping my note cards, but no one noticed. It had cast its spell over everyone . . . except Bree. The fact that she was spouting off about the evils of the Guild was proof she knew about the magic and was somehow immune to it.

I bent down and picked up my note cards. Bree had been wearing headphones during the presentation. She hadn't been listening to music just to screw around. She was protecting herself from the magic.

Bree finished her speech with a flourish, and the class whooped and clapped. It took Mr. Clemens several minutes to calm everyone down. He pointed at me.

I spoke in a wooden voice as wheels churned and clicked in my brain. Bree knew. She knew the Guild's real purpose.

I finished my speech, and Mr. Clemens nodded his approval. Bree and I took our seats, and another couple walked to the front of the room. I couldn't stop glancing at Bree. I suddenly remembered the way she looked at me when I told her that I wanted to switch sides in the debate . . . with more curiosity than I had ever seen in her.

My stomach bottomed out. She had looked at me that way because she had realized I knew about the magic. I risked one more glance at her. She was staring at me, face pinched, and as soon as our eyes met she turned away. I pressed my fingers to my forehead and rubbed. Not only did I now know one of Bree's secrets— she knew one of mine.

# CHAPTER SEVENTEEN

*The Possible Problem*

Mr. Salter's ancient, beat-up truck sat in our driveway when I got home from school. Figuring Lidia had invited him over for dinner, I trudged up the front stoop. Even before I laid my hand on the doorknob I heard Lidia's voice firing from the other side.

"—could you not tell me?"

I opened the door. Mr. Salter sat on the couch, watching my mother pace in front of him, her feet pounding on the century-old floorboards.

"I didn't know," Mr. Salter said. "How could I have known?"

"What's going on?" I shut the door and dropped my backpack to the floor.

At the thud, Lidia stopped pacing and marched toward me. "That power plant. Do you know where they're building it?" She jabbed her finger toward the woods. "Next door to our farm."

"I know." I slid my jacket off and hung it on the peg by the door.

"You know?" Lidia planted her hands on her hips and blocked my path. "How do you know?"

"I, uh, was at the presentation." I had been so wrapped up in how the plant would affect the Benandanti that I hadn't really thought about how it would affect my own home.

"I was there," Mr. Salter said. "I don't remember them mentioning where exactly the plant would be built."

*Of course not*, I thought, *because you were under a spell*. I bit my lip. "I had to do all this research for a debate in government class. Maybe that was where I saw it, then."

Lidia threw her hands up in the air. "Why didn't you tell me?"

"I-I guess I didn't really think it was a big deal." I picked my bag off the floor, letting my hair fall in front of my face.

"Not a big deal?" Lidia grabbed my arm and dragged me through the living room to the large window in the kitchen. Outside, the goats milled across the pasture, and the low sun spilled over the treetops of the forest beyond. "You see how nice this view is now? When we look out this window we will see a big, ugly building. All those trees will be gone." She let go of my arm so forcefully that I stumbled back against the island. "Not to mention the lights that will be on day and night and the noise. We might as well burn the farm down and move back to Italy," she yelled.

"I'm sure it won't be that bad," Mr. Salter said from the doorway of the kitchen.

I narrowed my eyes at him. Was he still under the influence of the magic? Its hold on me must have broken the moment I realized what it was. The Eagle said it was more of an influence than control.

"They have to do all sorts of environmental studies before they can get permission to build, don't they?"

Lidia's face was as red as the tomato sauce she had simmering on the stove. "They're not going to get that far." Her voice shook. "Not if I have something to say about it. Alessia, go get your markers."

I squinted at her. "Huh?"

"I think we have some old poster board in the guest room closet," she said, tapping her fingers on her lips. She pushed herself away from the counter.

I caught her sleeve as she brushed past me. "Mom, catch us up. What are you doing?"

"Making posters, of course." She shrugged away from me. I followed her at a jog as she headed upstairs to the guest room. "Protesting the plant. We'll put them up all over town."

Sometimes I wondered if Lidia had taken a backward detour from her traditional Catholic upbringing to the sixties. But I knew that once she set her mind to something it was hard to deter her. "Do we have to do this now?" I asked as she searched the closet in the guest room and produced a few sheets of poster board that must have been left over from a long-ago school project. "I have homework, and Jonah is coming over in an hour."

"You can help me after you've finished your homework." She bustled past me, poster board tucked under her arm. "Are you staying for dinner?" she asked Mr. Salter as she went back downstairs.

"I've got inventory at the store," he said, putting his jacket on. "Rain check?"

Lidia nodded and disappeared into the kitchen.

I rolled my eyes at Mr. Salter. "See what you started?"

He didn't smile. "I didn't start anything. Those people from the Guild came to see your mother. She called me in a tizzy. I was trying to calm her down."

"They came to see her?" A little throb started at the side of my head. This was why Mr. Wolfe wanted her to go to the second presentation. *Wait a second.* Mr. Wolfe must have used the same magic when he visited Lidia. That was why he wanted to meet with her personally, so she'd agree to the plan. How had the magic not worked on her? I opened the front door. "Uh, thanks, Mr. Salter."

"Let me know if I can help." He rested his hand on the doorknob, then turned back to me. "I just don't understand why I didn't make the connection when I saw the presentation."

"I didn't, either," I said in what I hoped was a reassuring voice.

"Ah, well." He opened the door. "Hey, I may need your help at the store in the next few weeks. Are you up for it?"

"Definitely," I said, nudging the door closed a little to encourage him out. He jogged down the front steps. I closed the door and went straight to the kitchen.

Lidia bent over a piece of poster board on the table, tracing large letters in pencil.

I leaned against the doorway, twisting my fingers together. An image swam to the surface in my brain. The list of possible problems, my mother at the top. "Maybe you should hold off on putting these posters up."

"Oh? Why?" She paused her writing and looked at me.

"Because I think—I think these guys, the Guild, are pretty powerful." I touched her arm. "Maybe being the fly in their ointment isn't such a good idea."

"Well, someone has to do it. And sometimes you have to take a risk to be that someone." She patted my hand and finished the letter she was tracing.

"But is it worth the risk?" I pressed my palms on the edge of the table. "Who knows what their reaction will be. What if they come after us, after the farm?" In my head I heard that unseen voice on the teleconference phone. *Take care of it, gentlemen . . .*

Lidia pursed her lips and shook her head. "They can't do that. This is America." Even after fifteen years of citizenship, she still spoke the name of her adopted country with awe.

"Yeah, but I don't think these guys play by the rules."

"Alessia, I cannot sit and do nothing." She put her hand on my arm and looked me in the eye. "Your father wouldn't sit and do nothing."

She was right; my father would plaster a sign on Mr. Wolfe's front door if it came to that. I swallowed and ducked my head.

Lidia squeezed my fingers. "Now go do your homework before your boy gets here."

I backed out of the kitchen and went up to my room. The throb started again in my temple, like someone chiseling words that didn't belong there. How could I make her see how serious this was without jeopardizing my own secrets? I sank onto the bed with my copy of *Wuthering Heights*, but the print blurred on the pages in front of me. Wouldn't it be worth breaking rule number one if I could protect my mother?

*Protect.* I dropped the book onto my pillow, went to my desk, and opened the top drawer. Stashed in with a mishmash of playing cards and old date books was the amulet I had found in the basement. I'd put it here after the mystery of the Benandanti had been solved and forgotten about it.

I pulled out the amulet and held it in my hand. *This house is under the protection of the Benandanti.* It was, indeed. Had the amulet blocked Mr. Wolfe's magic with its own?

Downstairs, the bell rang.

I tucked the amulet back in the drawer and slammed it shut. If there was anything that could distract me and lighten my mood, it was Jonah. I only hoped Lidia was as charmed by him as I was.

With a deep breath, I answered the door. "Hey."

He held up a covered plate. "I come bearing gifts."

I opened the door wider to let him in. As he passed into the living room, I noticed that the wildness of his hair had been tamed a little, and he was wearing a neat sweater and jeans under his peacoat. I smiled. "Thanks for coming."

"Thanks for saving my life in advance," Jonah said, shrugging out of his coat. "My mom was attempting beef Wellington for dinner. I wouldn't be surprised to go home and find my entire family poisoned."

I laughed and led him into the kitchen. Lidia had abandoned the posters for cooking; the poster board was stashed in the corner by the door. That was a relief. "Mom, Jonah's here."

Lidia shut the oven door and came toward us, wiping her hands on her apron. "*Buonasera*," she said and held out her hand. Lidia always laid on the Italian when she was trying to impress—or intimidate—someone.

"Thanks for having me," Jonah said, balancing the plate of cookies in one hand as he shook Lidia's with the other. "My mom made these."

"*Grazie.*" Lidia took the plate and set it on the counter.

"How long 'til dinner?" I asked.

"About a half hour. We're having chicken *parmigiano*." She eyed the two of us standing side by side. "Why don't you set the table?"

"Actually, I thought I'd show Jonah around the farm," I said. I tugged him toward the back door. "We'll be back in fifteen minutes, okay?"

"Take the lantern—it's dark out," Lidia called after us.

I flicked the outside light on just before I closed the door and slid my hand into Jonah's.

"She seems like she's gotten over being mad at me," Jonah said.

I squeezed his hand and leaned into him. "The real test will be at dinner. If she starts talking to me in Italian, you know you've been blackballed."

"I knew I should have taken Italian instead of French."

We were at the barn. I opened the door and stepped into the calm warmth. A lantern hung on a peg beside the door, and I clicked it on, illuminating the earthen floor and stacks of hay with dim golden light. Jonah walked in behind me and closed the door. The goats rustled in the pens, bleating softly as they sensed humans in their midst.

"*Buonasera*," I said. "That means 'good evening.'"

Jonah put a hand on my waist. "*Buonasera*, Alessia."

"You might hear my mother call me *cara*," I said. "That means 'dear.'"

"*Cara*," Jonah murmured. It sounded completely different on his tongue than my mother's.

I leaned into his hands and turned my face up to his. I had never realized the barn could be so romantic.

Jonah lowered his head to mine. "Teach me another," he whispered.

"*Baciami*," I said. "Kiss me."

He obliged and walked me gently backward until we hit one of the wooden posts that framed the pens. I molded myself against him and twined my fingers in his hair.

"Ahem."

Wild horses couldn't have dragged us apart faster. Before I knew it, Jonah was on the other side of the barn.

I hugged myself. "Hi, Heath."

"Hi yourself," Heath said. His gaze shifted from me to Jonah and back again.

"This is Jonah," I said.

"We've met," Jonah said. "You, uh, have a knack for interruptions."

"One of my many talents," Heath said, his voice easy.

I thought that would be the end of it. I smoothed my shirt down and followed them back to the house. But as Jonah faded out into the darkness, Heath gave me a look that nicked me to the quick. "We'll talk," he growled and stalked over the hill toward his cabin.

I stopped in my tracks. Crap. What had I done wrong *now*? Pressing my cold hands to my flushed cheeks, I hurried in through the back door.

After Lidia had dished out heaping plates of chicken *parmigiano*, she sat down and sipped her wine, eyeing Jonah over her glass. "So, how was school today?"

I nodded at Jonah. "That's to you."

Jonah swallowed. "Oh. Um, fine, I guess."

"What's your best subject?"

"I do pretty well in French," Jonah answered.

I choked back a laugh. French was one of the only classes Jonah made a regular appearance in.

Lidia ran her finger along the rim of her wineglass. "Did Alessia tell you she won a writing competition last spring?"

"Mom . . ."

"What? I can't be proud of my only daughter?"

"She did tell me," Jonah interjected. "I think it's really cool that she loves to write."

"Do you like to write?" Lidia asked.

Jonah shook his head. "I'm more of a reader."

"You should see his room," I said. "It's wall-to-wall with books."

"I guess you've spent some time in his room, then?"

Busted. I shoved a pile of chicken into my mouth.

"Alessia's really helped me out in biology and math," Jonah said.

I shot him a grateful look, but I didn't think his defense would help me much.

"Alessia is a model student," Lidia said. She set her wineglass down. "I would hate to see that change in any way."

"Me too," Jonah said. He smiled at my mother, and I saw her face soften a little.

"I'm pleased we agree," Lidia said and picked up her

fork. "So, how's the chicken?"

"Delicious." Jonah took another bite. "Way better than anything my mother cooks."

"I'm sure she does her best," Lidia said. Modesty about her cooking was not one of Lidia's virtues. "And what does your father do?"

I dropped my fork. How did Lidia not know who Jonah's father was? My mind scrambled over the weeks since Jonah had moved here. Lidia hadn't been to a town meeting in months; in fact, she was so busy on the farm now that she rarely went into town at all. Grabbing my fork, I said, "He's just a businessman—"

But at the same time Jonah said, "He's a vice president of the Guild."

"*Scusi*?" Lidia narrowed her eyes at Jonah. "What's your last name?"

"Wolfe," Jonah said, a little muffled over the chicken in his mouth. "My dad is here working on the hydroelectric power plant they're building."

A flush crept up Lidia's throat. "And do you know where they're planning on building that plant?"

"Mom, don't—"

Jonah's gaze shifted between Lidia and me. "Sorry. Am I missing something?"

"Right next to our farm!" Lidia's face was mottled and blotchy.

I pinched the skin of my forehead together. "Mom, please. Not now."

A nerve pulsed at the base of her clenched jaw. "Then when? Someone needs to stand up for the *piccolo ragazzo* . . . the little guy."

Jonah nudged me. "Seriously, fill me in."

I turned in my chair to face him. "Your dad came to see my mom today about the plan. They're building the plant in the woods right at the border of our property." I pointed out the large window, even though it was too dark outside to see the forest.

"Wow." Jonah whistled low between his teeth. "That sucks."

"That sucks?" echoed Lidia. "That's all you have to say?"

I glared at her. "What is Jonah supposed to do?"

She waved her fork in the air so hard I was afraid it would fly into Jonah's eye. "He could talk to his father. Tell him to build it somewhere else."

"Believe me, I would if I thought it would make a difference," Jonah said. "But he barely talks to me."

"Besides, maybe it won't even happen," I said. "Like Mr. Salter said, they probably have to do a ton of reports and studies before they can build anything."

"I don't know about that," Jonah said, mopping up the last bit of sauce on his plate with a hunk of bread. "I think I overheard him saying that they're almost ready to break ground."

Lidia drank the rest of her wine and slammed her glass down on the table.

I kicked Jonah under the table.

"Ow!" He rubbed his shin.

"I know it's not your fault, but could you at least be a little indignant on our behalf?" I said.

"I am." He laid his hands, palms up, on the table. "But what do you want me to do? Chain myself to a tree when the bulldozers come?"

"For starters." Lidia grabbed his empty plate and reached for my half-full one.

I pulled it closer to me and started shoveling in as much chicken as I could chew.

Jonah took a long gulp of his water before Lidia snatched the glass away from him. "Look, I'm really sorry. It totally sucks that the plant is so close to you. But it could actually turn into a good thing."

Dishes clattered in the sink as Lidia started to clean up. "Oh? How is it good to chop down half a forest?"

"It's going to provide clean energy for this entire region," Jonah said. "And the Guild will replant most of the trees. They have a great environmental track record."

I pushed my plate away and tucked one leg up against my chest. "That's not what Bree says." Was it possible that Jonah was under the same spell as the rest of the town?

Jonah heaved a dramatic sigh. "Yeah, Bree says a lot of things she doesn't mean. She gets off on playing devil's advocate." He touched my knee. "There are a lot worse companies than the Guild."

If he only knew. Unless . . . I clutched my leg tighter

to me. Could it be that Jonah was defending the Guild because he knew exactly what their real purpose was? And unlike his twin, he agreed with it? I looked into his deep green eyes, my heart skittering.

"Hey." Jonah took my hand. "What's wrong?"

I shook my head to smooth out the suspicion that rankled my thoughts. Heath was right; it was driving me nuts. I didn't want to doubt every single person in my life. I squeezed his hand. "I'm fine."

The plate of cookies banged onto the table, breaking us apart. Lidia stood behind Jonah. She plucked a cookie from the plate and bit into it. "*Ha bisogno di più zucchero,*" she said and refused to speak English for the rest of the night.

I had never been hung over, but the next morning, I was sure I was. As I headed out to the barn, my brain felt broken into a million pieces that I couldn't quite fit together. With a heavy sigh, I hauled open the barn door and grabbed my basket.

"What the hell are you doing?"

Heath's voice made me drop the basket. I whirled to face him. The blue light of dawn seeped in through the cracks in the barn walls. I stepped into a weak shaft of it, so I could see Heath's face, half lit and half in shadow. "What do you mean?" I knew exactly what he meant, but I wanted to hear him say it.

"With that boy. What are you doing?"

"Well, we were kissing. Kissing is when—"

"Cut the crap." Heath folded his arms. "I didn't ask what *were* you doing. I asked what *are* you doing."

"What do you mean?" I asked again, genuinely confused.

"After what we found out about his father, you're still hooking up with him?"

I retrieved my basket. "It's totally separate."

"No, it's not." Heath grabbed my arm as I strode past him. "Alessia," he said, his fingers digging into my bicep, "this is not a joke. Mr. Wolfe could pose a real threat to the Benandanti, and you're dating his son? This isn't something to take lightly."

I wrenched my arm out of his grip. My skin burned where he had held it. "The Stag told me to keep pumping my source for information. Who do you think that source is?" Clutching my basket, I headed for the back door of the barn.

Heath followed me so close I could feel his breath on my neck. "That's a bullshit excuse and you know it. Especially since you haven't gotten any more information out of him since you saw the plans."

"That was four days ago. Give me some time." I flung open the door. The hillside was drenched in mist shot through with the pink beginnings of sunrise. I breathed in deep and let the cold, clean air fill my lungs.

"We don't have time. We need to act *now*." Heath

took my wrist, his hold much more gentle this time. "I'm not trying to be a hard-ass." He turned my palm up and gazed into it as if it held the secret of the future. "You may think you can keep them separate, the part of you that is of this world and the part that is Benandante." He raised his eyes to mine, his blue pupils clouded with trouble. "But you can't. They intertwine, and you'll find yourself lying to everyone you love, and it will eat you up inside, and eventually you'll have to choose." Heath swallowed. I watched his Adam's apple work up and down. "There was a girl in Italy. I—"

"Oh, please," I said. My whole body shook with impatience and frustration. I yanked my hand away from him so fast that he stumbled forward a step. "I am not you. Just because it happened to you doesn't mean it will happen to me." I spun away from him and ran to the first hen trailer.

The hens sensed my distress, their nervous clucks and restless wings filling the close confines of the trailer. As I moved from one nest to the next, a couple of eggs slipped through my fingers. They hit the floor with a loud smack.

"Damn it!" I put the basket down on the hay-strewn floor and pressed my palms against the wall, pushing with all my strength. I breathed in and out through my nostrils, filled my body with the scents of hay and chicken droppings and feathers. *Just because it happened to Heath doesn't mean it will happen to me.* I repeated it over and over in my head until I was whispering it. The mantra stopped me from shaking, and I was able to collect the rest of the eggs without dropping any more.

Heath was waiting for me outside when I emerged from the trailer. I blew out a breath of annoyance and looked up to the lightening sky. "Look, I hear you, okay? But what am I supposed to do, not get close to anyone? Hold myself apart from the world? Not ever fall in love?"

Heath stared at me without speaking, his eyes locked on mine. I saw into their depths, how much pain they held, and my breath caught. That was exactly what Heath had done. I had never seen him out with anyone. I had never heard him talk about any friends. He lived alone. He worked on our farm, but that was only because he had been sent here to be my Guide. He had nothing else in his life except being a Benandante.

I shook my head with such vigor that my ponytail came undone and my hair fell into my eyes. "No, I can't live like that. I can't do it."

"I hope you don't have to. But you must remember, if you ever have to make that choice, the mission is what matters. You accepted the Call; you cannot turn your back on the mission now. The Benandanti are your family." Heath launched himself away from the trailer and walked toward me. "They will always be there for you. They will always take you in." He stopped in front of me, just inches from my face. "Can you say the same for Jonah?"

# Chapter Eighteen

*The Construction Site*

I didn't want Heath to be right; he couldn't be right. He was just jealous. He was alone, so he wanted me to be too. But his words swirled in my head. Keeping my two lives separate was as exhausting as trying to outrun a tornado.

I ate with the girls at lunch, listening to their chatter as though from a distance.

The next period, Jonah actually showed up to biology.

I moved to his table at the back of the room and perched on a stool. "Hey."

"Hey." He looked at me through a beaker, the glass enlarging his green eye to a cartoonish size. "Where were you at lunch?"

"I ate inside with the girls. Jenny's been bugging me about it."

"Oh." He set the beaker down and ran his finger around the rim. "It's not because of last night, is it?"

"What? No." I laid my hand on his arm. "I'm not mad about last night. My mom can be a total freak sometimes. It's not your fault."

The bell rang, and everyone started getting their equipment ready for the lesson.

"I guess I have to sit through this class now, don't I?"

I laughed. "I'll help you. If you want, I could come over after school and catch you up on stuff."

"Stuff?" Jonah raised an eyebrow, a sly grin pulling at his mouth.

"*School*," I hissed, but I touched my foot to his under the table. It was better that he thought I wanted to come over to make out in his bedroom than the real reason. I didn't like the idea of spying on Jonah's father, but if it got Heath off my back for a while, it was worth it.

As Jonah and I made our way up Main Street with the girls after school, Jenny pulled up short on the sidewalk. "What is this?" she said, pointing to a red-and-black sign that screamed, "Stop the Destruction of Our Wildlife."

"Oh no." I stared at the sign, thoughts of spying pushed right out of my head. "She is unbelievable."

"Who?" Jenny said.

"Lidia." I shook my head. "She's all up in arms about the power plant."

"How come?" Carly came up behind me and peered at the sign over my shoulder.

"It's going to be built in the woods right next to our farm." I tugged at the edge of the sign, but it was stuck to the lamppost. Why couldn't she listen to me for once in her life? Hadn't I told her the Guild was dangerous?

"Are you kidding?" Carly knocked my hand away from the sign and smoothed out the corner I had wrinkled. "I never would have argued for it in class if I'd known that."

"I know. No one really knew," I said. I looked at the back of the sign to see what Lidia had fastened it with. Maybe Mr. Wolfe hadn't seen it yet. If I could only get rid of it . . .

"Leave it," Carly said. "I'm sure other people want to know about this."

"But—" I swallowed and glanced at Jonah. I couldn't voice my fears and bad-mouth his dad, not without compromising myself.

"My parents are going to have a field day with this," said Jenny. "And your farm has been here a lot longer than the Guild. Right, Wolfe?" she added, turning to Jonah.

"Don't look at me. I didn't tell them where to build it."

We crossed the street, Jenny and Carly bickering with Jonah until Carly turned off to go home. At the next corner a blue-and-white sign greeted us: "The Guild Wants to Build in Your Backyard. Will You Let Them?"

"Your mother better take these down."

I turned around.

Bree stood behind us. "If she knows what's good for her."

"What's that supposed to mean?" I stepped in front of Jonah and crossed my arms over my chest.

"Just that she shouldn't make enemies with the Guild." Bree hoisted her bag higher on her shoulder and brushed past us. "It might not be good for her health."

"Are you *threatening* me?" I started after her.

But Jonah caught my arm. "Ignore her. Your mom has a right to say whatever she wants. I don't think it'll do anything, but she can try."

We followed Bree at a distance, Jonah stroking my wrist in an effort to calm me down. It didn't help. By the time we got in his front door, I was ready to storm into Mr. Wolfe's office and rifle through all his papers in plain view of the rest of the family. But instead I sat in the kitchen with Jonah and his mom, eating her cookies, my knee bouncing up and down.

Finally, his mom stopped chattering at us, and we escaped upstairs. I managed to keep Jonah on task with homework for quite a while before he got distracted by my neck.

"Do you want to pass biology or not?" I teased, dodging out of the way as he tried to kiss me.

"Your lips are worth a D," he said, trying to pull me onto his lap.

"My lips are an A+, and don't you forget it." I wormed away from him and headed to the door. "Be back in a minute."

"Hurry." When I made a face he put his hands up. "Hey, I'm just dying to know the difference between plant and animal cells. Really, I'm on the edge of my seat."

"Ha-ha," I said and ducked into the hall. The door to the upstairs bathroom was closed, and the smell of nail polisher remover wafted through the crack at the floor. Well, that gave me a good excuse to use the downstairs bathroom, conveniently located right across from Mr. Wolfe's office.

I started down the hall, then froze outside Bree's room. Her door was half open, displaying her unmade bed and cluttered desk where a laptop sat in sleep mode. I glanced at the bathroom door, then at Jonah's room. One minute. Minute and a half tops, if I found anything interesting.

I slid into her room, heart pounding. Clothes were strewn on the floor; lipsticks and nail polishes littered the top of the dresser. What was I looking for? A big banner proclaiming, "I know about magic," hanging from her ceiling? Not likely. I stepped deeper into the room, tiptoeing over tank tops and cardigans, and eyed the stack of books on her nightstand.

The top two books were best-selling thrillers. The bottom two had their spines facing inward. Carefully, I picked up the thrillers and raised an eyebrow. *Lady Chatterley's Lover*. Definitely not on the approved reading list at Twin Willows High. I lifted it to reveal the last book.

*Witchcraft of Italy* by Summer Grimaldi.

It wasn't a banner, but it was pretty damn close. I set the other books down and flipped through Ms. Grimaldi's book. It opened in my hand to a folded-down page. There was a break in the middle of the text, with the heading THE BENANDANTI AND THE MALANDANTI.

The words swam on the page. I didn't need to read what it said; I already knew more than any book could ever tell me. But Bree had sought this out for some reason. More than that, she had known what to look for. She knew about the Benandanti. She knew what we were.

A loud ringing filled the room. I dropped the book on the floor with a snap. Bree's phone was blaring and vibrating on the nightstand. No way could she not hear that from the bathroom. With shaking hands, I restacked the books on the nightstand and dodged out of the room.

The second I was clear of the doorway, Bree emerged from the bathroom, walking on her heels because of the separators in between her toes.

"*Finally,*" I said, hoping my voice sounded normal. I circled around her and into the bathroom, shutting the door as she turned away to answer her phone.

I leaned against the door and drew a shaky breath. It was not a coincidence that she had marked the Benandanti section of that book. The pieces of the puzzle were adding up. But what the final image would reveal, I had no idea.

I debated telling Heath what I'd found, but then I remembered how much he had wigged out over the website. He'd flip out over this too, and I wasn't sure if it was worth flipping out over yet. Even if Bree knew about the

Benandanti, it wasn't like she was running around town telling everyone.

Still, the whole thing gnawed at me for the next couple of days. By the time patrol duty came around, my mind felt like an apple eaten inside out by a worm. I thought I would hate patrolling, but actually it calmed me. Besides giving me a night off from training with Heath, it was one of the few places where I was completely alone and I could hear only my own thoughts.

As the clock ticked toward midnight, I opened my window and lay on my bed, beckoning the shift to happen. When it did, I flew out of the house and through the woods to the sacred place.

I soared over a ring of pine trees, their needles glistening with frost. The sound of the Waterfall rumbled in my ears before I could see it, growing louder and louder as I angled my way around the trees. But there was another noise coming from the Waterfall. Something different. Something . . . wrong.

Floodlights ringed the Waterfall, casting an unearthly glow over the trees. The lamps reached almost as high as the tall pines at the edge of the stream and arched over the water. An eerie shimmer rose from the surface, a bright and ghostly light that prickled my feathers. I pitched over the Waterfall, following the luminescent trail that the lamps let off, a sickening feeling inside me as I saw the pool below.

The water, which usually reflected the sky above,

now held the image of a squat building. I whirled in the air and found the source of the reflection. A sleek rectangular trailer sat at the edge of the water within the magical barrier the Malandanti had erected. The dark mist of the barrier swirled around the trailer, and the trailer's silvery walls mirrored the forest around it. I peered at myself in it. My reflection was fractured and distorted.

Several trees had been flattened to make room for the trailer, which was elevated by four spidery legs that arched away from the structure. A wide landing fanned out from the doorway, with stairs leading to the ground. The noise I had heard was the constant whirring of a huge raised fan on top of the trailer. The sound shattered the stillness of the forest. The trees left standing seemed to lean away from the trailer, as if they knew it didn't belong. Everything about the structure was out of place, wrong, and unnatural.

I had just enough time to read "Guild Inc. Headquarters" on the little sign on the side of the trailer before the door banged open.

Pumping my wings in the air, I took refuge in the dense branches of a pine tree. From my bird's-eye view, I could now see the roof of the trailer was decorated with a huge imprint of the Guild insignia. It had been painted on with some kind of light-reflecting paint and looked bright enough to be seen from space.

"Three in total." Voices floated up to me from the landing. "Another one across from this one and the third at the top of the Waterfall."

Needles shed from the branch where I perched as I dug my talons in. They were putting up *more* of these heinous things?

A figure stepped farther out onto the landing. It was Mr. Wolfe. He pointed across the water. "We'll have to bulldoze that cluster of trees, but that will only take a day."

I snapped my beak, fighting the urge to claw the back of his neck.

"Good. The board doesn't want any more delays." Pratt Webster came into view. His pin-striped suit clashed with the muted green and gold of the forest around him.

Mr. Wolfe pursed his lips. "Did you see those signs in town?"

"Yes." Pratt pulled out his BlackBerry. "I'm handling it."

What did that mean? I fluttered down to a lower branch. My wings hardly made a sound, but Pratt looked up, his fingers hovering over the keypad for a moment.

Mr. Wolfe's pocket buzzed. He took out his own BlackBerry and, after checking the message, glanced around. "We're done for tonight, then."

"You could be a little less obvious," Pratt muttered. He slid his phone inside his jacket and stepped down from the trailer. "Set that bulldozing up for Thursday. We want the other trailers here by the weekend."

"*You're* supposed to be the assistant," Mr. Wolfe said.

Pratt gave him a look that could have withered

wildflowers and stalked away, his lip curling at the mud that clung to his designer shoes.

Mr. Wolfe leaned against the rail at the edge of the landing and watched the Waterfall. His shoulders were hunched, defeated.

I unfurled my wings and glided away from the pine tree. What did he have to be upset about? He . . . they . . . *the Malandanti* . . . were winning.

Anger fueled my speed, searing through my veins, as I nose-dived at the trailer. I slashed at the insignia, my talons scraping against the metal with a screech that tore through the silence of the forest.

Mr. Wolfe spun at the sound and clutched the rail.

With every fiber of my heart, I wanted to strike him, slash his skin, and tear down that horrible trailer. But more than anything, I wanted him to transform into the Panther and show me who he really was.

Mr. Wolfe's breath came in little shallow puffs of white in the chilly air.

I locked eyes with him, willing him to transform. *Come on. You know you want to.*

He blinked, fear flashing in his dark irises.

I pumped my wings. Dark eyes. The Panther had green eyes . . .

Across the water, something rustled and snapped.

I broke my gaze from Mr. Wolfe's dark eyes.

From out of the tangled undergrowth, the Panther

emerged, its silvery aura casting glittered shadows on the forest floor.

I glanced back at Mr. Wolfe. If he was here, wide awake, there was no way that he was the Panther. The Lynx had been right.

Mr. Wolfe took advantage of my distraction and scrambled to the ground. His clumsy footsteps echoed through the trees long after he disappeared into the darkness.

I turned to the Panther. *We don't confront the Malandanti*, I remembered the Lynx saying. *We stay hidden and observe.* Well, it was too late for that—the Panther had already seen me.

Under the black velvet sky, the water glistened between us. The Panther crept forward, its paws right at the edge of the pool where the earth turned muddy. The thought of it touching the water filled me with such red-hot heat that my aura flamed outward. My sight fixed on the Panther, I careened toward the magical barrier of black mist.

Too late I remembered the barrier was there for a reason: to keep me out. I hit it with a loud smack. The barrier looked ethereal, but it was very, very solid. An electric jolt blew me backward, throwing me to the ground. I righted myself and launched into the air, ruffling my feathers.

The Panther leapt to a rock in the center of the pool

and tracked me. I flew high over the water, frustration mounting inside me. The barrier shielded the site like a bubble, and every time I got too close it shimmered with anticipation.

I landed on a rock at the top of the Waterfall, just outside the barrier. The Panther watched me. I examined the filmy magic, looking for any weakness, knowing it was useless. The Benandanti had combed over this site, trying to find a way in through the barrier. I stiffened. They had been searching for a way *through* the barrier. What if the way through was *under* it?

Before I could question my sanity, I dove into the water and let the stream carry me toward the barrier. The second I hit the surface I realized this wasn't the best idea; I wasn't a duck. But I had to know if my instinct was right.

From below, the Panther let out a belly-deep roar and bounded up the rocks that lined the Waterfall.

The pull of the rushing water grew stronger and stronger. When I reached the barrier's border, the air felt cleaner, sharper. I took a deep breath and plunged under. Beneath the surface, the water was crystalline clear, not a touch of the murkiness from the barrier. Just as I was about to tip over the edge of the Waterfall, a sharp pain pierced my wing, and I was yanked upward.

I broke the surface, twisting and screeching. The Panther had me in its mouth, dragging me away from the barrier. I struck out with my talons and met its nose.

It let me go with a howl, and I rocketed up. The Panther lunged at me, its fierce green eyes glowing in the darkness. Beating my wings with all my strength, I buffeted out of the Panther's reach.

As much as I wanted to fight, I forced myself back. My wing stung with pain, and my lungs felt tight from being underwater for so long. I rose higher over the Waterfall, the Panther crouched below. My heart stopped for a second as I looked down.

The barrier was gone.

The Panther had stepped outside of it.

At the same moment I plunged, the Panther realized its mistake. It leapt over the rocks, stretching its sleek black body. By the time I reached the Waterfall, the barrier was back, the Panther inside, holding it in place with its presence. I swerved just in time to avoid another electric shock and flew to the sturdy branch of an oak tree at the edge of the stream.

The Panther sat on a rock, its aura flickering, as though it was nervous. As though it knew it had done something wrong.

I tried to calm my racing heart as I fixed my gaze on the spot where the bottom of the barrier met the Waterfall. I had breached a weakness there. That was the only reason the Panther had risked leaving the bubble, in order to prevent me from getting in.

Still, it didn't make sense. Even if I had gotten inside, there was a good chance the Panther would have been able to take me down before the rest of my Clan could get here, and it wouldn't have had to risk leaving the barrier to fight me. I remembered how still the Bobcat had sat during our failed attempt to regain control, not even moving a muscle toward the barrier's edge. It never would have made the mistake the Panther had.

The Eagle had noticed that the Panther was new. What if the Panther wasn't only new to the Twin Willows Clan but to the Malandanti in general? What if the Panther was as new as I was? Because the way it had acted, rashly, without thinking, was something that someone with less experience, less training would do. It was just like something I would have done. Hell, I *had* done that, by attacking the Panther tonight to begin with.

I stilled on my branch, cold wind whispering around me. The Panther wasn't just new. It was a kid, like me.

# CHAPTER NINETEEN

*The Bad Influence*

"There's an opening at the edge of the Waterfall; I'm sure of it," I told Heath the next morning. "I could feel it, the way the water changed. I think I got underneath the barrier for just an instant before the Panther pulled me out."

The Panther had woven itself all through my restless sleep last night. I kept seeing different kids from my school transform back and forth into that sleek-bodied beast. This had gone beyond driving me nuts; I had crossed into full-blown crazy land.

"Did you tell the Stag?" Heath asked as we neared the pasture gate.

"Yes, the minute he showed up for patrol." I opened the latch on the gate to the pasture to let the goats in. "He said he'd be in touch. It better be soon; the Guild is moving fast. You should have seen that trailer."

Heath shuddered. "Not looking forward to that."

One of the goats ran over my foot. I stepped out of their path, wincing. My body ached from the Panther's bite last night. "And that Pratt guy is 'handling it'—*it* being my mother." I ran my hand through my hair. "I'm worried."

"I am too." Heath secured the gate after the last goat passed through. "But we're on top of it."

I blew out a breath, tousling the loose strands of hair around my face. "It's so frustrating. We need to go back in *now*."

The frosty grass crunched beneath our feet as we headed toward the house. "We can't do that until we have a solid strategy. You saw what happened last time when we didn't." Heath clamped his mouth shut as Lidia emerged from the kitchen door, wrapped in a heavy woolen shawl.

"You two look thick as thieves," she said.

I stepped away from Heath. "I was just—asking him a question about French."

"You've been pestering Heath a lot lately, Alessia. Let him do his work."

"I don't mind," Heath said quickly. "Is that bacon I smell?"

"*Sì*," she said. "Let's go in and eat. I have to leave for the farmers' market soon."

I hunched my shoulders. "I'm going to Joe's for breakfast. With the girls."

"Don't forget your chores this afternoon."

"I won't." I tugged the ends of her shawl away from her and wrapped them around us both. "I promise."

She laughed and kissed my forehead. "Keep your cell phone on."

"Do I ever turn it off?" I gave her a peck on the cheek, dashed through the house and out the front door. Lately I had spent my Saturday mornings at Joe's with Jonah instead of Jenny and the girls, but Lidia didn't need to know that.

Joe's was crowded; it seemed everyone in Twin Willows was here for breakfast. The smells of fried eggs and French toast washed over me as I stood inside the door, scanning the restaurant for Jonah. I spotted the crown of his familiar raven-haired head at the counter and sidled over.

But when I arrived at his side, I found myself looking down at Bree. "Oh, it's you." I stood on my tiptoes and looked around. "Is your brother here?"

Bree reached into her purse and pulled out a pack of cigarettes. "Man, I did have you pegged from the start," she said and lit a cigarette. "Now that our assignment is over and you've got Jonah, you don't want anything to do with me."

I glared at her. "The trouble with that theory is that you didn't want anything to do with me to begin with. You took one look at me and decided you hated me. I have no idea why, and I couldn't care less. So why don't you go your way and I go mine, and we'll be fine. Okay?"

"Except that you keep getting in my way," Bree said, shaking the cigarette at me.

"How?"

"Are you kidding?" Bree took another pull on the cigarette. "Jonah."

"What is this obsession you have with me and

Jonah?" I waved cigarette smoke out of my face. "You really need to get over it."

"You're the one who needs to get over it," Bree said, her voice raised enough that the diners around us looked over curiously. She dropped her volume a notch. "Look, I'm actually trying to be nice. With my brother . . . you could get seriously hurt. Do yourself a favor and end it now before you get in too deep."

"You have a funny definition of nice," I said. "Why on earth should I believe you?"

"Fine, don't believe me," Bree said, inhaling a mouthful of smoke. "Ask him. Ask him about Fairfield."

"Fairfield?" I shook my head and made to move past her. "Yeah, okay. Thanks for the tip."

She grabbed my arm so hard that I gasped. "I'm serious," she hissed. "I'm telling you, leave my brother alone."

"Or what? What are you gonna do?" I wrenched out of her grasp. "Face it, Bree, you can't control me any more than you can control him."

Bree's pale face turned beet red, her lips white around the butt of her cigarette. Her emerald-green eyes were luminous.

I stumbled back a step. That ferocious expression . . . I had seen an echo of it last night . . . on the face of the Malandanti Panther. I clutched the counter to stay upright.

At that moment, Sally, one of the waitresses, appeared. "You can't smoke in here."

"Says who?" Bree retorted.

"Says Joe," Sally said, jabbing a finger toward the bright red No Smoking sign over the counter.

"Fine." Bree grabbed her purse and, with a toss of her shiny black hair, stormed toward the front door.

Through the huge glass window I saw her halt outside the coffee shop, drop her cigarette, and grind it into the sidewalk with her heel. It was another piece of the puzzle, but they still did not all fit. I watched her walk down Main Street until she was out of sight.

"You okay?"

I took a deep breath and turned to Sally. "Yeah. Thanks."

"That girl comes in here every Saturday and sulks for hours, reading weirdo books and ordering nothing but coffee. Never tips, either." She grinned at me. "I think what you're looking for is in the corner."

All the way at the back of the restaurant, I spotted Jonah in a small booth. He took a sip of steaming coffee and darted his gaze around before noticing me.

In spite of my still-shaky breath, the sight of him made me smile. Later I would try to put all the puzzle pieces of Bree together, but for now I just wanted to be with my boyfriend. I smoothed my hair and shimmied through the tables to reach him.

I slid into the seat opposite him. "What the hell is wrong with your sister? She will not let up with me."

Jonah stared into his coffee cup. "I know. I know. She's a bitch. How many times are you gonna bug me about her?"

"Excuse me?" I leaned back into the deep leather cushion of the booth. "Good morning to you too."

Jonah looked at me. I noticed his cheeks were unusually pale. "Sorry," he mumbled.

"What's wrong with you?"

He sighed heavily and crossed his arms over his chest. "What's wrong with *me*? You're the one obsessed with Bree."

That hurt, probably because it was true. But I couldn't tell him the real reason why. I slid out to the edge of the seat. "I'm gonna sit with Jenny. Come get me when you're in the mood to be human."

Jonah reached under the table and grabbed my knee. "Don't. I'm sorry. Stay."

"Then tell me what's wrong," I said, inching back into the booth.

A long moment passed. "I got into a fight with my dad," he said finally.

"That sucks but it's nothing new." I wasn't quite ready to be fully sympathetic. "What was it about?"

"I don't really want to talk about it."

"Are you ready to order?"

I started and turned in the direction of the overly cheery voice. It was Sally. "Uh, can you give us a minute?"

"Sure." Sally looked from me to Jonah, shrugged, and bounced away to the next booth to refill their coffee.

I turned back to Jonah, who had slid farther into the seat so that he was now smushed into the corner. "You don't have to tell me what happened. But it's not my fault, so don't take it out on me, okay?"

He leaned forward and reached for his coffee. After a long sip he said, "You're right. I'm sorry."

"Apology accepted." I grabbed a menu and waved Sally over to order pancakes and bacon.

"So what did Bree do now?" Jonah asked after Sally had left.

"Oh, just the usual." I toyed with my silverware. "She said to ask you about Fairfield."

Jonah was still for a long minute while I stared at the table. His silence was answer enough that something had happened in Fairfield, something I wasn't sure I wanted to know.

He took a deep breath. "Alessia . . ."

I shivered involuntarily; I loved the way Jonah said my name.

He touched my hand, and I finally looked up. "What happened in Fairfield . . ." His gaze shifted past me, and he pulled his hand away. "Jenny's coming over here."

With a sigh, I twisted in my seat and watched her thread through the tables, her long blonde hair flouncing over her shoulders. "Hey, Jenny."

"Hey, yourself." Jenny leaned against the edge of the table. "A bunch of us are going to the beach tomorrow. You know, one last bonfire before the weather gets too cold."

I laughed. "It's already like forty degrees."

"Well, we'll have the bonfire to keep us warm. I

think we're heading over around noon." She pointed at my throat. "Hey, your necklace broke."

"What? Oh." My locket had fallen into the collar of my shirt. I pulled it out and squinted at it; the ancient chain was broken, and the clasp dangled uselessly. "Thanks. I'll have to get a new chain for it." *Right away*, I thought.

"Anyway, I would really love it if you came. You know you owe me," Jenny teased. "Both of you should come," she added with a slightly reluctant nod toward Jonah.

Someone called her name from across the restaurant.

"I gotta go—my dad wants to order." She spun away, a blur of golden hair and flowery perfume.

Sally came with our food and poured more coffee for both of us.

I watched Jonah smear egg yolk on his toast while my food got cold. "So about Fairfield?"

He reached across the table and traced my palm with his thumb, sending tingles up and down my spine. "Listen, I want to explain. About Fairfield. But I don't want to do it here. Not with all these people around. Meet me in the graveyard tonight?"

"What is it with you and the graveyard? It's getting kinda cold to be meeting there all the time."

Jonah took my hands and raised them to his lips. "I'll keep you warm." He kissed each knuckle. "It might not be the most romantic place, but it's like our place. And no one will ever intrude on us there."

"That's true." I swallowed. "I'll have to sneak out."

"So sneak out." His eyes bored into me.

Smiling, I half stood and leaned across the table. "You are such a bad influence on me," I whispered before my lips met his.

# Chapter Twenty

*The Confession*

Lidia went to bed at nine thirty, so sneaking out of the house was simple. It was so easy, in fact, that I wondered why I hadn't started doing it years ago.

Dead leaves swirled over the ground as I headed toward the bench where Jonah and I had first kissed. He stood under the huge willow tree that hung over the bench, its branches bare and forlorn. I studied his profile, the graceful arch of his neck, the slope of his nose. He was more beautiful than any of the angels carved into the nearby headstones.

A little beat thrummed inside my chest, and I finally had to confess to myself that I was in love with Jonah Wolfe. I knew there were a hundred strikes against him and maybe a hundred and one after what he had to tell me tonight. But despite all that, I loved him. After all, I had some strikes against me too.

I took a step, little twigs breaking under my feet.

Jonah turned. He smiled, bringing sunlight into the dark night, and stretched out a hand to me. "Wanna sit?"

"Sure." I took his hand, and he pulled me into his lap as we sat on the bench. Cold wind swept around us, but Jonah opened his coat and wrapped me against him so that we were both warm. I buried my face in the side of his neck and breathed in the slightly spicy scent of his skin. "Jonah, I don't really care about your past."

Jonah tilted his head back, his gaze fixed on the stars above us. "Even if that's true, you deserve to know." Through our thick layers I felt his pulse racing. Against my cheek his Adam's apple worked up and down. Without looking at me, he said, "Fairfield was the last place we lived. I told you about it once—the place where everyone wore khakis."

"I remember." I thought back to that night outside Pizza Plus. It felt like a million years stretched between then and now.

"There was more to it than that. Everyone was so bored there. Bored with their own lives but too comfortable and lazy to do anything about it. They all lived in these big beautiful houses and drove big fancy cars, but underneath it all was this . . . I don't know . . . *rage*." Jonah turned his head to look at me. "That's what it was. Rage. It seethed under everything. It's different here. People are pretty much what you see is what you get."

I pulled away a little bit. I wasn't. If you looked at me, you saw a normal girl, and I was anything but.

Jonah tightened his arms around me. "Don't worry. I like that. It's a good thing."

"I guess." My heart thudded. I could only hope that if he ever found out I wasn't what I seemed he'd be able to accept it.

"Anyway, we lived there for almost six months. That's longer than most places we've lived. I think the company was going to keep us there but then . . ." His voice trailed off. I felt him shiver, but I didn't think it was from the cold. "The longer we lived there the more I felt that same rage build in me." He fell silent, staring into the darkness at something I couldn't see.

I stroked his cheek with my finger. "What happened?" I asked gently.

Jonah bit his lip. "The rage was too much. I started drinking a lot to dull it. There were parties every night at some rich kid's mansion. I'd drink so much that I'd still be drunk at school the next day."

"That must have gotten exhausting," I said. I had never been drunk, but I wasn't a prude about drinking. There were several bottles in Lidia's liquor cabinet that looked full but were severely watered down after Jenny and I had gotten to them. It was only good luck that Lidia hadn't discovered this.

"Yeah, it did." Jonah's tense arms relaxed a little around me. "But every time I tried to stop, my mind would just go into overdrive, thinking about all the things I hated about my life."

"And your parents didn't know?"

"They were clueless," Jonah said. His fingers flexed

and opened on the back of my jacket. "Bree knew, though. She was worried. She tried to say something to me, but I wouldn't listen."

"She's protective of you," I said, thinking about some of the things she had said to me. Maybe that was why she treated me with such hostility.

"To a certain extent," Jonah said. "But there comes a point where she gives up and that's usually when—when I—"

"Self-destruct?" I supplied.

"Yeah." Jonah blew a hard breath out. "And I really self-destructed in Fairfield."

Part of me wanted him to stop talking, to stay that boy I had seen under the willow tree earlier, pure and beautiful. But he had opened this door, and it was too late to slam it shut now.

As if he could sense this, Jonah ran his words into each other as he talked. "Most of the parties I went to Bree would go with me to keep an eye on me. But that night she didn't. I was already buzzed by the time I got there and got drunker as the night wore on. I left after midnight with a girl I was kinda dating." He glanced at me, but I only nodded so he rushed on. "Emily liked to drink too—that was the only thing we had in common.

"I don't even know how I made it out of the driveway," Jonah continued. "For that matter, I don't know how I got the key into the ignition. But less than a mile from the house, I lost total control of the car. We went flying off the road. We were going so fast that we crashed through the guardrail and—and—finally—slammed into a tree."

"Oh, my God," I breathed. I pressed my hands to his cheeks and made him look at me. His eyes were haunted and far away. "Were you okay?"

He laughed, a harsh bark of a laugh that cut me inside. "Oh, I was fine. Hardly a scratch. But Emily . . . she . . ."

I could barely breathe. "Is she—did she die?"

"No," he whispered. "Her legs got pinned under the dashboard. They had to amputate both of them."

My stomach bottomed out. I pushed myself off his lap and moved to the edge of the bench. Jonah reached for me, but I held my hand up. "Just give me a minute."

He dropped his arms and twisted his hands in his lap. "It was horrible, and I wasn't sober enough to really know what was going on. The ambulance took her away . . . and then the police took me . . . They put me in the county jail, and my parents came in the middle of the night to get me. I'll never forget the look on my dad's face . . ."

His voice sounded muffled and far away to my ears. How could he have been so stupid, so reckless? He had destroyed someone else's life because of his own selfishness. I shuddered, not sure I could look at him, but I forced myself to. He was in profile again, his hair wild from the wind. A teardrop poised at the corner of his eyelashes. He was still the same Jonah, the same marble angel. A fallen angel now, maybe, but who wasn't?

I had caused destruction too; all those people on the bridge had died because of me. Even though I knew it was really the fault of the Malandanti, they destroyed the bridge to take me—and only me—down.

"—Dad's company bailed me out—"

I snapped back to what he was saying. "Wait. What?"

"My dad's company. They kinda swooped in and handled everything. They got the charges against me dropped. I have no idea how but they did. They also made us leave Fairfield—told my dad that if we didn't they would ruin his career. My parents were so mad at me—still are—because they thought Fairfield was it. Bree was furious." Jonah leaned forward, elbows digging into his knees. "As if I cared about moving again or any of it . . . I mean, I should be in jail for what I did, and I got off so freaking easy, and Emily . . . she has to deal with this the rest of her life." He covered his face with his hands.

My mind was jumpy and fractured as I watched him. The Guild—the Malandanti—had bailed him out. Of course Jonah had no idea how, because I was sure they had used magic, the same mind influence Mr. Wolfe had used to fool everyone about the power plant.

I sucked in a breath. No wonder Jonah had defended the Guild the other night at dinner. It had nothing to do with the Malandanti or the Waterfall or the power plant. They had saved his life. And Jonah, free from the law, was shackled to this guilt for the rest of his life, the same way the kernel of guilt from the bridge collapse would always live in me. I touched his shoulder. "Do you still drink?"

He dropped his hands away from his face. His eyes were clear. "No. I haven't had a drop since that night. I don't think I ever will again."

"Good."

He swallowed. "So you—you still want to be with me?"

Maybe it was strange, but that had never been in question. "Jonah." I put my other hand on his shoulder and circled my arms around his neck. "I'm not saying what you did wasn't awful, but we all deserve forgiveness." I scooted closer to him. "Your family came to Twin Willows for a new start, and that's what you get."

He snaked his arms around my waist and lifted me onto his lap. I rested my head on his shoulder, and he stroked my hair, my neck, my back. He didn't say anything; he didn't need to. We stayed like that for a long time before I raised my head. "Was that what the fight was about with your dad?"

"Yeah." Jonah leaned back against the bench, bringing me with him. "I guess I deserve to have him throw the accident in my face, but when he goes on and on about how I don't have ambition or direction or anything—how does he know? All he cares about is his job. He doesn't pay attention to what we want. I do have a direction, and there are things I want, more than he'll ever know."

My breath hitched in my throat. "Like what?" I whispered.

He looked at me, his eyes glittering like a thousand emeralds. "Like you," he murmured and kissed me softly.

I clung to him, wanting to wipe my brain clean and surrender, but my skin itched with guilt. He had shared his secret with me. It wasn't fair that I couldn't share mine with him. A battle raged inside me . . . *tell him* . . . *rule number one* . . . and I saw again the blueprint of the power plant. Whatever his dad and sister knew, it was better if Jonah knew nothing, so there was no risk of anything getting back to them.

Jonah circled his thumbs against my collarbone. "Every day, I think I can't like you any more than I already do, and then you do something even more amazing." He shook his head. "I really thought you'd run like hell after I told you about the accident."

"For that? Nah." I traced his lips with my finger. "For making me freeze another night in this graveyard, maybe."

He smiled softly. "I adore you. I've adored you since that day in the office when you switched my schedule with Bree's, so we'd have all those classes together."

My fingertip paused on his bottom lip. "You knew about that?"

He bit my finger gently. "Yeah. I thought it was really cute." He slid his hands from my shoulders down my back. "You are totally not the type of girl I wanted to like. You work in the school office. You're the kind of girl

I can actually introduce to my parents. I wanted to like someone who wears way too much black eyeliner and has piercings in unmentionable places."

I laughed.

"Then I got to know you and realized you're just as much of a freak as I am. You just wear it on the inside."

My heart went cold. "What do you mean?"

"You get it, like me. You get that there's more to life than this place, and you aren't satisfied to be put into a little box." He ducked his head to kiss me. "You're an explorer, like me."

*You have no idea*, I thought, but I let him kiss me until my mind was empty. I felt him lose himself in me, and it was a relief to lose myself in him, too . . . and let the world outside the ancient wrought-iron gate disappear.

The moon was starting to descend by the time Jonah walked me to the street. We stood in the shadow of the gate for one last kiss good night that neither of us wanted to end. Jonah held me close, and I felt a tug in my chest, a pull at my heart so strong I thought my ribs would break open. I buried my face in his neck and clung to him, trying to breathe. As Jonah's lips moved behind my ear, the pain in my chest quickened and spread, and my whole body felt pricked with needles.

With a sharp intake of breath, I knew what was happening. I pushed Jonah away with more force than necessary.

"What's wrong?" he asked.

"Nothing." I gasped and clutched my coat tight to my throat, as though it could somehow keep the transformation from happening. "I-I should really be going."

"I'll walk you home."

"No! I mean"—I forced a smile—"it's okay. You live just around the corner, and it's freezing. It's not like there's some serial killer lurking the streets of Twin Willows. I'll be fine." I gave him a peck and pushed him gently in the direction of his house. "See you tomorrow."

I waited until he had faded into the darkness and then took off toward my house, running full tilt. The Call tugged at me; I ran faster but only made it to the top of my driveway before my body gave out under its power.

# Chapter Twenty-one

*The Message*

Even as I soared toward the stars, my mind was pulled down to earth by thoughts of Jonah. Against the black night, my aura flickered. I stuffed Jonah into a box and shoved it back to the corner of my mind. I was a Benandante right now, and my other life couldn't cross into this one . . .

The moon was hidden behind a bank of clouds, shrouding the world below in darkness. I opened my mind, searching for Heath's thoughts. *What's going on?*

*Clan meeting. At the birch trees.*

*Are we going in again?*

*How should I know? I'm not the one in charge.*

Why was *he* in such a pissy mood? *I* was the one who had my date cut short.

As I neared the birch trees, I heard the thoughts of the other Benandanti. I landed on a branch next to the Eagle. On the ground below the rest of the Clan gathered, our auras overlapping in the small copse.

The Stag looked around at each of us. *I'm sorry, but*

*I have to start this meeting off with bad news. We've lost control of the Redwood site.*

Shock and grief flooded into my mind from the others. I turned to the Eagle. *Redwood—as in California?*

*Yes.* She blinked, her golden eyes bright in the darkness. Briefly I wondered if her eyes were the same unusual color in her human form, just as mine and Heath's were. *We've controlled that site for decades.*

*What's the magic there?*

*The power to heal, even fatal wounds. Including wounds done to your human form while you are transformed and vice versa.* She tucked her wings in close to her side. *It means the Malandanti are virtually indestructible now.*

I turned back to the rest of the Clan. *So there's only one site left under the control of the Benandanti?* I felt cold inside.

*Yes.* The Stag paced in a circle around the birch trees. *We have no time to lose. We have to act before they break ground on the power plant. That's why I called us all here tonight.*

*Are we going in?* The Lynx stood up, his ears pricked forward.

The Stag shook his head. *Tonight we're going to come up with a strategy—*

*—which thanks to the Falcon should be a lot easier,* Heath interjected.

*Well, yes.* The Stag paused beneath my branch. *While the Falcon acted rashly by attacking the Panther, she discovered some vital information. So . . . good work.*

*Thanks.* I ruffled my feathers, but there wasn't time to feel proud. Not with everything else that was going on. *How soon will we attack?*

*I have to take our plan to the* Concilio Celeste *first,* answered the Stag.

Everyone protested at the same time, a mess of thoughts in my brain.

The Stag stamped his hoof. *Look, I screwed up last time, and I'm not going to let that happen again. We have only one shot at this, and I want all our bases covered before we go in. So the* Concilio Celeste *will have the final word.*

The Eagle and the Lynx continued to grumble a bit as we devised a plan of attack.

At the end of the meeting after we had a strategy, the Stag looked each of us in the eyes. *I need everyone on board with this. Okay?*

One by one, we agreed.

The Eagle flew toward the Waterfall to patrol. I wheeled toward the farm, my head buzzing with plans and battle tactics. And in the back of my mind was still the jumble of puzzle pieces about Bree, not to mention the bomb Jonah had dropped in the graveyard. I was so distracted that I almost missed the ball of silvery light in the corner of my eye.

I turned lightning fast, my body tilting. The Malandanti Raven disappeared into the trees, its aura visible amongst the bare branches. I looked down and realized I was above our pasture, the hillside empty and quiet with the goats shut away in the barn for the night. What was the Raven doing near my home?

I followed it into the forest, opening a channel in my mind, direct to Heath. *I just spotted the Raven coming from the farm.*

*That can't be good.* Heath's glowing white form appeared below me.

I didn't think there was any chance the Raven wouldn't see us, but I floated above the treetops, keeping an eye on the telltale shimmer of the Malandante's aura.

The aura went out.

*What the—how did it do that?* I snapped to Heath.

*That's advanced magic—*

The Raven collided with me, knocking me out of the air. Night enveloped its black feathers so completely that I couldn't see it. I free-fell for several feet before pulling myself up, then glided low to the ground.

*Are you all right?* Heath asked.

*I think so.*

Dead leaves crunched, and the Boar slammed through the brush, flattening bushes and small trees under its weight.

Heath stumbled backward. I circled in the air, and the invisible Raven bashed into me, slicing a talon across my back. White-hot pain seared my flesh.

Down below, the Coyote joined the Boar and danced around Heath, jaws snapping.

*Get out of there*, I told him.

*You think?* Heath shot back.

The Coyote lunged for him, creating a narrow space through which Heath streaked, his aura like a fiery tail behind him.

I scanned the ground. The Coyote and the Boar ran in the opposite direction, toward the Waterfall. The Raven had disappeared again. *Why aren't they following?*

*I don't know.* Heath jumped over a boulder. *I don't like it. Let's separate and meet at the barn.* He headed east, away from the farm.

I detoured in the direction of town, then turned back toward home. As I swooped low over the road, I suddenly remembered my body was not in my bed. It was at the top of the driveway where I had collapsed after leaving Jonah.

The darkness was broken by a set of headlights from a car parked where the driveway met the road. The driver's side door was open, and the lights pooled on the ground, revealing a figure bending over my lifeless form.

It was Jenny.

Heath's words flashed in my mind: *If anyone turns your body while you're transformed, your soul cannot return.* And the locket that was supposed to protect me . . . sat with its broken clasp on my nightstand.

I plunged toward Jenny. As I came closer I heard her calling my name. She grasped my human body by the shoulder and heaved.

I screeched, the sound ripping across the still night.

Jenny fell back and looked up. The headlights illuminated the fear on her face.

I rushed her, flapping my wings, and she threw her arms up in front of her face. In that instant, I dissolved into my body and rolled over, gasping for air.

"Lessi!" Jenny crawled to me. "Are you okay?"

I sat up and took her by the wrist, trying to slow my breathing. My whole body trembled. "Yeah, I think so. What happened?"

"I found you lying here." Her eyes were wide and glinted with tears. "Oh, my God, I couldn't find a pulse. I thought you were—"

I reached out and hugged her. "I'm all right. I tripped on something. I must have blacked out for a few minutes."

"And then there was this huge bird—did you see it?" She scanned the sky for the falcon I knew she wouldn't see.

"I think I heard it. Did it screech or something?"

"It made a horrible noise, like a scream. It must have flown away." She took a deep breath and squeezed my hand. "That was really, really freaky. But I'm so glad you're okay."

"I'm fine," I assured her. The pressure of her hand in mine helped slow my body's shaking. "But, um, what are you doing here? It's, like, three in the morning or something, isn't it?"

"I was out with Seth. Missed my curfew." She

grinned, her eyes sparkling. "Oops."

I forced a laugh, my nerves still on edge at almost being caught. Not just caught, I realized. Killed. It wasn't just the Malandanti who could kill me; a simple loving gesture could also end my life forever. If Jenny had turned me over . . . I drew a shaky breath and tried to focus on what she was saying. "What?"

Jenny jiggled my arm. "I said, we're going to the bonfire party together tomorrow."

"Oh. I take it you talked to Carly?"

"Yeah, she's fine with it." She punched me lightly. "If you'd been at lunch with us yesterday, you would have known that."

"Sorry. But Jonah and I are definitely coming tomorrow, and we'll have some girl time, I promise."

"Good." Jenny looked over my shoulder. Her grip on my arm tightened. "What is that?"

I turned. An unearthly red glow shone from behind the house, flickering against the darkness. Pulling Jenny with me, I ran down the driveway. When we rounded the side of the house, I slid to a stop, gravel sputtering under my feet.

The barn was on fire.

Flames poured off the roof and licked at the walls. Wind gusted, stretching the fire down around the barn door. Black smoke billowed high into the air, blocking out the stars.

I let out a cry and whirled in a little circle, trying to

organize coherent thoughts. "Call—," I said.

But Jenny was already punching numbers on her cell phone.

I heard the other line click and answer, "This is 911. What's your emergency?"

"There's a fire at my friend's farm," Jenny said. Her voice teetered on the edge of breaking. "At 826 Route Seventeen . . . No, the barn." She covered the receiver with her hand and said to me, "It's unoccupied, right?"

"The goats—" I choked out and started toward the fire. A wave of heat hit me. I covered my face with my hands, pressed my fingers deep into my skin. Then I remembered. Heath. *Let's separate and meet at the barn.* I pushed through a cloud of smoke that billowed into the air. "Heath! Heath!"

"Lessi!" Jenny screamed. "You can't go in there!"

"Heath might be inside," I shouted. The inside of my nose itched as smoke swirled around me. I took my jacket off and pressed it against my mouth. Sparks showered down, hissing and spitting as they hit the air and burned out. Through the thick blanket of smoke, the door to the barn yawned open. I inched toward it. Heat prickled my skin, made my eyes water. Fiery shadows danced on the walls. "Heath?"

"Get out of the way!" His voice echoed back to me, accompanied by bleating and nickering.

I jumped to the side as a stampede of goats flooded out of the barn, colliding with one another in their frantic quest for fresh air. I raced up the hillside and threw open the gate to the pasture. The goats tumbled in through the gate, bucking and whining. Ash covered their coats and whirled into my nostrils as they ran by me. Coughing, I clung to the fence post, my eyes watering. When the last goat had galloped in, I locked the gate and stumbled down the hill.

Heath crouched on the ground several feet from the barn, coughing so hard I thought his lungs would come out.

I bent over him. "Are you okay?"

He nodded and grabbed my hand to pull himself up. His fair skin was blackened with soot, his light hair singed brown.

I looked around. "Where's Jenny?"

"She—" He coughed again and wiped his mouth. "She went inside to get us some water."

In the distance, a siren wailed.

I clutched Heath's hand as I watched the fire devour the roof of the barn. His skin was hot as a fever. "It was the Raven," I said, voicing the thought that had hit me the moment Jenny and I had come around the house.

"We'll deal with that later," Heath said and jerked his chin toward the house as the back door opened.

Lidia flew at us, the tails of her bathrobe fluttering around her, while Jenny followed, carrying two glasses of water.

"*Mi Dio!*" Lidia cried and flung her arms around Heath and me. "Thank God you are all right."

I hugged her hard, burying my face in her shoulder for a moment to hide my view of the dying barn.

Heath broke away and took a glass from Jenny, downed it in one long gulp. "I got the goats out," he said. His voice was raspy and ragged from the smoke. "But . . ." He stared at the fiery structure. A huge hole gaped in the roof, and flames engulfed all four sides.

Lidia pressed me closer. "We can replace the barn," she said, reaching out to touch Heath's arm. "But we cannot replace you." She looked past him toward the hillside where the goats now grazed. "*Grazie mille*. For the goats. Tom loved those animals." She squeezed my shoulders as her eyes filled with tears.

The siren grew closer, red-and-white lights flashing as the truck barreled into view. The four of us backed away as the firemen unraveled the long white hose. Water arced onto the roof and quenched the fire within minutes, leaving the barn a twisted shadow of its former self. Wisps of smoke spiraled up from the smoldering mess, singing my nostrils with the smell of burned wood.

One of the EMTs examined Heath, making him breathe deep through a mask attached to an oxygen tank.

Jenny handed me the other glass of water. I drank with small sips.

We watched the firemen circle the barn, dousing water here and there on patches of embers. One of them came over to us. "Any idea how it might have started? Was your hay wet?"

I glanced at Heath.

Lidia sighed. "I don't think so. But it's possible, from the rain we had last week."

The fireman took off his helmet and ran his hand through his choppy hair. "Most of these barn fires are caused by hay. My guys and me are gonna look through the remains to see if we find anything. We might be a while."

"I'll make some food," Lidia said. It was just like her to cook in the middle of a crisis.

"Much appreciated, ma'am. Glad no one was hurt." He walked to the barn, his boots crunching on the dirt and gravel. ·

The kitchen felt clean and comforting. I shook out my balled-up jacket and hung it by the door.

Jenny put the empty water glasses in the sink and turned to me. "I better get going. I'm not—" She shot a look at my mother and pressed her lips together.

"You shouldn't be out this late." Lidia wagged a finger at her.

Jenny scuffed her shoe on the floor. "No, Mrs. Jacobs."

Lidia came around the island and put an arm around Jenny's waist. "You're a good girl." She pushed Jenny toward the door. "I'll tell your parents what a help you were to us."

"Thanks. Maybe they'll ground me for the rest of my life instead of eternity," Jenny said with a grimace. "I guess I won't see you tomorrow at the beach," she said to me.

"What? Oh, man, I totally forgot." I folded my arms over

my chest. "No, probably not. I should hang around here."

"What are you talking about?" Lidia asked.

"The bonfire party I told you about," I said. "Don't worry. I'll skip it."

"Oh, *cara*, I know how much you were looking forward to it." Lidia started to take down mugs from the cupboard, counting how many she needed for the firemen.

"It's okay, Mom. You'll need help here tomorrow."

"We'll figure it out in the morning."

"I'll call you tomorrow," I told Jenny.

"It *is* tomorrow," she tossed over her shoulder as she bounded out the front door.

I helped Lidia carry a tray of coffee and sandwiches out to the firemen. The sky was just beginning to lighten, a faint grey mist shrouding the hillside. The paramedics gave Heath a clean bill of health, and he followed us into the kitchen.

Lidia dropped into the chair next to him and rubbed her eyes. "Tom was always so careful about the hay."

All the emotions that were balled up inside me burst. "It wasn't the hay. Don't you get it?"

Heath swiveled in his chair. I ignored the heat of his gaze.

Lidia stared at me. "What are you talking about?"

"The Guild." I circled around the back of the island and pressed my palms against the edge, pushing the counter as though I could topple it over. "I told you not to put those posters up. I told you those people were dangerous."

Lidia stood. "You think they started the fire?"

"Of course they did!" I kicked the island and marched to Lidia so that we were face-to-face. "They had the whole town on their side about the power plant until you put those signs up. This is their way of shutting you up again."

Lidia shook her head. "They're a big company. Why would they do something so—so—drastic for a few little signs?"

"It's not just about the signs. They want to send a message—"

"What message?"

"To the Ben—"

Heath stood up so suddenly his chair fell over.

I clamped my mouth shut and breathed in sharp through my nose. I had said too much, almost spilled my secret.

Heath turned to Lidia. "To the town. They don't want anyone to stand in the way of the plant."

I looked at the floor. Although what Heath said was probably true, I knew it was the Malandanti that wanted to send the message. Even though they didn't know my identity, my connection to the farm, they wanted the Benandanti to know that any attempt to block the power plant would be met with brutality, even against innocent civilians. I put my hand to my throat where my locket should lay and massaged the skin there. How could I make Lidia understand without telling her everything?

Heath touched Lidia's arm. "I know I've only been working here a short time, and I have no right to give you advice. But I think you should listen to Alessia. For your safety, for all our safety, I think you should take the signs down and back off."

"But if what you say is true," Lidia said, tightening her fingers into a fist, "we can't let them get away with this."

"And we won't," Heath said. "We'll find another way. One that doesn't endanger our lives. Or our livelihood."

Lidia looked from him to me. Dark circles smudged the skin under her eyes. "You really think the fire was on purpose?"

"Yes," I answered without hesitation.

"Even if it wasn't," Heath said, glancing at me with narrowed eyes, "we need to be careful."

Lidia pressed her knuckles to her mouth. After a moment she nodded. "*Bene*. Okay. I'll take the signs down. For now."

There was a knock on the back door. Lidia smoothed her hair away from her face and answered it.

The head fireman stood with his helmet tucked under his arm. "Have a minute?"

"Of course." Lidia grabbed her coat from the peg by the door and put it on over her bathrobe. She followed the fireman to the barn where the other firemen looked to be wrapping things up. I watched them walk around the fractured frame and didn't turn when I heard Heath's chair creak. He came up behind me, so close I could feel his warm breath on my neck.

"It was the Malandanti," I said, not looking at him. "There's not a doubt in my mind."

"But you can't tell Lidia," Heath said. "You know that."

"I know but—"

"But nothing, Alessia. *You must not speak of the Benandanti.*"

Outside, Lidia stooped and picked up a half-melted lantern, misshapen and deformed. My heart ached as she tossed it aside and wiped her eyes.

"We have to retake the Waterfall," I said. "Like now."

"Yes," Heath said. "We're all at risk until we do. Not just the Benandanti but anyone who gets in the Guild's way. But you heard the Stag. The *Concilio Celeste* has to give the okay." He sighed, the force of his breath trickling down my spine. "I'll contact them and tell them what's going on. That's all I can do, but hopefully it will convince them to send us into battle sooner rather than later."

I turned so fast a crick seared through my neck. "I thought only the Stag could communicate with the *Concilio Celeste.*"

"He's not the only one who's got connections." Heath squared his shoulders and pushed past me, heading toward the Cave.

I shivered and hugged myself, looking at the barn. The fireman shook Lidia's hand and patted her on the shoulder. She stood still as they climbed onto their truck and maneuvered it out of the driveway. When they were gone she walked slowly back to the dark, smoky ruin.

My gut twisted into twin snakes of sorrow and anger. The Waterfall and now the barn. They were striking at the very heart of me, shredding me from the inside out. I punched the doorframe, ignoring the burst of pain across my knuckles. They wouldn't get away with it. No matter what it took, they would pay.

# CHAPTER TWENTY-TWO
### *The Bonfire*

Mr. Salter brought a posse over in the morning—so many people, in fact, that Lidia told me she had enough help and I should go to the bonfire.

I felt guilty for leaving her, but my spirit was craving a day to be a normal girl. I called Jonah to come pick me up.

He arrived fifteen minutes early, carrying a foil-covered dish. "My mom sent over a quiche. Don't worry. I think it's safe to eat."

"Thanks." I stepped out of the way to let him inside. "You told your parents about the fire?"

"Actually, our neighbor is a volunteer fireman, and he was telling my dad about it this morning," Jonah said.

*As if your dad didn't know all about it already,* I thought but clamped my lips together. I had decided that I wouldn't say anything to Jonah about my belief that the Guild was behind the fire, and I had asked Lidia not to, either. After all, I had no solid evidence that the Guild was involved. I could only imagine how that conversation would go. *Well, see, there was this Raven . . .*

I led him into the kitchen where my mother sat at the table, talking on the phone with papers spread all around her. She waved to Jonah and mouthed, "Thank you" when he set the quiche on the counter.

We walked out back to where the barn should have stood. Heath had joined Mr. Salter and the neighbors as they sifted through the ruins and hauled away sodden garbage.

Jonah whistled low and long. "Holy shit . . . the whole thing is gone." I leaned against him, and he put his arm around me, pulling me close. He kissed the top of my head. "I'm just glad you're okay."

"For now."

"What do you mean?" he asked, brushing a strand of hair off my face.

"Well, winter's coming, and it's going to start snowing soon." I twisted my locket in between my fingers. I'd replaced the chain with one from another necklace—no way would I ever be without it again. "You haven't lived this far north. Once it snows, it doesn't melt until spring. Which means we won't be able to rebuild it for months."

Jonah gazed at the hillside where the goats milled and grazed in the cold autumn sunlight. "What about the goats?"

"We have to board them at other farms." I nodded at the house. "That's what my mom is doing in there, calling all our other farmer friends to see if they can take in the goats. I think that will work out, but while the goats aren't here . . ."

"You can't work the farm," Jonah finished for me.

I stared at the ground, trying to swallow the lump that had formed in my throat.

"Will you guys be okay?"

I shrugged and squinted, my vision blurry. "I just wish my dad was here," I whispered.

Jonah threw his other arm around me and pressed me into him, holding my head against his chest. He stroked my back, and I let myself cry for a few minutes.

"Are you sure you want to go to the beach?" he asked. "We can hang out here if you want."

I hiccupped and smiled at him. "Thanks, but no, I want to go."

The beach was only a few miles from my house, but I hadn't been there since the start of school. I liked going this time of year, when the sand was cold on your feet and the water too icy to swim in. Not that the water was ever balmy in Maine, but something about the deep autumn chill made the sea seem more wild to me, the way it should be.

A small group of people clustered around a burgeoning fire when Jonah and I arrived. The sun's rays shimmered orange and gold on the water. I breathed in deep and let the salt air fill my lungs. When I was young I thought there was no problem the ocean couldn't cure, and as I stood there, listening to the waves, I could believe it again.

I slipped my hand into Jonah's. "I love the sea," I said, my gaze fixed on the endless horizon. "It's my very favorite thing about living in Maine." I looked up at Jonah. "Don't you love it?"

"I like to look at it from this distance," he said. "But I don't like to go in it."

"Really?" We walked over the little bluff at the edge of the beach and descended toward the group. Jonah held my hand as we picked our way over the rocks. "You don't like to swim or sail?"

"I don't swim very well. I'm kinda—well . . ." Jonah tugged me to a stop. "I'm sort of afraid of water. I almost drowned when I was a kid."

I stared at him. "Seriously?"

He nodded. "I was eleven. It was pretty bad. A riptide yanked me under on a family vacation in Mexico. My mother pulled me out."

"Where was your dad?"

Jonah snorted and squinted at the sun. "Talking on his cell. He barely even knew what had happened until the medics arrived."

I opened my mouth, unsure of what to say, but at that moment Jenny bounded toward us, her blue eyes sparkling like the sun on the ocean. "Lessi, I'm so glad you're here."

I hugged her hard. "So your parents didn't ground you?"

Jenny made a face. "I have to do a bunch of extra work around the house, but no, I'm not grounded. Apparently Lidia called them to sing my praises this morning. I guess I owe her a fruit basket or something." She grabbed my hand. "How are things at your house?"

"I don't want to talk about it," I said. "I just want to have fun today."

"I'm down with that," she said.

We walked toward the bonfire. Music was streaming through someone's iPod.

"We're roasting some hot dogs, and we've got marshmallows for later. Did you bring a blanket?" Jenny asked.

Jonah held up the faded tartan blanket we had taken from my house.

"Awesome. Make yourselves cozy," she said with a wink.

I rolled my eyes, and we followed her to the edge of the fire. The smell of the smoke took me right back to last night, and I shied away, tears stinging my eyes.

Jonah caught my hand. Shadow and light moved over his face, and his eyes glowed in the firelight. The strength of his profile silhouetted against the twilight made him look like a painting from another era. The sight of him pushed the thoughts of the fire to the corner of my mind.

"Let's find a good spot for our blanket," he said, squeezing my hand.

We found a spot a little ways from the fire that was in the shadows but close enough to garner some heat from the flames. I spread the blanket out while Jonah went to find us good sticks for roasting.

Kids kept arriving by carloads. I settled myself on our blanket and waved to Carly and Melissa as they spread a blanket out not far from ours. Up at the parking lot, Josh Baker's Hummer pulled in, pumping music with the bass turned up so loud I felt the earth shake. The passenger door opened and out jumped . . . Bree.

"Oh, great." Jenny sat on a blanket next to ours with Seth.

"What is she doing with Josh Baker?" Carly asked. She and Melissa had come over to join the conversation. "I thought he only dated cheerleaders."

"And I thought she hated people," Melissa said.

"She doesn't hate people," Jonah said quickly.

"She certainly doesn't hate guys," Jenny said.

I glared across the bonfire where Bree was draped all over Josh, a smug little grin on her face. It wasn't my problem if she made a fool of herself over the biggest player in the school. I just wanted to know exactly how much she knew about the Benandanti, the Guild, and the magic. I watched them carry their blanket toward our group, my thoughts darkening with every step they took. If Bree knew the Guild's real intentions, how much of a leap was it to think she was in even deeper? I couldn't stop seeing her fierce look in the coffee shop, so like the Panther's . . .

*That's insane*, I thought. Lots of people had green eyes, Jonah included. But nobody else knew about the magic . . .

"Careful where you put those hands, Baker," Jonah said as Josh and Bree walked past our blanket. "That's my sister."

"I can handle myself, brother dear," Bree said as Josh's hand moved from her waist to the curve of her hip. She shifted her gaze to me. "Sorry to hear about your barn."

"Yeah, right," I muttered.

"Alessia." Jonah touched my knee. I looked at his hand for a second before the seething inside me boiled over. Shoving his hand off, I stood up. "Just admit it," I said, stepping practically nose to nose with Bree. "You're not sorry. Not at all."

"Control your woman, Wolfe." Josh laughed.

I felt Jonah stand behind me. "Go back to the fifties, Baker."

He laid a hand on my arm, but I didn't turn. I dug my gaze into Bree, breathing heavily. "You can act like you're above it all," I said in little more than a whisper, "but you and I know better."

Bree's lip curled. "I have no idea what you're talking about."

"Oh, I think you do," I said, my voice rising. "I think you know plenty."

"Let's go for a walk," Jonah said to me.

"I'm watching you," I snarled before I let him drag me away.

"What is wrong with you?" Jonah asked when we

had gone down the beach, away from the bonfire. Jenny, Carly, and Melissa walked over, casting worried looks at me. "Look, I know you don't like Bree, but she *is* my sister. It would be nice if the two of you weren't mortal enemies."

I peered into his face, lost for words for a moment. I didn't believe that Jonah knew anything about the Guild, but it still burned me that he would defend Bree. "She threatened my mom. She said to take down those signs or else."

Jonah threw his hands up. "She was just messing with you. That's how she gets her kicks."

"My mother put those signs up, and less than a week later our barn burned down." I swiped angry tears off my face.

"Whoa." Jonah held me by the shoulders. "You can't seriously think that Bree had anything to do with the fire."

Swallowing hard, I looked from him to the girls. I realized how I must appear to them, my eyes wild and my voice hysterical. "I'm being paranoid, aren't I?"

Jonah slid his arms around me and kissed the top of my head. "I think we can forgive you," he whispered in my ear. "I know you're worried about the farm, but it's going to be okay. And maybe my dad's company can help."

I nodded, not looking at him. *They've already done enough.*

Jenny stepped forward and touched my arm. "My turn, Wolfe." She pulled me into a hug. "Stop being such a conspiracy theorist. Who do you think you are, my parents?"

I forced a laugh. "You're right. I'm sorry, you guys.

I'm just really upset about the fire."

Carly and Melissa joined our hug, crushing me in the middle.

"Air, air!" I laughed, for real this time.

They glanced at each other. "We'll give you air," Melissa said and grabbed my arm. She and Carly dragged me to the water's edge where they tried to throw me in the water. But we were all laughing too hard and collapsed into a heap on the sand.

"That's for breaking the Girl Code," Carly gasped.

"And being a paranoid freak," Melissa added.

Jenny dove in the middle of the pile, and we shrieked, kicking sand at one another. We sat up, facing the ocean, still tangled together. Their love surrounded me on all sides, like a fortress against the mess the rest of my life was in. I held tight to them, wishing I never had to leave the safety of their walls.

Jenny squished up next to me, laying her head on my shoulder. "Don't worry. We'll help. We'll bring over food—"

"We'll carry lumber and hammer nails," Melissa said.

"And my dad already said he'd get some of his guys to work for free," Carly said. Her dad owned a construction company. "We're all here for you."

I smiled at them, warmed inside despite the chilly salt-sea air.

Jonah ambled toward us, hands shoved deep in his pockets.

I turned my head and kissed Jenny on the cheek. "Thanks, you guys."

"You don't have to go through this alone," Jenny said.

And just like that, the fortress crumbled. I knew they meant well, that their words were filled with good intentions, but they had no idea. Despite this close circle of friends around me, I was utterly alone.

# Chapter Twenty-three

*The Snowstorm*

The little bell over the door to the hardware store dinged when I entered. Inside, it was warm and smelled like fresh-cut wood, newly made keys, and turpentine.

"Morning, Alessia," Mr. Salter greeted me from behind the counter. He stacked some brochures and set them at the corner by the register.

"Hi, Mr. Salter. Smells like snow outside," I added.

He rubbed his hands together, grinning. "Oh, good. We should be busy today, then, with everyone rushing in for last-minute snow supplies. I'm glad you were free today."

"Me too," I said, smiling as I shrugged my coat off. I hadn't put in any time at the hardware store in weeks—since before I had learned I was a Benandante—and I had missed it.

"There's fresh coffee." Mr. Salter pointed toward the back office where he kept an ancient coffeepot. "And I brought doughnuts."

"You really went all out," I teased as I threaded through the aisles to the back. The bittersweet scent of coffee wafted out from the office, and my stomach rumbled. I took a chipped mug with a picture of a moose on it down from the shelf and poured myself a cup, then took a doughnut from the open box on Mr. Salter's cluttered desk. The doughnuts were from Joe's and still warm. I carried my coffee to the front counter and joined Mr. Salter behind it. "What do you need me to do first?"

"Finish your doughnut, then make sure we have all the snow shovels in stock out front. There might be some in the storeroom that you'll need to bring out." Mr. Salter cracked open a roll of quarters and poured them into the register.

I broke off a piece of doughnut and popped it into my mouth. While the glaze melted on my tongue, I surveyed the current mess on the counter. I could hear Dolly, chiding Mr. Salter for not keeping it tidy. I set my mug down and started to sort the piles of papers on the shelf under the counter. "Do you need these?" I asked, holding out a stack of junk mail.

"I've been meaning to go through all that," Mr. Salter said with a sigh. "You don't have to do it."

"It'll just take a minute, and then we'll have this whole mess cleaned up," I said cheerily and dumped the junk mail into the wastebasket tucked in the corner.

"Dolly used to take care of all this," he muttered, his face turned away from me.

I put my hand on his arm. "I know. I miss her too."

He covered my hand with his own and gave a little squeeze. "She loved snow," he said with a sad tilt of his head toward the wind.

"So did my dad." We both looked outside through the glass. There were no flurries yet, but the sky looked grey in the way that foretold snow. After a long moment we glanced at each other.

Mr. Salter shook himself and smiled. "How's your mom?"

"Since last night? Fine," I said. Mr. Salter had been over almost every night since the fire, helping around the farm. We had gotten the last of the goats over to their temporary homes yesterday, and the farm felt empty without them. "Thanks for all your help this week."

"Well, your mom has been so good to me since Dolly passed. It's the least I can do."

We had a steady stream of customers until the early afternoon, by which time several inches of snow covered the world outside. One by one the customers paid for their supplies and left to hurry home to their warm and cozy hearths.

"I think we'll close early," Mr. Salter said. "I'll give you a ride, so you don't have to walk home in this," he added, peering out the window beside the register. "It's really coming down."

I gazed out the window, thinking about tomorrow when the snow would be fresh and untouched over the hillside behind the house. Jenny and I would go sledding, and Lidia would have her homemade hot cocoa waiting for us when we came inside. I could almost taste the chocolate on my tongue.

The bell over the door interrupted my daydream. I peeked out from behind the now-meager display of snow shovels.

Mr. Wolfe stood in the doorway. Behind him, Jonah was dwarfed by his father's imposing size, made all the larger by the enormous puffer coat Mr. Wolfe was wearing.

My stomach flip-flopped. I leaned on one of the shovels against the wall. I loved that the unexpected sight of Jonah still gave me butterflies.

"Afternoon, Wolfe." Mr. Salter came out from behind the counter and crossed his arms over his chest. "What can I do for you?"

I stared at Mr. Salter. A hard edge tinged his voice, something I had never heard. His gaze was dark and pointed at Mr. Wolfe. I clenched my fist at my side. Had Lidia said something to Mr. Salter about our suspicions? Even after I asked her not to?

Mr. Wolfe surveyed the store as though he had just planted a flag on the top of a mountain. "A bag of salt and a shovel." He squinted at Mr. Salter. "You got those?"

"Yeah, we got those." Mr. Salter pointed to the few shovels that were left. "Help yourself." He watched Mr. Wolfe select a shovel, his shoulders stiff and tense.

Jonah shot me a look, tilting his head toward Mr. Salter.

I shrugged as though I had no idea what was going on.

Mr. Wolfe leaned his shovel against the counter and turned toward the bags of salt piled at the door. He bent over to pick one up, then straightened and cocked his head. "You think you could help me?"

"You think you could leave my town alone?" Mr. Salter stepped toward Mr. Wolfe.

I hurried between them. "I'll help you."

Jonah rushed to my side and lifted the bag to his shoulder. I held the door open for him and followed him outside.

Jonah dropped the bag into the back of his dad's SUV with a thud and turned to me. "What's all that about?"

"Nothing." I forced a smile and tilted my face up to his, hoping to distract him with a kiss.

Jonah reached out and took my face in his hands. When his lips touched mine, I closed my eyes, feeling snow on my lashes.

"Next *week*? Fat chance. You'll never get away with it." Mr. Salter's voice bled through the closed door.

"Watch me." Mr. Wolfe's voice boomed so loud I swear I saw the glass window shake.

I broke away from Jonah and opened the door to the store.

Inside, the air sizzled with tension as the two men stood inches apart, glaring at each other.

"I have half this town on my side," Mr. Salter growled. "And I can get the other half like that." He snapped his fingers like a whip crack.

Jonah leaned into me. "What the hell is going on?"

"He's mad about the power plant," I murmured.

"I'd like to see you try," Mr. Wolfe said.

I froze. The effortless threat in his voice sent chills running up and down my spine.

"We at the Guild have a way of getting what we want." He strode to the counter, plunked down two twenties, and seized his shovel. "Come on, Jonah."

Jonah rolled his eyes and grabbed my hand before he followed his dad out. "Call you later."

"This ain't over, Wolfe," Mr. Salter shouted just as the door swung shut with such force the bell clanged violently. "It ain't even begun!"

I watched the SUV back away, the tires spinning on the slippery surface of the road, before rounding on Mr. Salter. "What were you thinking?"

"I'm thinking someone has to stand up to them." Mr. Salter pushed past me and flipped the Open sign to Closed.

"Yeah, my mom did that, and our barn burned down." I tagged close behind Mr. Salter as he crossed the store and moved behind the counter. "These people are serious. You can't throw threats around like that."

Mr. Salter banged the register open and snatched the cash from the drawer. "And you're dating his son? What are you thinking?"

"Jonah is not the enemy." I pressed my palms flat on the counter. "His dad is."

Mr. Salter locked the register. "Like father, like son."

He tucked a stack of papers into a bag and turned off the lights in the store.

"Jonah is nothing like his father." I followed him out the back door to his truck. "You have no idea how not like his father he is."

We climbed into the cab of the truck. Mr. Salter slid the key into the ignition. I placed my hand on the steering wheel. He stopped and looked at me. "Mr. Salter, if I really thought Jonah had anything to do with the Guild's plan to build a power plant next to my house or the fire in our barn, I would stop seeing him. Immediately. Come on. Give me some credit."

Mr. Salter sighed. "You're right. I'm sorry." He turned the key, and the truck rumbled awake. "Just be careful, okay?"

"Okay," I said, facing forward as Mr. Salter threw the clutch in reverse and backed away from the building. I stared through the windshield at the snow-covered street. "But I know what I'm doing." The lie tasted sour on my tongue.

"I'm sure you do," Mr. Salter said quickly.

We pulled into the street, driving slowly in the deepening snow.

Something niggled at me. "What did you mean when you said, 'next week' to Mr. Wolfe?" I asked.

"That's when they're planning on breaking ground on the plant." He clenched his jaw. "Hopefully this snow will hold them up."

I clutched the door handle tight. The heat was on full blast in the truck, but I felt unbearably cold. Next *week*? No, the snow wouldn't hold them up. The only thing that would stop them was if the Benandanti retook control of the Waterfall and raised our own magical barrier to keep them out. Where the hell was the *Concilio Celeste* with their go-ahead?

We turned into the farm's long driveway. I took a deep breath. The *Concilio* had to know what they were doing—that was why they were on the council, right? They had to be preparing to send us into battle again any day now. Still, they were cutting it close.

The black roof of the house was white with snow. Light glowed through the windows of the house, reminding me of candlelight on a deep winter's night. Mr. Salter rolled the truck to a stop. When I jumped out, the snow came up to my shins. It was coming down harder now. Heads bent against the wind, we bustled to the front door.

A fire burned in the hearth in the living room. The scent of Lidia's homemade sauce, mixed with the sweeter smell of melting chocolate, wafted from the kitchen. "Hello?" I called out.

Lidia appeared in the doorway to the kitchen. "Oh, good—I was getting worried," She came forward to take my coat as I shrugged it off. She shook snow onto the floor, where it melted instantly to form a small puddle on the hardwood. "You'll stay for dinner of course," she said to Mr. Salter as she hung both our coats on the pegs by the front door.

"Fine. You talked me into it." He laughed.

We followed her into the kitchen. I pulled up short when I saw Heath at the table, his hands wrapped around a steaming mug.

"It's like a snow party," Mr. Salter said, putting out his hand.

Heath shook it with a smile. "I was still working out back when the snow started. Couldn't pass up Lidia's offer of hot chocolate, could I?"

"No sirree," Mr. Salter said and accepted a mug from Lidia as well.

We sank into the overstuffed couch and armchairs in the living room, a perfect New England picture on a snowy afternoon. If only I felt that calm on the inside. I wished I could tell Heath about the Guild's plan, but there was no way to get him alone without raising suspicion.

I sipped my cocoa and let its sweetness distract me. Outside, the snow clung to the trees in the front yard. A crow picked its way from branch to branch, its glossy black figure a stark contrast against the crystalline snow. I imagined being a Falcon right now, hunting under the snowdrifts for a morsel to eat, searching for a cozy tree hollow to take my rest.

A knock on the front door made us all jump.

"Who on earth can that be in this weather?" Lidia said. She set her mug down on the coffee table and got to her feet.

A blast of snow and cold air swirled into the house when she opened the door. Jonah stood framed by the door, his dark hair lightened with snowflakes, his long coat drenched so that it molded to his form.

I nearly dropped my mug and bounded to my shocked mother's side. "Jonah, what are you doing here?"

"I came to see you," he said and glanced at Lidia. "I hope that's okay?"

My mother came to life with a shake. "Did you walk here? Come in. Come in. You must be freezing."

"Thanks." Jonah stepped inside. His coat dripped on the floor, and he peeled himself out of it.

"I'll hang it in the kitchen." Lidia took it from him. "Can I get you some hot chocolate? You look like you could use it."

"I'd love some," Jonah said and looked down at me when she walked away, his eyes dancing and glittering with mischief.

I raised my eyebrows and stared at him, shaking my head slightly. Part of me wanted to know what he was up to, but most of me didn't care; I was happy just to see him. I slid my hand into his, wincing a little at his chilly skin, and led him to the spot on the couch that was closest to the fire. Being with Jonah was enough to put all my worries about the power plant out of my head.

I could feel Heath watching me, but I ignored him.

Lidia came back with a mug for Jonah, and we all sat in an awkward silence that Jonah seemed oblivious to as he grinned at me.

"So, Ed, what were you saying? About the mayor?" Lidia asked. The conversation sparked again.

I tucked an arm through Jonah's, snuggled up to his side, and rested my head against his shoulder.

Jonah stayed for dinner, and by the time we had gorged ourselves on my mother's homemade meatballs, the snow had risen to the windowsills outside.

Lidia peered out the windows at the dark storm and turned to Jonah and Mr. Salter with a sigh. "You two will have to stay the night. No way you can go out in this." She lifted the phone off the receiver and handed it to Jonah. "Tell your mom I'll take good care of you."

I watched carefully as Jonah dialed a seven-digit number and had a one-sided conversation with a closed pizza parlor. "Sure, Mom. I'll call first thing in the morning." He glanced over at Lidia. "Love you too. Good night."

Lidia nodded approvingly and turned to Heath. "I don't think you'll even make it over the hillside. You should stay here too."

"It's a slumber party," Mr. Salter said.

"Great. We can braid each other's hair and get into a pillow fight," Jonah said.

Lidia scowled at him and put me to work on the sleeping arrangements. Jonah would get the big extra bedroom over the garage, Mr. Salter would take the guest room in between my room and my mother's, and Heath would take the pullout in the living room.

It wasn't lost on me that Lidia put Jonah in the room farthest from mine.

We scurried back and forth making up beds, and when I passed Jonah in the hall I leaned in close. "You planned this, didn't you?"

His only answer was a grin that matched the devilishness in his eyes.

I pressed my face to the window in the upstairs hallway and peered out into the darkness. The light from inside the house reflected onto the snow outside. Drifts nearly buried the fence that ringed the hillside and covered Mr. Salter's truck in the driveway. We were well and truly snowed in.

Lidia banked the fire in the living room, and we retired to our respective beds. I stood in the middle of my room, staring at my neatly made bed. I knew I should be a good girl and get under the covers, but Jonah was down the hall, twenty feet away. How could I be expected to behave under such conditions?

I glanced out the window. There was something romantic about a snowstorm, I had to admit. I pulled the quilt half off my bed and messed up the sheets, so it looked like I had been under them. Then I listened to the sounds of the household. My mother's door closed, and the bedsprings of her old four-poster creaked. Downstairs, the shuffling in the living room quieted. I cracked my door open.

Darkness covered the house. I stepped into the hall,

careful to pick my way over the creaky floorboards. On tiptoe, I rounded the corner to the room over the garage and laid my hand flat against the door. My heart beat fast. Was I really doing this? I pressed my fingers to my throat and felt the flutter there. Every nerve in my body was alight, every hair on my skin on end. I could feel Jonah on the other side of the door, his presence burning my hand that lay on the piece of wood that separated us.

I slid into the room and closed the door behind me, let my eyes adjust to the moonlit darkness.

Jonah sat up in bed, facing me. "I was hoping you'd come, but I would have understood if you hadn't."

"Why wouldn't I have come?" I asked.

He lifted the covers, and I climbed underneath them. We curled into each other under the quilts, and the world outside fell away. We had made our own private world where no one—not the Benandanti or the Malandanti, the Guild or our parents—could come in. I wanted to live here forever in this moment, safe inside Jonah's arms.

We kissed until we both lost our breath.

I pressed my face into the side of his neck and felt his pulse against my cheek. "Your heart is racing," I whispered.

He touched the skin over my heart. "So is yours."

I raised my head and looked into his eyes. "My heart always races when I'm with you."

He slid his hand to the back of my neck and pulled me into a kiss, his lips fierce and possessive. "You are my heart," he murmured into my mouth. "I love you, Alessia."

My mind whirled; I clung to him to steady myself. He loved me . . . Jonah loved me . . . My throat tightened and my eyes felt hot. I blinked to keep tears from coming to the surface. I didn't want to be a sap, crying the first time a boy told me he loved me. Swallowing hard, I pulled back from him a fraction of an inch. "I love you too," I said, my lips grazing his.

We fell into each other. My body felt boneless with relief and joy; we were on the same page, both of us in just as deep as the other. For a moment I forgot everything else as he kissed me, and the world disappeared around us.

But too soon a hot thread of guilt and fear snaked its way from my belly and wrapped itself around my chest. How could I tell Jonah that I loved him and not tell him who I really was? As long as I kept my secret from him, there would always be a barrier between us. I didn't want those walls. I wanted to be his, free and clear and honest.

I broke the kiss and ducked my head, pressed my face into his naked chest. "I have to tell you something," I said, then clamped my mouth shut. *You must not speak of the Benandanti.* How could I betray that? And yet, how could I not, and betray Jonah by not telling him?

Jonah stroked my back. "What is it?"

Tears leaked out of my eyes, and I tried to wipe them away without Jonah noticing.

He lifted my chin. "What's wrong?"

I peered into his eyes, shining in the darkness. "There's something I want to tell you." I swallowed, and it felt like knives in my gullet. "But I can't. I can't."

"Why not?" He held my wrists and tugged me upward so that we were both sitting up, facing each other on the bed. "I told you about the accident, and you didn't freak out. Don't you think I'd do the same for you?" He ran his hands up and down my arms. "I love you. You can tell me anything. *Anything.*"

I touched his face. "Okay." I sighed with relief, and the sigh reached into every corner of my body, churned within me, and centered itself over my heart.

An instant later, a familiar tug pulled at me, and I knew the *Concilio Celeste* had finally given the go-ahead. "No," I whispered and scrambled backward toward the edge of the bed. "No, no, no, no!"

"What is it?" Jonah stared at me, his eyes bright with alarm.

I clutched the locket that dangled between my breasts, trying to dispel the stretching, aching feeling that was pulling me apart.

"What's wrong?"

I struggled to speak, but all that came out were gasps of air. I fought the shift, and it fought me back, iron bands around my body as I shook and fell to my knees. At last I managed to gasp, "Open the window," before I collapsed on the floor and soared up into the air in one singular, fluid motion.

# Chapter Twenty-four
*The Battle*

The look on Jonah's face as I rose toward the ceiling, my wings beating against the air, squeezed my heart so tight that I thought I would break apart in a thousand pieces. I wheeled in the air toward the window and hovered in front of it, turned my head to Jonah, and cried out softly.

Like he was unaware of his movements, Jonah climbed out of bed and walked to the window, his jaw hanging loose, his eyes wide and fixed on me. He unlatched the window and wrenched it upward. The frame crackled with the cold, and ice broke away as it opened. Snow dusted the floor. Jonah backed away from the window, still staring at me with shock etched on his features. His eyes held every emotion that I never wanted to see there—horror, disbelief, disgust. I plunged out the window.

Why, why, why? Why did it have to be tonight? My human mind sobbed inside my Falcon body. I wavered in the air, my feathers rustling in anger and frustration. Why did Jonah have to see me like this? *If you had told him, you would have had to show him*, a quiet, rational voice inside me said, but I brushed it aside. That would have been on my own terms, not against my will like what had just happened.

I opened my mind and sought out Heath. *Why tonight?* I felt him recoil with the force of my thoughts.

*You know why.*

*I was in bed with Jonah! He saw me transform!*

Heath shut his thoughts off, leaving me terribly alone.

I whirled in the air, scanning the snow-covered ground below for the other Benandanti. Shimmering blue figures moved in between the white trees. I pitched toward them, weaving in and out of the icicle-laden branches. I tuned out their chatter as I listened for Heath to come back to me.

At last, he did. *I warned you, Alessia. I said you had to make a choice, but no, you thought you could have it all. And now look what's happened.*

*Screw you,* I screamed in my mind and out loud, a piercing cry across the night sky. *I love him. And now he'll hate me forever.*

There was a pause in which I could hear both our minds heaving into calm.

Finally, Heath said, *You don't know that. He might very well accept this. There's always hope.*

I turned the idea of hope over in my mind. The look on Jonah's face when he opened the window . . . I closed my eyes and flew blind until I could sense the other Benandanti near me.

*But right now,* Heath said, *the mission—*

*—is what matters,* I finished for him, then alighted on a branch. I hopped the length of the branch for a moment, my feathers brushing the snow off its surface as I moved restlessly along it. I knew I had to compartmentalize, but I couldn't focus. Emotions collided inside me, making it impossible for me to stay still. I fluttered my wings in the air and took off again.

I leveled off at the treetops. *Concentrate on the task at hand,* I told myself. I tried to shut my mind off to what had happened, but images crept back in. The way the moonlight shone on Jonah's skin, the light in his eyes as he lowered his head to kiss me. The look on his face as he watched me soar out into the night. I rose in the air, my aura flickering as if I could shake that last image out of my brain, but it remained there, frozen in time forever.

On the ground below, Heath called to me. I opened my mind to him. *Are you okay?*

*No. What a stupid question.*

I felt him sigh. *I know. I know you're not okay. But can we count on you?*

*Isn't that why I'm here instead of back home with Jonah?*

*You're right. I'm sorry. I just need to know that, in the midst of battle, you won't go AWOL on me.*

I didn't answer. The truth was, I didn't know that I wouldn't go AWOL. My frame of mind felt so fragile that I just wasn't sure. *Is the Clan meeting first?*

*At the birch trees. You remember the plan?*

*Yes.* I veered toward the Waterfall and rounded the copse of birch trees, their thin white trunks glistening in the moonlight. The whole forest was white and black and grey, shadows and cold light.

One by one, the Clan gathered on the ground, and the Eagle arrived from the east.

Just outside the copse, the bushes rustled violently, and the Stag crashed into view, a dark ribbon of blood streaming down his neck. *They know we're here.*

In that instant, I opened a channel to Heath alone. *You can count on me,* I told him. *Never doubt that.*

He didn't have time to reply. With a great roar, the Malandanti burst out of hiding. In one frightening, maddening moment, the two armies clashed, body to body, jaws snapping, rumbling growls echoing through the forest. For a moment I watched the battle from outside myself, paralyzed in the air. And then the human part of my brain surrendered, and the Falcon took over.

Without the element of surprise, our entire plan was thrown out of whack. But I knew my part. Inside the barrier, the Raven was on duty, circling the pool. I dipped low and skimmed the water to the top of the Waterfall. Before any of the Malandanti could see what I was doing, I plunged into the water and let the current take me over the edge. I felt the air change and soared out of the water, droplets shedding from my feathers.

I was inside the barrier.

The Raven dropped several feet in the air, its aura flickering with shock.

The memory of chasing it over my farm seared my brain. I swerved and met the Raven head-on, my beak at its throat. Blood glistened on its feathers. Screaming, the Raven vaulted away from me. I chased after it and caught one wing in my talons. It fought back, trying to reach me with its beak, but I thrashed in the air, too quick for the weakened attack. I squeezed my talons harder and harder until I felt the delicate wing bones snap.

The Raven cried out, the harsh sound rippling over the water. I let go and the bird fell, vainly trying to keep aloft with one wing. I plummeted and caught the healthy wing. The Raven whimpered as though it knew what I was going to do.

I broke its other wing and clutched the crippled bird tight in my talons. It twisted in my grip, but I held fast. I mounted the air, climbing up the Waterfall toward the hidden opening in the barrier. The water was icy cold on my feathers as I dove in, dragging the Raven with me.

The instant I emerged from the water with the Raven, the glittering light of the barrier went out. The Malandanti froze in surprise, and in the moment it took them to recover, the Benandanti rushed to the Waterfall. I set the Raven down in the snow and followed. But before I could reach my Clan, something sprang out of the water and blocked me.

I halted in midair, my whole body shaking. The Panther's green eyes pierced through me. Was Bree behind those eyes? Screeching, I plummeted, talons outstretched, but it dodged to the side, avoiding my strike.

*Leave it,* Heath shouted at me. *Get down here before—*

I was too late. The other Malandanti had already made their way down the Waterfall. With a cry, I faced the Panther and dove with impossible speed. I didn't just want it out of my way; I wanted it out of commission. I slammed into its side, knocking it back into the water. It roared in pain and sprang up. Those green eyes never left me.

The Panther crouched, its black fur sleek and dripping with water. The wind sang through my feathers as I shot toward it. But instead of combating me, it pounced to the side. I tumbled off-balance, unable to control my speed.

*I said, leave it!* It wasn't just Heath guiding me; it was an order. I tore my attention away from the Panther and soared over the Waterfall. Down below, the Malandanti were fighting to stay in control, but they were outnumbered.

*She's here,* Heath told the rest of the Clan as I leveled off. *We have to get the entire Clan here to complete the magic—*

*But the Malandanti—*

*They're missing two so it will work.*

In the corner of my wide vision, I spotted the two in question. The Panther bounded down the rocks, holding the flightless Raven in its mouth. If they reached the rest of their Clan, we wouldn't be able to enforce our magic. *Hurry, hurry!*

Heath raised his head and howled, the sound echoing into the sky. A stream of brilliant blue light snaked through the trees and danced above the water. It seemed to be made of a million perfect stars. It was the magic of the Benandanti, wrought by the *Concilio Celeste*. The Stag had told us what would happen, but I didn't know it would be so beautiful.

The Malandanti Bobcat yowled, but its Clan mates were blinded by the magic. Just as the Panther reached the bottom of the Waterfall, the entire world turned blue, the light shimmering over the whole forest. I felt the earth shudder all around me. The Malandanti inside the barrier were all blown back. The light cleared, leaving a ring around the Waterfall. The magical barrier now glowed with the celestial aura of the Benandanti, like a prism caught by the sun.

The forest fell quiet and still. The water below me was smooth and clear, all the murkiness gone. And the trailer had disappeared, a blossoming willow tree restored in its place.

Outside the barrier, the Malandanti Bobcat growled and pawed the ground. It rammed the barrier, which flickered upon impact. The Bobcat fell back, shaking with the jolt.

*Ladies and gentlemen*, the Stag said, *the Waterfall is ours.*

I closed my eyes and let the sweetness of victory flood me. The jubilation of the Clan filled my head. For a moment, all my despair about Jonah was replaced with joy and relief. I wanted to stay in that moment with my Clan. But all too soon, the celebration sobered.

*They'll be back*, the Stag reminded us. *Maintaining*

*control will be a constant battle.*

*I'll take first watch*, the Lynx said.

*So will I*, replied the Stag. *We should keep two of us on patrol at all times now. The rest of you, take care. We'll meet again soon.*

Heath splashed out of the water, and the Eagle disappeared past the treetops. I spent a long time getting home, flying in circles as I tried not to think about what waited for me there. Exhaustion weighted down my wings, and I finally turned toward the farm. The snow on the hillside glistened as the sky lightened toward dawn. I skimmed the ground, every beat of my wings an enormous effort. With the last of my strength, I flew through the garage room window.

My body lay on the floor in the same place where I had collapsed. I dissolved into it and sat up, gulping in lungfuls of air. I grasped the edge of the bed and hauled myself into it, pulled the covers up to my chin, and let the blood steal back into my body.

It took me a moment to realize the bed was empty. I glanced around the room until I saw him, sitting in the far corner with his knees pulled up to his chin. His eyes gleamed in the semidarkness of the room. He was watching me. "Jonah?"

"Don't." Fear and horror resonated in his voice.

I clutched the quilt. Wind swept in the still-open window, scattering snowflakes and shuffling papers on the desk in the corner. I slid out of bed and crossed to the window. The icy breeze cut my skin. I closed the window and turned, then leaned against the sill and looked at Jonah in the corner. He followed my every move, shifting slightly away from me when I knelt on the floor in front of him. I didn't dare touch him.

"Please," I said. "Please let me explain."

"Explain?" He burst out laughing, an angry sound that hurt my ears. "Explain? Alessia." He grabbed my arms, his fingers digging deep into my flesh. The silver bracelet on his wrist flashed in the moonlight. *You just turned into a falcon in front of me.* And you want to explain?"

I struggled against his grip, but he held me fast, his eyes like knifepoints on my face. "You told me about the car accident, and I forgave you. Please just let me tell you—what I am, what I can do—and you'll understand. You'll forgive me too."

Jonah let go of me with such force that I tumbled backward, caught myself on my hands.

He got to his feet and towered over me, his whole body dappled in grey light and shadow. "That's right—I told you about the car accident. And the whole time you were keeping this huge secret from me—about who—about *what*—you are." He shrank away from me and crossed to the closet where his clothes hung on the door. His back was stiff and his shoulders tense as he pulled his jeans and sweater on.

I fought for breath, but my lungs had shrunk to half

their size. I scrambled to my feet and dashed to him, tugged on his arm so he half faced me. "Jonah, please! Please." My voice was an octave higher than normal. I slid my hand down to his wrist. His skin was ice-cold, and my fingers trembled as I tried to hold on to him. "It isn't my fault. I can't help what I am," I whispered.

"Yes, you can," Jonah said. He shook my hand off him and backed away, his face turned so I couldn't see his eyes. At the door he paused, his hand on the knob. "There's always a choice," he said softly and left the room.

# Chapter Twenty-five

*The Mirrored Compact*

Frozen to the floor, I watched Jonah leave. I felt like someone had punched a hole in my gut, reached inside, and twisted everything into a bloody mess. His footsteps thudded on the stairs. The creak of the old wood uprooted me. I ran out to the landing. "Jonah!"

He pulled his coat from its peg by the door. "Just leave me alone."

"No!" I galloped down the stairs, too late forgetting that Heath was sleeping in the living room. He sat up, wide awake. I raised a hand to stop him from interrupting and grabbed Jonah's coat. "Just talk to me. We can work this out."

Jonah wrenched the coat away from me and shoved his arms into the sleeves. "I don't think we can."

A sob escaped my throat. "I thought you loved me."

"I did," Jonah whispered, "when I thought I knew who you were."

I reached blindly for him but only found air. He opened the door, and a blast of cold wind rushed inside.

The sun glinted off the snow, blurring my vision. Jonah plowed his way through the snow that hid the front steps. Another wintry gust blew the door shut behind him.

The click of the latch echoed in my brain. I pressed my hands to my head to make it stop. Everything around me went into soft focus; all I could see was Jonah's back, his dark coat in sharp contrast to the glittering white snow. This was not happening. It simply was not happening. The reality was slippery in my mind, just out of my grasp.

Strong, warm hands gripped my shoulders. "It'll be okay," said Heath. "Just give him some time."

"Let go of me!" I pushed him away, and he stumbled back, catching himself on the coffee table. "This is all your fault!"

"Alessia," Heath said, "you know that's not true."

The patronizing tone in his voice caused something to snap inside me. "If you hadn't come here—if you all had your act together and had never lost control of the Waterfall, this wouldn't be happening."

"But we did lose control, you were Called, and you said yes." Heath's tone had hardened. He stared me down. "If you couldn't handle it, then you should have refused the Call."

"I didn't know how much would be asked of me." I brushed tears out of my eyes. "You lied—"

"I never lied—"

"—and now I've lost everything!" I was shaking.

Heath softened and reached his hand out to me. "You haven't lost everything. You still have the Benandanti."

"Fuck the Benandanti," I yelled, hitting his hand away from me.

"What's going on?"

We both looked up. Lidia stood at the railing at the top of the stairs.

Heath ducked his head and sat on the pullout bed.

I glared at him, at his silence, and answered my mother. "Jonah just broke up with me." I stomped into the kitchen and put on my snow boots that sat by the door. Overhead I heard the stairs creak, and a moment later Lidia came into the kitchen.

"*Cara*—"

"Don't." I grabbed my coat and threw the door open. A huge drift of snow greeted me outside.

"Alessia, it's too cold out." Lidia gave me a small smile. "Why don't I make some hot chocolate, and we'll talk?"

I paused in the doorway. "Mom, this is something that hot chocolate can't fix."

Her eyes widened with hurt.

I turned my back on her and climbed on top of the snowdrift. It was hard and icy and didn't give much under my weight. I trudged through the snow, crawled when I had to, and fought my way from the house toward the hillside. A few times I looked back, but no one followed me. I saw again that look of hurt on Lidia's face. A red-hot ribbon of shame tied itself into a knot in my stomach.

The effort of getting through the snow took all my concentration, and I welcomed the distraction. Soon I was sweating under the heavy coat. The hillside loomed in front of me. If things were normal, I would be sledding down the hill right now. I swallowed hard and dug the heels of my hands into my eyes until I saw spots.

I rounded the hill and came to the Virgin Mary shrine. Her head and shoulders were piled high with snow. She looked like she was wearing a mantilla. I stared at her face. Her downcast eyes were fixed on her praying hands. I had never noticed before how sad she looked. I fell to my knees before her and pressed my hands against her base, the cold stone stinging my bare palms. "Why?" I asked her. "Why did you choose me? Why do I have to be extraordinary? Why can't I just be normal like everyone else?"

She was silent, her head bowed under the weight of the world.

I whirled away and pounded over the snow to the far side of the hill. I stopped in front of the door to the Cave. Snow had piled up on the overhang, but the doorway was clear. I tugged the door open.

Inside, the air was cool and damp but close and snug. I swung the door shut and breathed in deep. It smelled like milk and butter, like goats and grass, like all the scents that surrounded my life, like days of innocence and joy. It smelled like my childhood before my dad had died. As I thought of him, my throat tightened.

Would all this be happening if he were still alive?

I sank down to the floor, crawled under the big table, and curled up on my side. I let everything inside me spill onto the wide-planked floor. I cried until I was sure there was nothing left to cry about, and then I cried some more, and then my tears dried up and I lay in the fetal position, heaving.

Blood pounded in my ears, and my head ached. I sat up and wrapped my arms around my knees. Sniffling, I rested my cheek on my knees. All I could see in my mind's eye was Jonah's expression when he saw me transform. The grief of losing him overwhelmed me. Before I knew it, I was crying again.

I don't know how much time passed that I spent curled beneath the table, alternating between crying and thinking and crying again. It might have been fifteen minutes or three hours. But when the door creaked open, sunlight beamed into the room. "I want to be alone," I croaked, not even raising my head to see who it was.

"I know." The door closed, and I watched Lidia's feet shuffle toward the table. She crouched down. "But I thought you might be hungry."

Despite myself, I laughed. Typically Italian. Sniffling, I sat up.

Lidia crawled under the table with me and set a thermos and a plate of fresh homemade doughnuts in between us.

I unscrewed the lid of the thermos. "Hot chocolate and doughnuts."

"When you were a little girl, this always made you feel better."

I looked down at my lap, my brow furrowed. "I'm not a little girl anymore."

She made a noise, like a choked sob. I looked up at her. She brushed a stray hair away from my face, her fingers soft on my skin. "Oh, *cara*. You will always be my little girl."

"No. You have to let go. You can't protect me from everything anymore."

Lidia swallowed, her fingertips suddenly cold on my cheek. "I know that, Alessia," she whispered.

I stilled, watching as she dropped her hand and picked up a doughnut. She knew something; I was certain of it. I opened my mouth to say the forbidden truth, but Heath's voice was in my head. *You must not speak of the Benandanti.* More than that, it could put her in danger. Weeks ago Heath had warned me, and now I realized he had been able to see ahead. Unlike me. I touched her hand. "Thanks, Mom. For the doughnuts."

She squeezed my fingers. "Do you want me to stay with you?"

I shook my head. "I think I need to be alone."

Lidia slid out from under the table and was just about to pull herself up when she paused. "I'm sorry about Jonah."

"No, you're not. You don't like him."

She rolled her eyes heavenward. "He wouldn't have

been my first choice for you, but I know how much you care for him."

"Well, you can be happy now because it looks like he's never going to talk to me again," I said.

Lidia shrugged one shoulder. "You teenagers are so *caparbio*—so willful. Tempestuous. He'll come around."

My throat felt tight. "I don't think so."

After a long moment, she sighed. "*Ti amo, cara mia.* Don't ever forget that." Her footsteps padded away on the concrete floor, and the door closed heavily. I was alone again.

The silence in the Cave wrapped itself around me. I closed my eyes, listening to my heartbeat. Underneath its thump-thump, another sound came, so quiet at first that I couldn't tell what it was. It grew louder and louder, from a low growl into a roar . . .

My eyes flew open. The Panther crept toward me under the table, its belly slung low to the floor. I scrambled backward, cold sweat prickling my forehead. The Cave door was still closed. How had it gotten inside?

The Panther's jewel-bright eyes bored a hole in me. I froze, losing myself in their forest-green depths. Again I wondered if Bree was behind them, taunting me, daring me to fight back . . .

*Fight.* I pushed myself up to my knees and pressed a hand over my heart, willing myself to transform. But my body would not cooperate, and no matter how hard I thought of my Falcon form, the shift would not come.

The Panther swiped its paw at me, its razor-sharp claws missing my throat by less than an inch. I jumped up and ran to the door, but the Panther was there in less than a breath, blocking my path. It reared up on its hind legs and flung itself on me, its paws gripping me . . . almost like an embrace . . . I screamed and jerked away.

I was on the floor under the table, curled up in the same position I'd been in earlier. The Cave was silent. The Panther was gone. I blinked, trying to calm my racing heart.

What had happened? It was just like that vision I had had so long ago, before I knew what the Waterfall truly was. But I hadn't touched the water . . .

Throat dry, I clambered out from the table. I *had* touched the water. In the battle last night. And I wasn't the only one.

I opened the door and stumbled through the snow toward Heath's cabin. Halfway over the hillside I met him.

He wasn't wearing a coat, and his face was pale as the snow beneath our feet. "I didn't know they'd be that real," he choked out. His blue eyes swam, and he shivered, hugging himself.

I stared at him. What had he seen? I was dying to know, but it suddenly seemed much too personal of a question to ask. "Yeah," I said finally. "That's what they're like."

We stood on the hillside, not saying anything, until Heath shook himself and looked at me. "Are you back to the land of the living now?"

I snorted. "Did I ever really leave?"

Heath rubbed his arms to warm himself. His eyes looked faraway, like he was lost in the memory of his vision.

I opened my mouth to tell him about what I had seen, then clamped my lips together. I didn't need to tell him. I knew what the vision meant. The Panther—the first Malandanti I had ever seen and the one that somehow kept getting in my way—was someone I knew. And I had a very strong inkling of who that was.

School was cancelled Monday because of the snow. On Tuesday I went to French class on pins and needles, my gaze on the door until the bell rang. But Jonah never showed up. Thursday morning I overheard (okay, I eavesdropped at his office door) Principal Morrissey on the phone with Mrs. Wolfe, suspending Jonah for a week for ditching. I knew he'd catch hell from his dad, but I was relieved I wouldn't have to deal with seeing him for several days, and then it would be Christmas break.

The girls fortressed around me, plying me with chocolate and you're-better-than-him platitudes. I was vague about the reasons for the breakup, and they didn't push me. It was a relief to be with them, rather than at home where the atmosphere was thick with anxiety. Lidia and I kept our conversations to small talk, and whenever she wasn't cooking she was at the kitchen table with a calculator and a spreadsheet of the household finances.

"I'm sure Mr. Salter will give me some more hours at the store," I said, sitting next to her with a cup of post-dinner coffee in my hands. "I can do evenings and weekends."

"No, I don't want you to neglect your schoolwork." Lidia put her hand on mine. "We'll be fine. We'll figure this out. We always do."

I was thankful for her optimism, but the next morning on my way to school, I went to talk to Mr. Salter anyway. But when I got to his store, it was shut and locked up tight. I stared at the Closed sign on the door for several minutes. The only other time I'd ever seen his shop closed was the day of his wife's funeral. Maybe he'd gone away? I'd have to ask Lidia if she knew anything.

Jenny joined me on the sidewalk, and we huddled together as we passed Joe's with its usual early-morning crowd.

Pratt Webster sat alone at a table against the huge plate-glass window, a half-empty cup of steaming coffee in front of him. Wincing, he flexed his fingers and picked up his BlackBerry, grimacing as he jabbed at the keyboard.

My nostrils flared, and my breath felt like jagged glass in my lungs. I hadn't seen him since the day he had said he would "handle" my mother, and twenty-four hours later our barn had burned down.

I turned away from Jenny, heading for the coffee shop, but she caught my elbow. "What are you doing?

The first bell is in like five minutes."

Taking a deep breath of cold morning air, I let her drag me across the street toward school, glancing over my shoulder at Pratt. He was in the thick of it all, I knew that for sure, but as with Bree, I couldn't prove anything.

"Josh Baker is having a party at his house tonight," Jenny said as we jogged up the steps to school. "His parents are out of town."

"But we hate Josh Baker."

"So what? There'll be so many people there we won't even see him." She nudged me with her elbow. "It might cheer you up. We'll go together, and if it's lame we'll go get a pizza. Okay?"

"Yeah, maybe." It *was* my off night from patrolling. I waved good-bye to Jenny as she went to first period and stood in the middle of the lobby. I was supposed to work in the office, but my exhaustion from patrol ruled that out. I headed for the auditorium to catch up on some sleep.

The auditorium was warm and quiet. I made a little nest in one of the alcoves with my coat and was drifting off to sleep when one of the heavy doors banged open. I lay still, hoping whoever it was would just pass through, but then I heard giggling, followed by a bag hitting the floor.

"Shhhh," hissed a deeper voice. The distinct sound of kissing took over.

I squeezed my eyes shut and tried to ignore it.

"Come on," murmured the deep voice, and footsteps neared my alcove.

I sat up as Josh and Bree tumbled into view. Her shirt was askew, her hair a mess. Josh had lipstick on his neck. I crossed my arms. "Hi."

"Guess this spot is taken," Josh said, tugging Bree away.

She didn't budge. "I thought Goody Two-Shoes worked in the office first period."

"Not today," I said.

"Come *on*," Josh said again, pushing her shirt up to touch her bare skin. "I bet the music room's empty."

Bree let him drag her away a few feet before glancing back at me. "I'll tell Jonah you said hi."

Josh pulled her against him. She shrieked with laughter as he lifted her and carried her away, her legs wrapped around his waist.

My face burned. There was no way I was going to get any sleep after that encounter. I grabbed my coat and headed toward the door. Halfway up the aisle Bree's bag lay on the floor, its contents spilled on the moss-green carpet. I stepped over them. Something glinted and caught my eye. Crouching down, I saw it was a silver compact, its catch sprung open. The mirror side reflected off the lights, but the other side wasn't filled with powder or blush or lip gloss.

It was filled with a leathery dried-up piece of skin.

# CHAPTER TWENTY-SIX

*The Suspect*

The minute I got home, I went to find Heath.

"He's gone to Bangor to meet with some vendors," Lidia told me. She set a plate of cookies out for me, but I was too jumpy to eat. "By the way, are you going to Josh's party?"

I stared at her. "What? How do you know about that?"

"Barb told me. She came over this afternoon." Lidia took a cookie and sat at the kitchen table. She picked up a stack of bills. "I think you should go. It will help get your mind off things."

Things being Jonah. I was sure Lidia didn't know that Josh's parents were away; she wouldn't be so eager for me to go if she did. "Yeah, okay." It was better than sitting around here all night, watching Lidia pay bills we could barely afford while waiting for Heath to come home.

Jenny came over before the party and performed an impressive makeover. When I looked in the mirror, I barely recognized myself. She had completely covered up the dark circles. My eyes looked luminous against my pale skin.

We drove through town in Lidia's car. Josh lived at the end of a dirt lane surrounded by woods. Before we even saw the house we heard music pulsating up the driveway. I parked in between an oversized SUV and a snowdrift. Jenny and I held on to each other as we walked down the icy driveway, our shoes slipping on iced-over mud puddles.

Clouds of smoke—cigarette and otherwise—fogged up the front porch. I coughed as we made our way to the front door and inside the huge Aspen-style house. The foyer and stairs were crammed with kids. We sidled through the crowd to the kitchen.

"You want a drink?" Jenny yelled over the din, pointing to a large keg in the middle of the floor.

I shook my head.

She shrugged and grabbed a plastic cup from the counter. By the time it was full, she was in a lip-lock with Seth.

I wandered through the house, passing dimly lit rooms where shadows of kissing couples moved on the wall. A carpeted stairway led to the basement with a huge game room. Two guys from my English class were playing pool, half a dozen girls hanging on to the sides of the pool table, their skirts hiked up to their thighs.

A bunch of jocks and their bored girlfriends sat on deep leather couches, watching college football on a massive television. The jocks let out a roar in unison as an apparently amazing play went down. One of the girlfriends rolled her eyes and got up, revealing another figure that had sunken into the corner of the sofa. My heart skipped like a stone on the surface of water. It was Jonah.

He stared at the television screen as though he were blind, sipping from a cup of foam-tipped beer. I felt hot and cold all at once and unable to move, like an insect trapped in a block of amber. He glanced up, and our eyes met over the heads of the pool table girls.

I turned and fled up the stairs. A cluster of new arrivals blocked the front door, so I rocketed up to the second floor. On the landing I stopped and peered over the rail to see if Jonah had followed me. But the only people on the stairs were couples who couldn't find a private place to make out.

I went down the hall, deeper into the house. Half the upstairs rooms were locked, whether by Josh or by couples that had gotten first dibs on the bedrooms, I could only guess. In the middle of the hall a huge sunburst window looked out at the dark forest behind the house. I pressed my nose to the glass, my breath foggy. My heart was still jumpy. I had been so sure Jonah wouldn't be here, not with his suspension from school.

A soft light flickered on from the porch beneath the window. I peered down. Josh emerged onto the porch carrying two plastic cups. Bree followed him, her gait unbalanced. She swayed as she gulped down her drink.

I grasped the windowsill, remembering what Jonah had told me, about how Bree would look out for him at parties. Clearly, she had abandoned her post tonight. I gripped the windowsill harder, my knuckles white. What was she doing up here when her brother was one flight below, drinking for the first time since he'd maimed a girl in a drunken car crash?

Bree finished her drink and held out her cup to Josh, a lopsided smile on her face. Maybe she was trying to forget something too. Like how she had screwed up and lost control of the Waterfall for the Malandanti.

Josh ran his finger down her throat to her collarbone, took her cup, and disappeared into the house.

I stood frozen at the window, thoughts colliding in my head as I watched her collapse into an oversized lounge chair, her body limp and loose.

The synchronicity of events was too much to ignore. I whirled away from the window and galloped down the stairs, muttering apologies to everyone I bumped into along the way. Melissa tried to catch my sleeve as I ran through the kitchen, but I was too fast. I opened the sliding glass door and skidded to a stop on the porch. The cold air filled my lungs as I panted.

Josh had beaten me to the porch and sat on the chair next to Bree, trying to tug her shirt over her head.

"Hey!"

He looked up and smirked at me. "Really? This is getting a little old, Jacobs."

I stalked toward him. "Yeah, I'd say it is. You taking advantage of girls is getting really, really old."

Josh got to his feet with some difficulty; he seemed almost as drunk as Bree. "What are you going to do about it?" he slurred.

"Get out of my way." I brushed past him and bent over Bree.

She murmured something, her eyes half-closed.

"I'm taking her home." I hauled her up. She pushed at me a little but was coherent enough to stumble along with me as I supported her around the waist.

Josh watched us go, his body swaying on the spot.

"Sorry to spoil your fun."

I got Bree through the house and into the car before I thought of Jenny. She'll get a ride. Seth was here. And Jonah—*Jonah*—how long would he carry on his self-destructive one-man show before he realized Bree was gone? My chest started to ache, but I shut it down. *The mission is what matters*, I told myself and peeled the car backward out of the driveway.

Lidia was asleep on the couch, the television still on, when I got home. I stared at her for a moment, how her brow creased with worry even in her sleep. My throat tight, I turned away before the tears came.

I grabbed what I needed from the house and went back to the car to get Bree. The act of half carrying, half dragging her unconscious body across the farm to the Cave exhausted me. At the Virgin Mary shrine I had to stop and rest, panting to catch my breath. I avoided the Virgin Mary's damning eyes and hoisted Bree up again. I had no idea that kidnapping was such manual labor.

When I got inside the Cave, I sat her in the most cushioned chair I could find. I backed up a few feet until I hit the door and pressed myself against it, staring at Bree's limp form. *What if she's not what you think she is?* said the little voice of doubt inside me. "She is," I muttered. The caul in her mirrored compact proved it.

Several long minutes passed before Bree moved. Her eyes fluttered open. She scrunched her face up and glanced around at the tight, rounded interior of the Cave. "What the—?" Her eyes found me. She blinked rapidly, confusion distorting her features. "Alessia? What the hell?"

I crossed my arms. "I think we need to talk."

"And I think you need some serious therapy." She stood, wobbled on her unsteady feet, and sat back down.

Without a word, I handed her a bottle of water.

She downed half of it and stood up again. I moved out of her way as she reached the door and tried the handle.

My dad was a quirky guy. Although he could be the life of the party, he also loved his privacy something fierce. And so when he built the Cave, he fashioned the door to lock from both the outside and the inside. With a key. I held it up in front of Bree's face. "I said, we need to talk."

She sidled away from the door, her lips white with anger. "What are you playing at?"

"I think you know."

Bree threw the water bottle against the door. It cracked open, and water seeped out, staining the concrete floor. "You have got to be kidding. Is this about Jonah?"

The sound of his name was a knife through my middle. I took a deep breath and pressed my fist to my rib cage. "No," I managed to say. "This has nothing to do with him. This is between you and me. You know that."

She shook her head. "This is insane. It's called kidnapping."

"There are far worse crimes," I said. My voice wavered. "Like killing twenty-two innocent people."

Her eyes widened. "Killing—are you shitting me?"

"Stop acting innocent!" I slammed the table, sliding it an inch. "I know what you are."

Bree stalked toward me. "You don't know the first thing about me."

I took a step back as she came closer, then caught myself and held my ground. "Yes, I do. You know about the magic." I held up a finger. "That was my first clue."

"First clue to what?" Bree stopped. She braced herself between the table and the sink, blocking my path. "And how did *you* find out about the magic?"

I scooted around the other side of the table. "My second clue was the witchcraft book," I said, ignoring her questions. "Should've hidden it under your mattress."

"I *knew* you were snooping in my room. Who the hell do you think you are?"

"But still I wasn't sure," I went on. I dug into the back pocket of my jeans. "Until I found this," I said, tossing the mirrored compact onto the table.

Bree went still. "Where did you get that?" she whispered. Her face was mottled with rage as she swiped the compact off the table. "How dare you!"

"It fell out of your bag in the auditorium," I said. "Pretty careless of you. Don't you know a Malandante should never be without her caul?"

I watched her face closely. Her lips thinned, and her pupils dilated until her eyes were almost black. She swallowed hard, her breath so sharp that her nostrils flattened. "Malan-what?" she whispered, but I knew she was lying. She knew the word, and she was unable to hide her surprise that I did too.

I edged toward the door. "Don't play dumb. You know exactly what I'm talking about."

"No," she said through gritted teeth. Her voice was steadier now, but her eyes betrayed her fear. "No, I don't."

"You're lying." I reached behind my back and fumbled to unlock the door. "I didn't expect you to tell me the truth. But I know how to make you show me the truth." I opened the door a crack. Cold wind sighed into the Cave.

Bree dashed forward, but before she could reach the door, the familiar ache twisted my heart.

The force of the transformation blew me up against the low ceiling. My wings beat against the beams, aching for the endless height of the sky. Just below me, Bree stared upward, straining her neck as she twisted back and forth to look at my seemingly dead body on the floor and the Falcon that hovered just inches above her. Any minute now, she would become the Panther, and then we could fight for real, instead of skirmishing with words. Any minute now, any minute now . . .

I shot down to the table, catching myself on its edge, to observe her transformation at close range. But she remained human, staring at me with feral eyes.

Loose hair around her face fluttered with her quick, uneven breath. "Alessia, is that you?"

I let out a long screech. *Come on*, I thought at her. *Fight me. You know you want to.*

But Bree held an unbelieving expression. "Your aura, it's blue . . . You're the other side—the Benandanti—"

*Of course I am, stupid!* I wanted to shout. *What did you think this was all about?* I flew in a circle in front of her, the beat of my wings rustling her hair.

She followed my every movement, but still she did not transform.

I shot up to the ceiling, bumping my head with my out-of-control speed, dipped down and back up again. It was against the code of the Benandanti to attack Malandanti in their human form, but if I did, if I cut her just enough to make her angry, would she finally shift into the Panther? I pushed away from the ceiling, my talons reaching out toward Bree's pale skin . . .

The door to the Cave banged open.

I jolted in midair. The force of stopping tilted me sideways.

Jonah stood in the doorway, his tall form silhouetted by the dim light. He fixed his gaze on me, his green eyes sharp. "Leave her alone." His voice shook. "She's not the one you want." He slammed the door shut behind him.

"I am."

# Chapter Twenty-seven
*The Panther*

Before I could blink, Jonah's body lay on the floor, and the enormous ebony Panther appeared. His silver aura shimmered like mercury.

*No*, I thought. My body felt frozen. *No, it isn't true.* It couldn't be. I had found Bree's caul . . .

The chain-link bracelet Jonah always wore glinted on his lifeless wrist, the bracelet I had never seen him without. The bracelet containing his caul, just as his twin sister kept hers near at all times.

The Panther's green eyes glowed at me . . . Jonah's eyes.

In the space of a breath, the light of my aura went out, and I found myself back inside my human body. I gasped for air as I sat up, dizzy and nauseous from the rapid, unplanned transformation.

The Panther swung his head and slunk toward me, just like in the vision I had had in this very room . . .

Bree stepped in front of her brother. "Stop it. Just stop it right now. I can't take it anymore."

The light in the Cave flashed silver. When it cleared,

the Panther was gone. Jonah scrambled to his feet. "*You* can't take it anymore? What about me?"

I thought I might be sick. All this time, I had thought it was Bree, but instead it was the boy I loved. "I-I need to sit down." Bree moved aside to let me pass, but Jonah reached out to catch my arm as I stumbled toward a chair. "Don't touch me!"

"Well, this is quite a pickle." Bree's tone was sarcastic, but her fingers twisted behind her back, betraying her anxiety. "You two are a real-life Romeo and Juliet."

"Shut up, Bree." Jonah crouched down in front of me.

I held a hand up to keep him away and turned to Bree. "How did you know about the Malandanti?"

She tossed her hair back. "Because they came to me first. As if I wanted to waste what little social life I have on them."

I straightened. "You said no?"

"Yeah, I said no." She glanced at Jonah. "So they went after the next best thing."

"And you told her?" I tilted my head to Jonah, barely looking at him. "You're allowed to talk about it?"

"He didn't tell me." Bree held up her hand. "We're twins, and we were both born with the caul," she said, ticking down one finger. "Our father works for the Guild." She ticked down another. "And then that accident happened, and I knew he was ripe for the picking. It doesn't take a genius to put it all together." She looked me up and down. "Or maybe it does. Because you obviously didn't."

The wheels in my head whirred and clicked into place, like a watch being set to the right time. Deep inside, I knew she was right; I should have suspected Jonah all along, but I didn't want to. Even now, with the proof right in front of my eyes, I didn't want to believe it. I rubbed my hands over my face. "Bree, I need to talk to Jonah. Alone."

"No way." She pulled me out of the chair and pushed me away from Jonah. "I'm not leaving my brother alone with you."

"What do you think is gonna happen?" Jonah stood and folded his arms. "We're just going to talk."

"Yeah, I'm sure that's what they told Osama when they stormed his compound," she said. "*You two are at war.* You can't just talk this out."

Jonah and I locked eyes over his sister's head. In his gaze I felt a silent pledge; that even though Bree was right, we would not hurt each other. I gave a slight nod.

Jonah grabbed his sister's arm.

"Let go of me!"

"No." He dragged her to the door. "You can't protect me this time." He pushed her out into the night and threw his weight against the door before Bree could slide back inside.

The handle rattled. I ran forward and locked it.

Bree pounded and shouted for us to open the door.

I backed away, clutching the key.

Jonah stared at me. The flickering light cast long shadows, and I thought I could see the form of the Panther moving and writhing on the ground.

The door thumped one last time; it sounded like Bree had kicked it. "You both are freaks!" she yelled, her voice muffled from beyond the heavy wood. "You deserve each other!"

It grew very quiet. Jonah and I looked at each other across the wide wooden table.

"I guess this is easier for me," he said finally. "I've had a week to process."

My mind tumbled with thoughts and questions. For some reason, the most insignificant came out first. "How did you get back inside that night? Can panthers jump that high?" The roof of the garage, underneath the guest room window, was at least fifteen feet high.

"Normal panthers can't," he said. "But I'm not a normal panther. Just as you're not a normal falcon."

"No," I said, "I'm not. I am a Benandante. And you fought me at the Waterfall. Even after you knew who I was."

"So did you," he shot back.

"I didn't know I was fighting *you*."

"You broke the Raven's wings."

"I did what I had to do."

"So did I. The Raven is my Guide."

"Your *Guide* started the fire in my barn."

"No way. I don't believe that." Jonah ran his hand over his face, rubbing his skin so that his cheeks grew ruddy. "Why, Alessia? Why did you join *them*?"

"Why?" I croaked, words stuck in my throat. "Why did *I*? Why did *you*? The Malandanti are evil."

"What? No." Jonah stepped toward me.

I was frozen, knowing I should run but unable to move.

"The Malandanti aren't evil at all—"

"They tried to kill me!"

"They saved my life—"

"They killed all those people on the bridge," I cried.

Jonah jerked backward.

Silence rang over us, save for the wind that rattled outside the door and my gasping, sobbing breath.

His last words replayed in my head. "What do you mean, they saved your life?"

Jonah looked down at his feet. "In Fairfield. They saved me from going to prison. For what I did to Emily."

I breathed in deeply and let it out slowly. "Your dad's company didn't bail you out. The Malandanti did. Because they're one and the same."

"Yes and no." Jonah raised his head. "I can't tell you anything more than that."

"They guilted you into joining them," I said, balling my hands into fists. I wanted to hit something. "I wouldn't be surprised if they caused the accident in the first place to get you to join."

"No." His voice was like an animal snarl. "I was drunk. I caused the accident. They offered me a purpose, a way to straighten out my life."

"By killing innocent people." I pressed a fist against my mouth, afraid I might vomit. In my mind's eye, I could see the broken bridge, the cars in the water down below, the overturned bus. "And me. They tried to kill me on the bridge." I shook my head, trying to dislodge the memory from that awful night.

Jonah paced the length of the table in short angry strides. "My Clan went there only to prevent the Falcon from being Called."

"By killing me."

"And when they got there," Jonah said, ignoring my interruption, "the bridge had collapsed. Our *Concilio Argento* told us the Benandanti had done it."

"What?" I sprang forward. Every muscle in my body shook. "We did not. The Malandanti caused the collapse—for the sole purpose of killing me."

"Well, of course your Clan would tell you that."

"They didn't need to. I was there—I saw it happen."

"The Benandanti showed you what they wanted you to see," Jonah snapped. "They wouldn't want you to think you were working for the wrong side."

"How can you be so blind?" I yelled. "Wake up. You're being manipulated."

Jonah rounded on me, nostrils flared and lips white. "No. I am not an idiot. I can make decisions for myself."

In his face I saw all the years that he hadn't been allowed to decide for himself. No wonder Bree had called him ripe for the picking. "What does your *Concilio* say about us? How can they possibly justify themselves?"

"They don't have to." Jonah stopped, his eyes sharp like crystal shards. "You want to hoard all the magic for yourselves."

"We do not." My voice filled the small space. "Every time the magic is used, the planet gets a little weaker. We want to prevent that from happening."

"Oh, that's bullshit." Jonah waved his hand. "That's the lie the Benandanti come up with to explain their actions. You'll see—pretty soon your Clan mates will be using the magic at the Waterfall, and that excuse about the planet will disappear."

"That's not going to happen," I said. Everything inside me was on fire, raging out of control. "We are only protecting the magic. It's the Malandanti who want to abuse it."

"And who told you that?" He cocked his head. "Your *Concilio*, right? The same *Concilio* that told you we were responsible for the bridge collapse?"

I met his eyes. "Just as yours told you that we were." I tried to clear the remnants of thoughts that swarmed my brain. "I should have seen it. The clues were all there."

Jonah pressed the heel of his hand into his forehead. "Snooping around my dad's office. Why didn't I see it, either?"

"Because we didn't want to," I whispered. Tears spilled down my cheeks. How was it that I was still alive? In the last hour I should have died a hundred times. I tripped over to the chair and fell into it. I couldn't look at him anymore. He was my mortal enemy. But still . . .

I loved him. "What are we supposed to do now?" My voice broke in pieces at the same time my heart did, like the jar I had broken in the basement so many weeks ago, the day I had first learned the word *Benandanti*.

"Are we just supposed to sit next to each other in French class and pretend we don't know anything?" Jonah's breath hitched every time he inhaled. "I can't do that."

He reached for me and I let him. One hand buried in my hair, the other against the small of my back. I clung to him too, wanting time to stop and never move us forward. His head bent toward mine. Our lips devoured each other as though they knew it was the last time. His arms were the only things holding me together, and I knew the instant I left them I would fall apart.

With a gasp, Jonah pulled back.

"No," I moaned, my fingers grappling to pull him back to me. The pain in my heart was worse than any transformation. "Don't leave. Not yet . . ."

"I have to." His words were choked. He moved toward the door, leaving me cold and alone. "You need to let me out."

*I need to let you go*, I thought before I realized he meant that the door was locked and I had the key. Swallowing hard, I held the key out to him, my hand shaking. When he didn't take it, I looked up.

Jonah's eyes were wide, his hand pressed over his heart. "You need to let me out *right now*," he gasped.

He was being Called.

# Chapter Twenty-eight
## The Map

I fumbled with the lock while Jonah panted behind me. The instant I swung the door open, he took off running across the pasture. A minute later there was a flash of silver at the edge of the woods. He had shifted.

The night air numbed my face. If Jonah had been Called, he had to be headed for the Waterfall. Heath and the Stag were on patrol. I had to warn them. I backed into the Cave and pulled myself in two, leaving my body on the floor as I soared into the darkness.

*The Panther is coming,* I told Heath. *I'm on my way.*

*How do you know?* he asked.

I ignored him. I couldn't answer that question without giving up Jonah's identity, and I wasn't sure what to do about that yet. I winged with all my strength toward the Waterfall, keeping an eye on the ground below for Jonah's aura. Just before the birch trees, I saw it.

The treetops shivered in my wake as I descended. I heard the water before I saw it, gathering speed as I left the treetops shivering in my wake. As Jonah burst out of the trees, another ball of silver light joined him:

the Bobcat. I pitched forward and streaked the Bobcat across the back with my talon. It screamed and twisted upward to get at me, but I was too fast for its paws. *Where's the Stag?*

*He's running late.*

*He picked the wrong night for that.*

The Bobcat leapt into the air and smashed its enormous body against mine. We both tumbled to the earth, but it was faster on its feet than I was. It rushed at me, and I tried to scramble backward, but my wings felt stuck and heavy. The Bobcat opened its mouth in a huge roar, its long sharp teeth dripping with saliva, and still my wings would not work . . .

A loud crack forced our attention away from each other. Jonah had collided with the barrier. He yelped, limping backward.

My wings found flight again, and I burst upward. The Bobcat followed, swiping at me as it jumped from rock to rock. Just inside the barrier, I saw Heath creeping toward its edge. *Do* not *come outside. I got this.*

At the top of the Waterfall I hovered high in the air, facing the two Malandanti. The Bobcat snarled and lunged for me, but Jonah hung back. I dodged out of the Bobcat's reach. This was it. Would Jonah do his duty and attack me? My heart beat as wildly as my wings. It thudded inside my feathery breast, pounding like hoofbeats on the earth . . .

I blinked. Those *were* hooves, beating into the

ground as the Stag galloped toward us. The Bobcat snarled and slunk low as though to pounce, but the Stag sprang into the air, light as a cloud, and socked the Bobcat a blow to its cheek with his back hoof. The Bobcat stumbled away into the trees, its painful yowls echoing back to us as it disappeared into the forest.

The Stag rounded on Jonah, who took two tentative steps backward. His eyes lit on me. The Stag gathered his back legs as though to jump, but I swooped over his head, screeching as I stretched my talons toward Jonah. I squeezed my eyes shut before I reached him, hoping he understood what I was doing.

My talons met air, and my eyes flew open. He was gone; there was a speck of silver light in between the trees before all was darkness again. I shook with relief and landed on a nearby branch. *Nice timing*, I said to the Stag.

*Sorry about that*, he said.

*We're going to be under constant attack from now on, aren't we?* Heath said.

*Yes.* The Stag picked over the rocks and through the barrier, coming to rest on the shore beside the water. *We cannot let our guard down for an instant.*

Even though there was no way he could know, that seemed to be directed at me. I launched off the branch. *Do you need me to stay?*

*No*, the Stag answered. *We'll Call you if they come back. Besides, I need to talk to the Wolf.*

The wind was cold against my feathers as I flew to the Cave. I transformed and lay on my back, looking at the curved ceiling for several minutes before sitting up.

I turned off the lights and locked the door behind me. But I didn't go back to the house. Instead, I ran across the pasture and searched the edge of the forest until I found Jonah, lying still beneath the low-lying branches of a pine tree.

I knelt beside his body. Seeing someone else's body without his soul was completely different than seeing my own. I knew I couldn't touch him, but I rested my hand within an inch of his fingers. "Why?" I whispered. "Why did you choose them?"

The hard snow crunched behind me. I whirled to my feet.

The White Wolf stood a few feet away, taking in the scene. To anyone else, it would look like Jonah was dead, but Heath knew better. He growled and leapt past me, jerking his head in a clear indication that I should follow him.

With one last glance at Jonah, I obeyed.

We rounded the hillside to Heath's little cabin, where the door was slightly ajar. Heath nosed it open, and in a softly dazzling glow of blue light, he shifted back into his body and sat on the quilt-covered twin bed in the corner.

I closed the door behind me, my eyes adjusting to the soft lamplight that flooded the single room. The last time I had been in the cabin was to clean it just before Heath had taken residence. Now I saw that he had made it cozy and comfortable. Plush throw pillows littered the futon that served as a couch, and a sprig of dogwoods bloomed from a vase on the table. The shelf above the sink in the kitchenette was cluttered with spices, and the walls were covered with thumbtacked pictures. Several of them showed a beautiful young woman with dark curly hair. I pointed to one in which she was laughing, her face in profile. "Who is she?"

"Never mind." Heath got to his feet. "Jonah—he's the Panther."

I didn't answer, just stared at the floor. The wooden slats were unevenly laid.

"Isn't he?"

It was hard to deny. I nodded without looking at him, my hair falling across my face.

"How long have you known?" Heath asked, his voice hard as thick ice.

I snapped my head up. "I just found out. Right before the fight. I thought it was Bree," I whispered. I swallowed hard and told him what had happened at the party and afterward in the Cave.

He listened without expression until I stopped talking. Then he blew out a hard breath. "We need to tell the rest of the Clan."

"No."

"Are you kidding me? What makes you think he

isn't telling his Clan *right now* who you are? Jonah is your enemy."

"He can't be my enemy," I said, my voice low and even, "if I'm no longer a Benandante."

Heath froze, his blue eyes dark. "What do you mean?"

"I want out." I touched a burl in the wooden table. "We recaptured the Waterfall. Mission accomplished. I'll stay until you find my replacement, but then I'm done. I want my life back."

"Did you not hear what the Stag said? We are under constant attack. And you want out?" Heath ran his hand through his hair and down the back of his neck. "Sit down." He pulled a picture down from the wall and sat at the small table in the center of the cabin.

I slid into the chair opposite him.

He laid the picture out on the table, smoothing it flat with his palm. It was a hand-drawn map, like the one of Middle-earth at the beginning of *The Lord of the Rings*.

"What is that?"

"This shows all seven magical sites around the world," Heath said. He pointed to a little sketch of a Waterfall in the corner of the map. It was circled in blue marker. "This is Twin Willows."

I peered closely at the map. In the center was a drawing of a tree. I watched as Heath drew a large *X* across the tree. The black lines somehow looked vicious. "What are you doing?"

"When you first joined the Benandanti," Heath said,

"we controlled two sites. The Redwood site in California . . ."

"Which fell to the Malandanti."

"Yes. Then we regained control of the Waterfall, and we had two again." He pointed to a tree beneath the *X*. "The Olive Grove in Friuli, Italy."

"The birthplace of the Benandanti," I murmured, thinking back to that website.

"And the seat of the *Concilio Celeste*," Heath said. "It's the beating heart of the Benandanti. Ground zero for this war." He stroked the tree almost reverently. "Last night that site fell to the Malandanti."

I gasped, my hand curling into a claw on the table. "What—how?"

"We don't have the details. That was what the Stag wanted to talk to me about."

"Why didn't he Call a Clan meeting?"

"He was going to." Heath clutched at the amulet around his neck that held his caul. "I told him I wanted to tell you personally before he did that."

I splayed my hand across the map. "Why?"

Heath leaned toward me. "Because I could sense you wavering. Ever since Jonah broke up with you."

How had it been so obvious to Heath when I barely acknowledged it myself? I kept my gaze on the map. "Is the *Concilio Celeste*—are they dead?"

Heath shook his head. "They are all alive but they've fled Friuli. They have scattered to each of the sites."

The lines and circles on the map swam in my vision.

"So the Waterfall is the only site we control now."

Heath nodded. "And if we lose it and the Malandanti control everything, there is no doubt in my mind that they would use all that power to destroy us." He clasped his hands and brought them to his mouth. His eyes swam with jumbled emotions as he looked at me. "So you see, you can't leave. Not now."

I pushed away from the table and backed up until I felt the wall behind me. My legs felt watery. I slid down until I hit the floor. I was trapped here in Twin Willows forever, fighting against an enemy that I loved with all my heart . . .

Heath got to his feet and came around the other side of the table, crouched down to me. "But if we maintain control of the Waterfall and help the other Clans recapture the other six sites, maybe then you can have an out."

"That could take forever." The idea of defeating the Malandanti all over the world seemed impossible, like trying to keep a snowflake from melting. "I could die before that happens."

"You could," Heath agreed.

I glared at him through tears that formed on my eyelashes.

He tucked an errant strand of hair behind my ear. I tossed my head away from him, but he rested his finger on my jaw. "Or you could commit yourself so fully to the mission that we succeed sooner rather than later."

I turned my head. My vision blurred, softening the

edges around everything in the room. Instead of the table and chairs and bed, I saw in front of me everything I had sacrificed for the Benandanti. My schoolwork. My friendships. My family's safety. I swallowed hard. Jonah. "It isn't fair. I'm only sixteen."

Heath let out a rough exhale. "You think you're the only one who's given up their world for the Benandanti?" His gaze traveled to the picture of the dark-haired woman on the wall above me. "That's what I had to give up. Everyone has to make sacrifices."

*It isn't fair that anyone has to sacrifice anything*, I thought, but I didn't say it out loud. I swiped away tears that spilled onto my cheeks. "So what do we do?"

Heath grasped my shoulders and stood, pulling me up with him. "We fight the good fight. It's the only thing we *can* do."

I pressed the base of my palms into my hot eyeballs. Starbursts bloomed and shrank on the inside of my eyelids. I dropped my hands and took a deep breath. "Okay. Okay. Whenever the Benandanti Call, I'll be there." I pushed away from him and moved toward the table.

"He protected you."

Heath's voice stopped me, made me turn. "What?"

"During the fight just now. Jonah protected you."

I crossed to him. "How?"

"He threw himself into the barrier to distract the Bobcat."

I studied the gnarled wooden table, blinking hard to

keep the new tears from rising to the surface.

"Every battle is going to be harder for you from now on," Heath said. I looked up at him. His eyes had softened. "You have to maintain focus on your own Clan, or it might cost you your life."

We stared at each other, both of us breathing hard. "Are you—?"

Heath held up his hand. "I won't say anything. For now. But if we find out that he's told his Clan about you or he distracts you in any way, there will be consequences."

"Thanks, Heath." I walked out of the cabin and closed the door. Light spilled through the cabin windows, making golden pools of warmth on the cold ground. I shivered and turned away into the dark night. Somewhere in the distance, an owl hooted.

Everything I had learned in the last few hours was jumbled inside me, swirling like snow in a thick blizzard. I walked slowly to the Cave. So many things were uncertain, and I couldn't see anything clearly. But out of it all, I knew one thing for sure. Jonah was wrong. I believed that he thought the Malandanti were right and that he himself wasn't evil, but I knew, deep in my soul, that the Benandanti were the light and the Malandanti were the dark.

I pressed a hand to my heart, and even though I was exhausted, I beckoned the shift to come. When it did, I soared out over the hillside and away from the farm, leaving my body far behind in the soft light of the Cave.

I flew over the quiet streets of Twin Willows, the snowy rooftops of my neighbors and friends, safe in their beds without any inkling of the power that lay just outside their doors. The school sat dark and dormant as I winged over it. The bleachers, where I had spent so many happy lunch hours with Jonah, dripped with icicles big enough to see my reflection in as I went by.

At last I reached the ocean, the place where Maine came to an end and the rest of the world began. I swooped down and touched my talons to the white-crested waves, so constant and eternal. No matter what happened, the sea would always rise and fall. That, at least, I could count on.

I sailed upward, rocketing toward the stars, and let the wind take me where it would. Daybreak would come soon, and I would have to go back—to my body, to my home, to my other life—but for now, the moon, the stars, the night, and the sea were all I needed to let my soul take flight.

# AUTHOR'S NOTE

This is a work of fiction. But the Benandanti are real. They were investigated by the Roman Inquisition from the late sixteenth century to the mid-seventeenth century in the Friuli region of Italy. Although many people confessed to having the gift to separate their souls from their bodies, the Inquisition never convicted a single Benandante. They realized that the protection the Benandanti gave to their villages was too valuable to remove.

These investigations are the subject of Carlo Ginzburg's excellent book *The Night Battles*, which includes actual transcripts from the Inquisition trials that are fascinating to read. His book was the main source of my research for *Winter Falls*.

Although I greatly changed the mythology of the Benandanti to suit my story's purpose, the foundation is built upon the original legend. I encourage my readers to learn more about the real Benandanti by reading Mr. Ginzburg's book and by visiting my website, www.nicolemaggi.com, which includes a link to the Wikipedia page that inspired Alessia's journey.

*In bocca al lupo.*

# IN THE
# MOUTH
# OF THE
# WOLF

### THE NIGHT BATTLES
### RAGE ON

# NICOLE
# MAGGI

book 2 of the twin willows trilogy

# IN THE
# MOUTH
## OF THE
# WOLF

## NICOLE
## MAGGI

The Twin Willows Waterfall is now under the control of
the Benandanti, but for Alessia, the victory comes at a steep
price. And the arrival of Nerina, one of the seven Concilio
elders from the Friuli Clan, only complicates her life. Now
she's hiding a 450-year-old immortal on her farm, juggling
school and her increasingly frustrated friends, and trying to
keep the Malandanti from regaining the Waterfall. But it's the
passion that still lingers between her and Jonah
that really keeps Alessia awake at night.

After a fatal visit from the Malandanti's mage, Alessia
brings in Jonah's twin sister, Bree, to serve as a Benandanti
spy. Bree has her own reasons for wanting to bring down the
Malandanti, and soon she and Alessia find themselves in a
tenuous alliance. But not even the powerful magic that Bree
possesses nor the strong leadership that Nerina provides can
stop the vicious Malandanti. As the two Clans barrel towards
their inevitable collision, Alessia and Jonah are swept into the
devastation and forced to make the ultimate choice.

ISBN# 978-1-60542-619-8
TRADE / Young Adult
$9.99 US/CDN
JUNE 2015